A LIE FOR A LIE

Also by Ren DeStefano

HOW I'LL KILL YOU

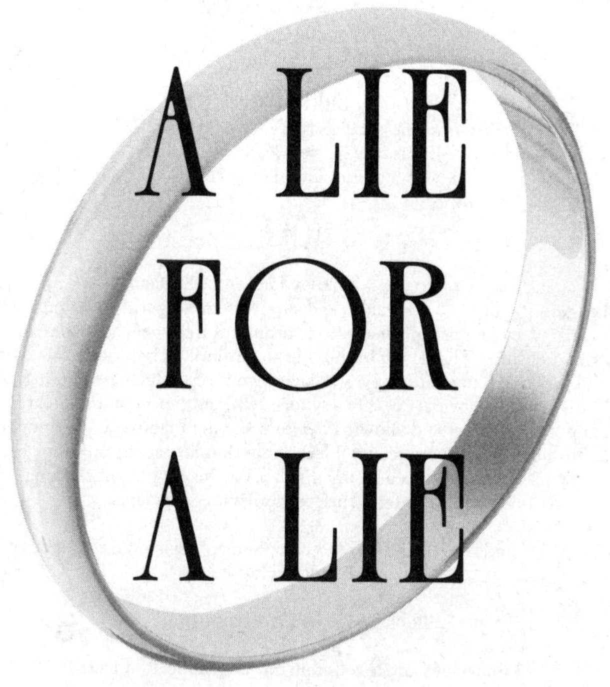

A LIE FOR A LIE

REN DESTEFANO

BERKLEY
New York

BERKLEY
An imprint of Penguin Random House LLC
1745 Broadway, New York, NY 10019
penguinrandomhouse.com

Book design by George Towne

Library of Congress Cataloging-in-Publication Data

Names: DeStefano, Ren, author.
Title: A lie for a lie / Ren DeStefano.
Description: First edition. | New York: Berkley, 2026.
Identifiers: LCCN 2025027616 (print) | LCCN 2025027617 (ebook) |
ISBN 9780593438343 trade paperback | ISBN 9780593438350 ebook
Subjects: LCGFT: Fiction | Thrillers (Fiction) | Novels
Classification: LCC PS3604.E7644 L54 2026 (print) |
LCC PS3604.E7644 (ebook)
LC record available at https://lccn.loc.gov/2025027616
LC ebook record available at https://lccn.loc.gov/2025027617

First Edition: March 2026

Printed in the United States of America
1st Printing

A LIE FOR A LIE

PROLOGUE

When I was a little girl growing up in rural Oregon, I thought the entire world was made up of acres and acres of green grass. I thought everyone's life revolved in some way around farmlands.

I would sometimes hear the distant sirens on the interstate, and it felt like a piece of a parallel universe was breaking into my sanctuary. I couldn't imagine that anything bad would ever happen to us.

Then the fire happened.

The lighter fluid spilled out of the bottle so easily. All down the white couch that my mother fastidiously vacuumed. It splashed against the coffee table and the wall. And I stopped, stunned, as the flame appeared almost like magic. It caught everything, swallowing it whole like a monster from a dream.

I heard my mother screaming in the bedroom. I ran to her, thinking numbly how backward it was that she was crying out to me for help. It had only been a few years since I'd stopped having bad dreams that woke me from my sleep, prompting me to call out for her. Now I was the one running to save her. Only this time, the nightmare was real.

The doorknob was white-hot, and I drew away, hissing in pain. Panic set in and I started to cry. No, I told myself. Think. In school, they made us do weekly fire drills. We assembled into a line and tried not to giggle and whisper too loudly, excited as we were to escape class for a few minutes.

But it wasn't something that could really happen, I'd thought.

I balled my nightshirt up and used it like an oven mitt to turn the knob. The door opened, but the air was pulled from my lungs and I reared back. The smoke was thick and black, and I couldn't see anything. It roared louder than the screams, everything blurring into one big sound.

I was twelve, and I remember stumbling out of the first-floor window. I found myself beneath the same clear, starry sky that had been looking over me all my life. Only now, the silence was punctuated by sirens. They weren't trilling on some faraway interstate, but racing toward my little ranch house.

My older brother found me, both of us standing in the darkness beyond the glow of the flickering lights. His eyes were wide, like he couldn't believe what was happening. But his hands were firm when he gripped my shoulders and turned me toward him.

"The police are going to come," he said. "They're going

to ask questions. Don't tell them anything. That's the only way I can protect us."

I was too stunned to ask him what he meant. I was too frightened to ask what had happened to our parents. On some level, I already knew.

Then he ran back into the flames.

ONE

The courtroom is packed.

Today, the highly publicized six-month murder trial comes to an end. At seven this morning, the jury announced that they had reached their verdict. Now we gather to hear the fate of the defendant, Emma Graham.

"Mom," Collette whispers, "I *can't* be late for school. I have a math test today."

At eleven years old, my daughter is going on thirty.

"It's fine." I wrap my arm around her shoulders, giving her a comforting squeeze. "Not everything is learned in the classroom. This is educational."

Collette cranes her neck to see over the rows of people seated ahead of us. We didn't get here early enough to sit directly behind the attorneys, but with the popularity of this case, it's a miracle we got in at all. Through the window, I can see that the sidewalk outside the courtroom is also packed with people, all of whom are huddled over smartphones waiting for the next update.

Collette was interested in this case because it fascinated her that this crime went down long before even I was born, but also because the murderer could still be found guilty. I explained the statute of limitations to her—how some crimes, like petty theft or even assault, have an expiration date. But murder never does. Even if they find you when you're a hundred years old and on your last days, justice will come for you.

I stare at the back of Emma Graham's head. Her gray hair is cut short, and her skin is still tanned from her long days spent on sunny beaches. Back in 1985, when her husband went missing, she was youthful and radiant, only thirty-two. She wept on the news and pleaded for her husband to return to her, safe and sound. She begged the public to be on the lookout. She alluded weakly to poorly planned-out and vague mental health issues, claiming he'd "been depressed" and that she'd "always known" he "might do something."

This didn't stop her from cashing the insurance check when his van was later found submerged in a river, with him at the wheel. No attempts to escape had been made, and it was deemed an accident. He'd fallen asleep at the wheel and perhaps hit his head, rendering him unconscious on impact.

That was forty years ago. Since then, she's remarried three times—no children—and retired to an upscale condo in sunny Florida. When her husband's death was ruled accidental, the case disappeared from public discussion. And because there are so many tragedies to fill the evening news, the world eventually forgot about her.

The room falls silent when the jury files into the room. Collette eyes them curiously. The jurors aren't shown on the cameras, so this is the first time she's having a look at them.

My husband, Waylen, would be angry if he knew I've taken our daughter here. Yesterday, when he caught Collette watching the trial recap on YouTube, which contained salacious details about Emma's affairs during her first marriage, he took her iPad away. He said the topic is too grown up for her.

But whether or not he wants to admit it, Collette is smart. She knows that criminals exist and finds it reassuring that they can be punished for their crimes. Like me, she's interested in how a grave injustice can be corrected. How criminals who thought they'd gotten away with it can finally be punished.

"You're a good mother," Waylen told me recently, during one of our hushed little late-night arguments while Collette was sleeping across the hall. "A perfect one, really. But you're trying to make her too much like—"

"Like me?" I'd pressed.

"Like an adult," he'd amended, with irritating calm. "Shouldn't she be—I don't know—collecting stickers and coloring books?"

"She's not five, Waylen."

"She's not thirty-five, either." He'd had to fight to keep his voice low. He didn't say the rest of it—the part we've hashed out a thousand times. He wants our life to be more . . . normal. My obsession with spying, he doesn't understand. "What are you trying to prove?" he's asked. But I can never tell him. There's only one person who truly understands, and that's Mr. X, who agrees with me.

Now I sit in the courtroom with Collette, who is eleven—and admittedly I do forget she's not thirty-five sometimes.

The teachers at Collette's esteemed private school would be horrified to know that I'm exposing her to this case. But I wasn't much older than she is when I was in a courtroom as a defendant and stood trial for murder.

I already know the verdict will be guilty. The head juror is a petite college student named Mira Hart, and she's working for me. If there was any evidence of jury tampering that led to this conviction, the courts would have to throw the whole thing out. But that won't be an issue.

Emma Graham sits tall and straight. Maybe she's trying to maintain her pride, or maybe she still thinks she can get away with the crime she committed forty years ago. It happened before they had things like DNA testing, and small-town cops thought a man was more likely to take his own life than his loving wife was. This was back when the news media lined their pockets with sad stories of pigtailed girls who were stolen from their beds or snatched from their bicycles.

I found Emma's story while browsing a thread on Reddit. "What's a solved case that you think the cops got wrong?" Investigators never looked into Emma's motives. Just two months after her husband was found, she cut all communication with her extended family and ran off with a man she'd been having an affair with. These could have been the actions of a desperate widow looking to escape her grief. But the case still intrigued me.

Someone on the forum claimed to have a taped confession. He was an Uber driver, and he'd recently shuttled an intoxicated Emma home from a senior center bingo night. She told the Uber driver that he shouldn't get too cocky about his good looks, because one day he would also be washed up and ugly, like the man she'd murdered for a fifty-thousand-dollar insurance settlement.

Most people assumed the post was a hoax. No shortage of those on the internet. But I reached out and obtained a copy of his dashcam footage. I took on the case—no easy feat—and was able to piece the evidence together.

But I'm not a cop. I'm not even an investigator. I am part of an organization that handles things a bit differently.

Dear Emma, I began my letter to her. Although nothing can bring your loving husband back, today you are given the chance to redeem yourself. In your backyard, below the seashell where you keep the spare key, you'll find a cassette tape of the night you confessed to positioning your sedated husband behind the wheel of his van, putting it in drive, and watching him roll forward into the lake. Some details the police never released, to prove that I'm serious: You'd given him Benadryl in a late-night smoothie, and he threw up on impact. You had tried to tape a rock to the gas pedal, but it kept falling off, so you had to push it yourself. You tell people that your husband was planning to leave you and that's why you were having an affair. But after the truth cocktail my contact slipped into your drink at the bar, you confessed. You don't remember this, but I have the proof.

By signing your latest dearly departed husband's pension checks over to the safe home for battered women and children, you can save lives like the one you ended and make things right. You will not go to prison if you comply.

I'll contact you soon with instructions.

Sometimes, the criminals I contact know a gift when they see it. Not Emma. She was used to the accusations—all of which had been proven false—and she must have assumed this was yet another hoax. She didn't shutter herself in the house or call an attorney like some have, but she did become increasingly paranoid. Looking over her shoulder when she sat at the seaside bar, jolting whenever the voices of strangers grew too close as she sunned herself in the sand.

Still, when the police finally showed up at her door, I imagine she was surprised.

Throughout the trial, Emma searched the faces of the jurors and sometimes turned to the people in the pews behind her, no doubt searching for her letter writer. No doubt wondering who was watching, who knew her darkest secret. But now that I'm here in person—rather than watching the recaps in my kitchen as I make dinner—she doesn't look for me. She's given up.

The judge, for her part, gives a passionate speech about the abhorrence of Emma's crime, and then she summons the head juror to read the verdict.

Mira Hart, twenty-one and with a melodic theater major's voice, reads from the paper in her hands. "To the charge of murder in the first degree, we the jury find the defendant guilty."

There are more charges, but that was the big one. Collette is perched on the edge of her seat, biting her lip.

When Mira finishes speaking, for a moment it's quiet enough to hear a pin drop. The judge has instructed all of us that we'd be removed from the courtroom if we caused a disturbance.

I wait until the room is mostly empty before I take Collette's hand and lead her outside. She's somber, but when we reach the last step of the courthouse, she leaps into a dancer's pirouette. "That was really cool, Mom," she says. "Thanks for bringing me. Now I can tell my friends I was sitting five feet away from a murderer. Her shoulders got all hunched up when they found her guilty."

"Maybe this should be our secret," I say, opening the door to the SUV for her. "Your father didn't want me to take you."

"Why not?" she asks. "It's not like she's going to kill me, too. They had her in handcuffs."

Collette has Waylen's gold hair and blue eyes. She has his prowess for art and science, and they both love to bake bougie French desserts.

But even though we don't match up on everything, Collette is more like me than she realizes. I knew it very early on. Waylen sees it too, and it scares the hell out of him.

"I don't want this life for her," he's whispered to me while we're lying in bed. He doesn't mean my day job as an interior decorator, or his salaried job editing manuscripts for a Big Five publisher. He means the thing we don't say. The life he gave up. The things I do when I disappear for hours at a time, and the reason Emma Graham will spend the rest of her miserable life in prison.

"She can do anything," he's told me. "Anything but that."

I arrive at the school twenty minutes late. As I turn into the driveway, I hand Collette the note that was tucked in the sun visor. "Give that to your teacher."

She reads it—the only child on earth to question a permission note that allows her to be late to class. "But we weren't at the dentist," she says. "Isn't that lying?"

"No, it isn't," I say, glancing at her in the mirror. "No plaque buildup. The technician said you did a perfect job."

She hesitates, tucks the note into her pocket.

She hates lying, which as a parent is a trait I appreciate. But I'm working on teaching her the subtle art of playing her cards close to the vest and knowing when to keep a secret.

"Collette, all of that 'honesty is the best policy' stuff you learn about in kindergarten isn't always applicable."

She unbuckles her seat belt. "What's 'applicable'?"

"It means sometimes the rules are bullshit." She doesn't flinch at my language, even though I don't talk this way often. She knows that this morning is special, one of those rare times when we're on the same level. And she knows that I'm going to answer the questions she normally wouldn't ask me.

"Why does Daddy get so mad when I watch trials with you?" she asks.

"You can't be too hard on him," I say. "He still thinks you'll be little forever. *That's* why he keeps buying you unicorn Squishmallows on your birthday."

"I still like them," she says. "I mean, a little bit." It is true that Waylen wants to preserve her innocence, but that isn't all of it. Really, it's that he doesn't want her to be like me. He doesn't want her to grow up and fall in love with someone like who he used to be when we met.

Collette opens the door, but before she can set foot on the pavement, a woman comes bursting through the double doors of the school's entrance. She paces toward us like a mad bull in pink heels and perfectly dyed platinum hair.

"Who's that?" I ask. Cynthia Nyugen does morning drop-offs, but seeing as we're late, I was expecting the drop-off to be empty.

"Mrs. Blevins," Collette groans. "Finnegan's mom."

"Who's Finnegan? I don't recognize that name," I say.

"The Blevinses just moved here," Collette says. "She's the *worst*."

"Which one is the worst?" I ask. "Mrs. Blevins or her daughter?"

Before my daughter can answer, Mrs. Blevins is knocking on my passenger-side window and motioning for me to roll it down, as though she's a cop pulling me over for a bank heist.

As the glass comes down, I give her my brightest smile. The one that Waylen says makes me look like a Miss America contestant whose onstage talent is dismembering a corpse. "Good morning," I say, in my best Stepford wife tone.

"This is the drop-off for students who arrive on time," she says by way of greeting. Her perfume floods the car, flowery and potent, like Natalie Portman's fever dream. I suppress a cough. "For tardy students, you're supposed to pull into the commuter lot and walk her into the main office so that she's not marked absent for the day."

"Is that really necessary?" I ask. "She's got a note."

"It's for everyone's safety," she says. Up close, it's infuriating how beautiful she is. Her makeup perfectly blended and contoured, not a single clump in her mascara, perfectly manicured nails. She exudes newness. Someone who understands the power of a first impression.

I can feel Collette's eyes on me, pleading for me to make this easy on her.

I extend a hand to Mrs. Blevins, my smile relaxing into something less robotic. "Margaux," I tell her. "My daughter has spoken so highly of your Finnegan. I'm just sorry that you've caught me on an off day."

She blinks, looking at me the way that new people often do, as though she's not sure whether I'm mocking her. But she takes my hand. "Elodie Blevins," she says. Then she nods to the parking lot in the distance, so full of BMWs, Lexuses, and Jeeps that I'll have to park in the nosebleed section. "Let's get your daughter signed in properly."

Collette closes the door. And for her, I wait until we've driven away before I mutter, "What a bitch."

It matters how I'm perceived by the parents at this school. Not just for Collette, but for my own reputation. It's a fragile dance with these people. "Just be yourself," Waylen will say. "People like you."

But "people" don't know me. Not even Waylen knows everything. He doesn't know about the fire that happened when I was a child, or how it impacted me. Although being a spy for hire rarely pays much, there was a time when it paid for my entire cost of living in a studio apartment, eating cheap takeout and cozying up to a space heater. It was a simple, minimalist life, and it was enough for me. I liked knowing that I wouldn't lose any valuables or loved ones in a fire—because I didn't have any left to lose. I only had enough money to pay for food and utilities, and that was enough. I didn't touch the inheritance I'd been left. Saving it for a rainy day, I suppose. I didn't need more than what I had.

It's a huge contrast to how I live now, in a stupidly large house filled with things none of us really needs. But this lifestyle makes Waylen and Collette happy, and that's why I don't mind it so much, even though I know I'd be happy to abandon the house and all the things in it tomorrow.

I believe that as adults, we become the person that we needed most as a child. Well, when I was twelve, I fantasized about an all-knowing and benevolent entity who had been spying on me for all the important events of my life. I imagined her to be a kind ghost in a mirror, holding a pen and a notepad. Whenever I was accused of something I hadn't done, or whenever I couldn't trust my own memory, she could lick her fingertip, flip through her records, and say, "Here it is. This is what really happened."

Now? I'm that person for people who hire me. I don't rest until I find the truth. Whether the people who hire me like it or not.

TWO

The decal on the rear window of my Bentley Bentayga reads *Blue New You Designs* in swirly periwinkle letters. A play on my last name, Blue, and my profession, interior decorator.

At least, by day. It's the perfect front because it pays very handsomely and the hours are flexible, giving me plenty of time for my true passion: being a spy for hire.

I pull in front of the house, a modular in a neighborhood of new construction. White faux-brick facing and black shutters that gleam like plastic in the daylight. I already know that the owner of this house will want neutrals. Gray walls, marble countertops, and vessel sinks.

My boss lines these up for me, and he deliberately picks the clients who are the least work. In Westport, there's no shortage of these gigs. Old money living alongside new money, and people with high-powered NYC careers who opted to live in the suburbs on the Connecticut shoreline.

Before I can turn off the ignition, my business phone rings. The name MR. X appears on the screen in bold white letters. My boss.

"Blue New You," I say in my chirpiest voice.

"Got a good job for you," Mr. X says. "Are you someplace where you can talk?"

"Just pulled in," I say. "What's up?"

"This one's going to require two of you," he says. "A plagiarism case. The victim spoke with me last week, and I've been doing my research. It seems worth our time."

"Plagiarism?" I say. "You do realize I've just put a murderer behind bars. Now you want to bust someone for stealing their college thesis?"

"Code, actually," he says. His voice is cool as ever. You never know what he's thinking, never know what he'll do. But I've known him a long time, and I can hear the slightest bit of excitement in his voice. "The victim's name is Erin Casimir. She contacted me because her brother stole the code she developed for a finance app. He's made billions off of it."

That word—*billions*—erases any apprehension I had just a moment ago. "This is more than white-collar Bernie Madoff stuff," I say.

"Bingo."

"But you said there are two of us for this?" I ask. "Who else did you get?"

"I got her on embezzlement a few years ago, at one of those pyramid scheme clothing companies based out in California," he says. "Seemed a waste to turn her in to the police. She's smart. Really good with numbers, knows how these sorts of crimes work. Let's just say I've held her on retainer because I had a feeling she'd be of use to us."

"And you trust her?" I know it's silly of me to ask. Mr. X is thorough. *Very* thorough. He keeps a Rolodex of former criminals and con men in his arsenal, and he makes sure they know what will happen if they screw him over. Even if they somehow avoided the lengthy prison time, they would have nothing left to return to when they were released.

"You'll meet her for yourself tonight," he says by way of answer.

Tonight. Dread sinks like a lead anchor in my stomach. Waylen already hates my secret career—the only way I can keep him on board is by conceding to his reasonable requests that we still function as a typical suburban family. Never missing dinner is one such condition.

Mr. X knows this, of course. That's why I don't say anything; he can read my silence.

I care about my family, and I love my husband. It isn't the sort of person I ever thought I'd be, but it's true nonetheless.

"M," he says, breaking the businessman facade he likes to wear. He's no longer the mysterious Bosley-type voice on the phone, addressing one of Charlie's Angels. He's appealing to the real me. "This domestic life isn't for you. You always said you'd rather end up doing life at Rikers than be a housewife."

Before I met Waylen I was wild. Take-a-pill-you-find-in-a-train-station-bathroom-and-see-what-happens wild. I'd gambled, stolen, even committed armed robbery once at a 7-Eleven, although that was accidental. I forgot I had a gun tucked into my belt loop when I was caught stealing a travel box of Tylenol for my massive headache. Let's just say the panic was overblown.

It was Mr. X who bailed me out that night. Told me how smart I was, that I was wasting my life. He said he was starting a new business, assembling small-time criminals who were interested in reforming themselves to right what he called "certain wrongs." I was going to jump out of the car, but he said he'd pay me. Give it a week, he said. Now it's been fifteen years. One husband and child later, I'm head of the props department at the elementary school production of *The Nutcracker*, and my daughter is angling to be head ballerina. I right injustices, wipe runny noses, and make a damn good cherry pie for the PTA fundraisers.

He thinks it's my fault that I turned out the way I did. Although it's been years since we've acknowledged that we're family, blood remains thicker than spy work. A traumatic childhood will do that to a person, I guess. After the fire killed our parents, I never recovered from it, and I learned never to speak about it, but it didn't matter because it still followed me everywhere I went.

Mr. X is the same way, but his coping mechanisms are different from mine. He started his spy business and gave us both a way to find some control in an uncontrollable world.

When Mr. X paired twenty-two-year-old me with twenty-two-year-old Waylen, the last thing he expected was that we would fall in love. Waylen was so—clean. He'd hacked into his college admissions database to secure a spot for a friend who'd failed the SATs and been rejected because she'd been caring for a sick father in hospice. A regular Robin Hood. Mr. X thought I'd eat him alive. But nobody was more surprised than I was when Waylen proposed and I said yes.

"We have a daughter, remember?" I tell him now by way of explanation. "But I can juggle. It's fine. I've got this."

"Perfect," he says, donning that Bosley demeanor again. "Then I'll send you the info for tonight's rendezvous."

I can't help but feel like I've played right into his hands.

THREE

The house smells like a French bakery when I step inside and throw my car keys into the art deco bowl on the ornate Pier 1 table by the door. It's carved out of fake jade, meant to evoke images of an ancient palace, but the price sticker is still adhered to the leg.

Collette is sitting on the living room floor, doing her homework on the coffee table. Music is blasting through her headphones. She says Beethoven helps her study. Sometimes I don't know where she came from. But then when I think on it, she's some version of me that I never got to meet when I was growing up. She makes the choices I would have made if my childhood had been comfortable and safe.

Waylen emerges from the kitchen, a bit of jam smeared on his cheek. "Hi, beautiful," he says, wrapping me in a hug. "I had a little bit of time, so I went grocery shopping and got a head start on dessert. Linzer tortes." His face changes when he draws back and sees the look on my face. "What's wrong?"

"I can't stay for dinner," I say, wincing sympathetically. I move into the kitchen, out of Collette's line of sight.

"What?" His voice is hushed, as though I've just confided something awful. "Why not?"

"Work," I say, glancing at the doorway just to be sure we don't have an audience, even though I can hear Collette's music from here. Our daughter doesn't know about my little side hustle. She doesn't know that her father used to do it too, before he traded it in for an editing job and a life of domestic bliss. He'll take her to the bookstore and point out the notable stories he's worked on. "It was my note to give Mr. Copper a pet dog in this scene. Initially it was going to be a nosy neighbor destroying his garden, but he already had one of those." Or "I talked them into naming the dog Mr. Pickles."

But rather than scroll through my Instagram page, featuring parties and events and homes I've decorated, I take Collette to a courthouse. She is eventually going to realize that my job isn't like her dad's.

We told Collette that we met in Paris while we were on respective summer vacations. I dropped my wallet and he sprinted across the café to return it to me before I climbed into my cab. It was love at first sight. She thinks that she was conceived well within the parameters of our holy matrimony, and that everything about our little family was planned.

In truth, Collette is what happens when two colleagues have a few too many margaritas and find each other too attractive to resist. Three months later, our mission was completed and Waylen and I were never meant to see each other again. Except I had a bathroom trash bin full of positive pregnancy tests, and Waylen was looking for apartments on Zillow. He says he fell in love with me the moment he knew I was carrying his baby, and his adoring commitment scared me more than the prospect of motherhood.

Mr. X was less than thrilled. "How are you going to play house and keep your head in the game?" he'd asked.

My response was simple: "Because it's not a game to me."

Waylen had fallen for my act. He told me I was sweet, that he couldn't see himself settling down with a better gal.

"I'm not good for you," I told him one night as we sat on the couch of our tiny apartment, huddled by the space heater that was shaped like a wood-burning stove. The electric glow of the fake logs lit up his face. "I'm not good for this baby, either."

I almost told him the truth about my past. All he knew was that I'd committed some small crimes in my teens and early twenties. But it was enraging how determined he was to forgive me.

"You were just a scared kid who'd lost your parents when you were young," he told me. "You *are* good. Better than good. If you don't believe it, I will."

"Are you quoting Hallmark movies to me, sir?" I'd said, and he laughed.

"Maybe I'm broke now, and this is all we can afford. But if you give me the rest of your life, I'll fill it up with everything you deserve."

I didn't tell him about my inheritance until we were officially engaged. I hated to talk about how I received the money. It meant reliving the night my parents died, and all that came after that. That night is a clean seam down the middle of my life, dividing it between Before and After forever.

Waylen—sweet Waylen—didn't force me to talk about it. He didn't ask questions. He didn't even ask to see the savings account where I was storing it. Instead, he kissed my forehead and told me he wanted us to build a life together, however that may look.

He's kept his promise. All these years later, he's so slick that he can even convince me sometimes that I deserve to be here, co-heading our little family. Sometimes, foolishly, I consider telling him the things he doesn't know. The crime that Mr. X had purged from the internet as much as was possible. The one I never speak of.

It would be enough for him to leave me. It dangles in the corner of my mind like an emergency rip cord. A way out. I think about pulling it every day, but I never do.

All these years later, Mr. X has given up on trying to coerce Waylen back into a life of vigilantism, but the strain on our marriage has been constant. A fact that is evidenced by the glare Waylen gives me now. "You promised, Margaux," he says. "You said this thing wouldn't interfere with family life."

"It hasn't," I say. "This is the first dinner I'm missing in months. You've missed dinner once or twice for work."

Waylen isn't reassured. In fact, this only makes him angrier. "So you just stopped by to say goodbye, then. What am I supposed to tell Collette?"

"Don't do that," I say. "Don't use our daughter to guilt me."

He crosses his arms across his broad chest. "If you're feeling guilty, it isn't because of me. Maybe that's just a natural reaction to—this." He nods to the air around us, as though it's filled with my misgivings.

My phone buzzes in my pocket, and even though I don't react, I know Waylen heard it. The tension is palpable.

I soften my voice. "I'll be back before midnight."

His arms are still folded and he says nothing. My husband cuts an imposing figure—tall and muscular, his hair already gone silver in his early thirties. But he's never been the confrontational sort. He doesn't say whatever he's thinking—a sentiment I'm sure isn't agreeable or kind. He only watches as I turn and head for the door. I stop to kiss Collette on the head, pull out one of her earbuds, and tell her I have to meet with a client for work, listen to your father, no iPad after nine p.m.

Once I'm out on the front steps, I wind my scarf around my neck to guard against the autumn chill.

"Wait." Waylen is sprinting after me, and he squeezes past the door before it closes. He turns me to face him. All the anger is gone from his features. "Be careful."

"It isn't anything dangerous—"

"I know," he interrupts. "But some of these people you meet up with leave a lot to be desired." He tucks my hair behind my shoulder and his fingers brush against my neck, warm against the cold night air.

We play the part of a normal, happy couple so well that I don't know where the truth and the facade intersect anymore. I love him, and that much is true. The rest—I'm not sure. This house is too big for us, and we spend a fortune on garden care. The rooms are painted in neutrals, decorated with faux antiques. I could leave it all tomorrow, go back to how it used to be in our tiny apartment with a shower that only gave us five minutes of hot water and only one working burner on the stove.

The house in the suburbs was Waylen's idea, once we were both making enough money to afford it. He thought that if he could give me a perfect life, I would ditch the vigilantism, but all it's done is give me a good front.

Still, he loves me. He sees who I really am, and that's worth something.

I push forward and kiss him, and I feel his muscles relax. "I'll be safe," I tell him. "Save me some dessert."

If I told him about my past—about the fire, and that Mr. X is my brother, he might understand. But he also might not. I don't like to entertain situations where I can't easily predict the outcome, so I clam up.

So many times, I've wanted to tell him why I do this, and why I continue my work as a spy. It's not for the paycheck. It's the act of piecing together a puzzle and watching a situation finally make sense. It's getting to the truth, which is always objective once it becomes clear. It's about feeling like I'm doing something good with my present and my future, to make up for all the things I can't go back in time and change.

Most likely, Waylen would tell me the fire wasn't my fault. He'd want us to go to couples therapy or something. He'd want to fix it. But I don't want to be a person who needs fixing—I want to be the one who fixes things.

* * *

I'm meeting my new partner at a commuter lot off the highway. It's well lit, close enough to the gas station that someone would hear me scream if I had to, but there are no security cameras. Mr. X sees to all the details, and I just oblige. I call him to let him know when I've arrived.

Before he started this Bosley vigilante gig, he was top of his class at MIT. He dropped out in his senior year, even though he was on track to graduate with honors. Never talked about why, but he isn't the sort who does well under pressure, and he's not one for structure. He does much better when he's free to go fully rogue.

It's been years since I've seen him in person, though sometimes I catch a glimpse of a car passing by, or the back of a familiar head in a crowded place, and I know that he's nearby. Watching out. Making sure I'm safe.

I lie when Waylen asks what I'm looking at. He's always found Mr. X's presence to be intrusive.

"Your new partner is pulling up now," Mr. X tells me. "The white Mercedes."

Like clockwork, the pristine SUV pulls into the lot. The windows are tinted, and there's a *Ballerinas Do It on Their Toes* bumper sticker on the rear.

"You're sure this is your genius?" I ask.

"Don't judge," Mr. X chides. "You hate it when people underestimate you. Don't underestimate her."

"I love being underestimated, actually. Makes it easier to strike."

He doesn't laugh at my joke. He only tells me, "Good

luck," and disconnects before I can even ask my new partner's name.

Waylen always worries for my safety on these missions, but I have a lot of faith in Mr. X's measures to keep all of us protected. Myself in particular, given what we went through in our childhood, after our parents died. I know that he's somewhere out of sight, watching everything. I know that he will know just what to do if things go south. That's if I don't stab any wayward assailants with the retractable knife I keep in my pocket first.

I step out into the night and rap a knuckle against the tinted window of the Mercedes. I never know what to expect from Mr. X's finds—Mira Hart had surprised me by being so unassuming and soft-spoken. Before that, a brawny home care worker who could lift you over her shoulder with one arm. And of course, Waylen, the one I ended up marrying. So, when the window rolls down, I'm prepared for anything.

Anything, that is, but the perfect blond curls and well-made-up face of Elodie Blevins.

She's just as surprised to see me, judging by her gaping expression. "Yes?" she says, perhaps thinking this is some sort of mix-up. I'm not the partner she's been told to expect—I must be here out of pure coincidence, she's thinking. Maybe I moonlight as a meter maid.

In response, I give her a timid wave, reminiscent of what Collette does when I drop her off at a classmate's sleepover party she didn't really want to attend. A wave that says *I'm doomed* and *Please save me* all at once.

Her gaze flattens. "You?" she says.

My phone buzzes in my pocket. I glance at the screen. A text from Mr. X reads: **Play nice.**

"I don't think we've been properly introduced," I say, flashing a smile that could never compare in brightness to Elodie's bleached teeth. I extend a hand through her window. "I'm Margaux. Our girls are in the same grade."

Elodie recoils as though she thinks I'll try to steal the tube of Milani Color Statement lipstick and mascara wand from her cupholder. Then she sighs. Her hand is buttery soft when she shakes mine with it. "Get in," she says. "I'll drive. After seeing how you park, I don't want to know how you operate a vehicle when it's in motion."

I don't make waves because I suspect this is what Mr. X wanted. I never know exactly where he's watching me from, but I can be confident he keeps a protective eye on all of his employees—all nine or ten of us. He has a small network of spies he trusts. I have no idea what he pays the others, but I know that it must come out of his own inheritance. He doesn't want the money. Like me, it makes him think about that awful night, so he only takes what he needs to keep his operation running.

Fifteen years in business and none of us has ever sustained so much as a workplace papercut. We are Mr. X's perfect chess pieces: He knows just where to place us, and he can anticipate every move we'll make.

I climb into the passenger seat of Elodie's SUV, overwhelmed by the chemical sweetness of her various beauty products. There are two car seats in the back row, which has been recently vacuumed and shows no sign of a single crumb, smudge, or spilled juice box.

She's too perfect. She reminds me of myself. I always make sure all the skeletons are in the closet before I entertain guests, too.

We ride in silence for a while. Then I ask, "What do you know about the client?" at the same time Elodie asks me, "How many kids do you have?"

"Collette's an only child," I say. What I don't add is that Collette wasn't part of my original life plan. Falling in love, getting married—none of this was in the plan. It just sort of happened, and here we are.

If Waylen and I had been able to restrain ourselves, we never would have had the one-night stand that conceived her. I would be living in an apartment somewhere, far from suburbs and yoga classes and social cliques. There was a time when I would have been happy with this—or at least, I would have told myself I was happy. But now that I have Collette, I can't imagine being without her. I could leave everything else behind, but not her. It's terrifying to love anything this much, and I'm in no hurry to double those worries.

"Oh," Elodie says, pityingly. "Fertility troubles? I get it." She plows right through formalities. "Todd and I had to do IVF the second time around, and that's how we got the twins." She laughs dryly. "So, *now* we're done."

"Have you been briefed about the client?" I try again. I've learned to change this particular subject seamlessly. The trick is to ask the other person a question that gets them talking a lot.

"Sister of some tech billionaire who claims he stole her idea and she wants revenge," Elodie says. "Between you and me, I don't know if there's even a case. It sounds like she's just jealous he's got all that money and she has nothing. Maybe he's bad at sharing."

"Mr. X vets his clients well," I say. "I'm sure there's something."

We roll to a stop, and Elodie glances at me. Her diamond ring catches the red of the traffic light and glows like blood. Everything about her is so . . . shiny. So practiced. It makes me wonder what she really looks like when she wipes her makeup off.

"You've worked for him a long time, right?" she asks.

"Since the beginning," I say, intrigued by what this small bit of seniority may get me. She seems interested. Every partnership has a power dynamic, and I know when to take the lead and when to hang back and wait for my turn to run point. With Mira Hart it was easy—she was meek, nervous, and eager to be done with things. Elodie, though, is type A and very green. It's a combination that could be catastrophic if not handled correctly. I'll need to make sure she doesn't get ahead of herself, but also be mindful not to come across as so bossy that she starts contradicting me to assert herself.

"He doesn't like to get his hands dirty," I go on. "But he knows what he's doing when he assigns us to a client."

The light turns green and Elodie glances at the map on her phone. We're headed downtown, and the route says there are twenty minutes left. Of course the client won't live close to us. There's a lot of corruption in the suburbs, but you don't play around where you sleep.

"I suppose he picked me for this one because I'm a people person," Elodie says. "I used to sell makeup out of catalogs way before social media. Had to do it in person on campus."

"That must be it."

Another glance as she appraises me. "What did you do, anyway? He said this is a onetime deal and then I'm out scot-free. What's he got on you that you've been working with him for all these years?"

"It was a string of petty crimes," I say. A partial truth is as effective as a lie, and twice as easy to manage because it doesn't require a good memory. "I paid my dues. I just like the work."

That much is true. I had the option to get out long ago. Waylen begs me all the time. It chips away at the fragile edges of our marriage like someone taking a chisel to the borders of a picture frame.

I could be like Elodie, fully committed to the PTA lifestyle, a helicopter parent, a traffic director for the school pickup lines. I could have a little whistle around my neck and write strongly worded emails to the parents whose SUVs have crude bumper stickers. Don't they realize that we're all trying to raise a generation of exceptional children?

A part of me wants it, but only as a facade. This life I'm living is the perfect place to hide, and the best part is that it doesn't rub off as easily as Elodie's makeup at the end of the day. It conceals the real me—the ugly, dark secret bearer who can never be redeemed, even if I did put in my time.

"Tell the truth," I heard when I was growing up. By my parents, and then by my social worker. And then by the court system. But I learned the hard way that telling the truth doesn't mean you'll be believed. Sometimes the truth needs a little embellishment in order to be accepted.

The conversation turns light. We talk about our daughters. Collette will hate me for it, but I set up a date for her to tutor Finnegan with her math. She's too much of a loner as it is, and she needs to learn the value of social allies.

I hardly notice that we've edged into an unsavory part of town until I see the worry on Elodie's face. "Next time we should use a rental car," she says. "I think it's one of these."

We've pulled into a complex of small brick condos in various stages of disrepair. Unit 5 is one of the few with any lights on inside. Once the car is parked, Elodie and I pull our phones out as they buzz in unison. Mr. X letting us know that he's tracking us and that he'll make sure we're safe.

I text him: **Don't let anything happen to Elodie's car. She'll quit on the spot.**

He replies with a thumbs-up.

"You ask the questions," I tell Elodie. I want to see how good she is at thinking on her feet. "If you need me to jump in, we should establish a code."

"I'll ask what time it is in London," Elodie suggests. "She's from England, right? So that'll be your cue to jump in and save me."

I nod. "Perfect."

Elodie strides ahead of me, but I can see by her posture that her confidence is shaken. While she takes a deep breath to compose herself, I reach past her and knock.

The door cracks open, tethered to the frame by a chain. A pair of the greenest eyes I've ever seen greets us, so vibrant and piercing that I feel like they're accusing me of something. The woman's eyes look at me and then at Elodie.

"Yes?" she says. Polite. British. "Can I help you?"

It's dark now, the Connecticut autumn sky a particular type of black that only happens this time of year. The flickering streetlamp does little to illuminate us.

Elodie stiffens her shoulders, mustering up some renewed confidence. "We were sent to help you address a complaint," she says. "I'm Elodie. This is Margaux. I believe you spoke with our supervisor earlier this week."

We never use last names—only first. At the start, Mr. X tested the use of pseudonyms, but it went bad when one client did an extensive online search and started calling a woman with the same first name, convinced she was one of us. Almost blew our entire cover when the woman threatened to call the police for harassment.

The door closes. Elodie gives me a quizzical look, but I grab her wrist when she tries to knock again. A moment later, there's the clattering of a chain, and then the door opens fully, revealing the woman inside the house.

Erin Casimir, our new client, is tall and thin and elegant against the backdrop of her cheap rental condo. It's evident that she was raised to carry herself with dignity and grace—it's not her fault that things all went to shit when she got older.

In our briefing, Mr. X told me that she's from an upper middle-class family in London. Her older brother came to America to study at Yale while she was working toward a medical degree in St. George's. After her brother hit it big, something happened. The specifics of that "something" are a question mark, but what we do know is that she dropped out of medical school, became estranged from her family, and ended up here.

"Come in," she says, peering briefly outside as though to make sure nobody is watching us.

Erin is our client, but I already suspect that her tech billionaire brother is where the real story lies. Does she think he's watching us? Is her condo being monitored?

Inside, it's clear that Erin is working on a serious budget. The couch is stained and secondhand, though she's made an effort to shampoo and vacuum it. The same can be said of the gray shag carpet. Someone is shouting on the other side of the shared wall. A door slams, and Elodie flinches. I wonder if she's going to be able to handle this.

I gauge Erin as she pours three mugs of hot water from a kettle on her tiny outdated stove and then steeps three tea bags for us and brings them to the couch on a cheap silver platter.

"Right," she says, sitting on the armchair across from us. "I trust you know the situation, then?"

Elodie leans forward. "Your brother invented a budgeting app, Budgie, a few years ago. It was featured on *Good Morning America*, and that's when it took off. Through a string of investments, it's made him very wealthy and he landed in *Forbes* for becoming a billionaire by age thirty-five."

"*I* invented the app," Erin says, and she appears startled by her own outburst. "And I did it all by myself, before this AI nonsense started to take over the tech world. Our parents wanted us both to be doctors—our father is a cardiologist. All our lives, he told us that the only way he'd support us is if we went into medicine. He has this perfect dream, I suppose."

I watch her cradle her mug of tea. Her hands are shaking.

Elodie has the sense not to speak; she sees that we're already getting straight to the point.

"I was always more into engineering and programming, but given my father's demands, I was forced to treat it like a hobby. But I had fun playing around with app ideas, and I even made a little money." Her eyes light up as she speaks about it, the passion coming back to her as she relives it. "A lot of big ideas start in a dorm room."

"Even for a hobby, it would be a lot of work," Elodie says, validating her feelings.

"It was." Erin sips her tea. "And I didn't expect it to be profitable. Most apps weren't back then. I never even tried to get Budgie in the app store. After a few months—well, I got inundated with school and I didn't have time to go back to it. But Bertram"—now her expression turns sour—"that's my brother. He stole my work and passed it off as his own. I had no idea he'd done it until suddenly it was everywhere. Imagine my shock when a friend linked me to an American talk show I'd never heard of, and there was my brother on the stage, making up some phony story about how he'd come up with the idea."

Her hands are shaking again, the rage barely contained in her thin frame.

I had worried about Elodie's ability to handle this, but now I see that she's exactly in her element with the opportunity to gossip. She effortlessly engages Erin by asking about her childhood—the overlooked younger sibling to a golden-child brother. He's a narcissist, Erin says—no, no, a sociopath. But do her parents see it? Of course not. They love him. The whole *world* loves him.

By the time Erin has finished her tale, she regards Elodie like they're old friends. "Can you help me?" she asks.

"Of course we're going to help you," Elodie says, clasping a hand over Erin's. "We'll make him pay."

"How?" Erin asks. The emotions are raw, and she's shed the cautious numbness she greeted us with at the door. Recalling all that she's lost has been too much for her to contain. It's not just the billion dollars her brother made off her hard work, but the love of her family, the respect of her peers. Even her own friends have distanced themselves, accusing her of being too angry, too obsessive, for not just letting it go.

"Hey, M," Elodie says, acknowledging me for the first time since this impromptu therapy session began. "What time do you think it is in London right now?"

"They're six hours ahead, at least until Daylight Savings," I say. "But I think we're better off keeping things local." I look to Erin. "Your brother lives here in the States, yes?"

"In the Atlantic Bay Towers in Westport," she says sourly. "He's got a penthouse where he likes to spend his winters."

I lay out my plan. It's just a little something I came up with while Erin and Elodie were commiserating. Bertram is private; all my Google searches this afternoon came up empty when I looked for personal details. There are no hints at what his private life is like. And I've never been to the Atlantic Bay Towers, but I have driven past the place, and I know that it's a tacky modern skyrise with a waterfront view and guards at the door. No worries. Mr. X will be able to get me in.

"We'll show up as reporters writing a story," I say. "Elodie will be my supervisor. I'm a new hire trying to prove my worth at the paper so I can get hired officially. While I'm interviewing him, Elodie will make some excuse to leave the room. She'll look for anything usable in his computer."

"How will you get into his computer?" Erin asks.

"We have our ways."

"I'll bring a dummy laptop to replace his, and we'll steal the real one?" Elodie guesses. It's a genius idea, though I'm not sure if we'd be overpromising to agree to it. We don't even know the model he has, much less where to get another one. But I like her confidence, and I've never been one to let semantics get in the way.

"We'll adapt to what's available and find a way," I promise her.

Erin looks skeptical. "What if you don't get what you need?"

"We will," Elodie says. "We've never failed before." She's so good at acting confident, I would never believe this was her first job if I didn't know better. On the drive here, she was nervously scrolling through notes she'd typed out on her phone to prepare.

"He will have an opportunity to redeem himself," I say. "I have to tell you that, in the name of full disclosure. That's how we operate. Once we have the proof that he stole your idea, we offer him a chance to come clean. If he takes it, he can redeem himself by giving you back the credit for your idea and returning the money to his investors. And if he doesn't—he rots in a federal prison."

Even as I say this, I'm struck by what a simple job this

will be. Two spoiled rich kids duking it out over a family fortune. It should be easy enough to solve in under a week. I can't imagine why Mr. X thought it was worth our time. He always goes for the challenges—the true puzzles of the world that can't be solved by a simple police investigation.

Mr. X doesn't exactly advertise his services. He works purely by word of mouth on the dark web, and he only accepts payment when the work is completed, leaving us off the hook if we can't complete a job—which has never happened to me.

Erin seems satisfied, though. To her, this will mean the world. She'll get her life back, or her reputation, at the very least. Maybe Mr. X has a particular soft spot for her, or maybe he's getting soft as time goes on. Although Mr. X stays objective in all his jobs, something feels personal about this one. He has always loved technology, and while Budgie may not be of any special interest to him, he holds a special disdain for what billionaires are doing to the world. Nailing Bertram Casimir can satisfy some of his repressed rage.

When we were kids, he was obsessed with electronics, especially computers. He wanted to do something to better the world, my brother. In his own way, he is. But I know that he'll never think he's doing enough. He scoops one bucket from the ocean, and it starts to rain.

"Oh, there's one other thing," Erin says, just as I'm reaching for the doorknob. Elodie and I both turn, and I think Elodie feels the same shift in the air that I do. Erin's face has gone very sober. "When Bertram moved here, he wasn't alone. He was dating a dear friend of mine, Annie. She disowned me during my spat with my brother, but we'd known each other and been close like sisters since primary school and I still love her anyway."

"You want revenge against her, too?" Elodie guesses. "She was part of this?"

"No." Erin shakes her head earnestly. "It's just that nobody's heard from her in months. I've checked with her family and it appears I'm not the only one she's cut out of her life, but I think it's more than that. Nobody has heard from her at all, and nobody has seen her. I think—" She hesitates. It takes effort for her to spit out the words, "I think something awful may have happened."

"Awful?" I ask, although I'm beginning to understand. There it is. The real reason Mr. X sent us out here. It isn't just some stolen app and a greedy billionaire. Still, I need her to say it. "What do you mean 'awful'?"

"I think—" She's wringing her hands, once again the nervous shut-in who first greeted us. "I can't believe I'm saying this. I hate my brother, but I'd never think him capable . . . I just, I think he's done something to her. I think she may be dead."

FOUR

"Holy shit," Elodie says once we're back inside her SUV. "Holy *shit.*"

I don't answer right away. I'm too busy replaying everything about Erin's demeanor. She was strange, although that isn't unexpected. Living in one of Connecticut's wealthiest suburbs, I've met my share of quirky rich people, though Erin is the first to have lost everything. She must really believe she's right if she was willing to lose her family over it. If she just called her parents and admitted fault, they'd welcome her back.

"Do you think he's a murderer?" Elodie asks.

"I don't think anything yet," I say. "I have to meet him."

She taps her finger against the steering wheel. "How are you so calm about this? What if he tries to kill *us?*"

"In a secure building filled with security cameras? I wouldn't worry about that. Besides, you forget that we're always being watched. We'll be safe."

She shakes her head. "You sound awfully confident."

I stare pensively through the window as we pull out of the driveway. My phone is buzzing in my pocket. Mr. X will want to know how it went, and what we're planning, so I'll have to spend the ride thinking about my strategy.

My phone buzzes again. I slide it out of my pocket and look at the screen. His latest text: **Give E a chance. Let her in on whatever you're thinking.**

The message couldn't be clearer. I do have a habit of taking over these missions—but only because Mr. X pairs me with the green ones. God, Waylen was so sweet and clueless when we did ours together. But he proved himself to be more than meets the eye. There's an edge underneath the surface that only I can see. He tries to pretend it isn't there, but I know. It's part of why I said "I do."

Still, Elodie did prove herself by handling that interview with Erin. It's only fair that I give her a chance. "You've heard of 'good cop, bad cop,' right?" I ask her.

She snaps to attention. "Huh? Yeah, sure. Of course." She's still reeling from the chance that our mark is a murderer.

"We'll need to go in there with a strategy when we interview him," I say.

"So, good reporter, bad reporter?" Elodie asks.

"Not exactly. More like super confident, cocky reporter, and bumbling, nervous assistant reporter."

Something about this makes her smile. "Sounds like the script for a Meryl Streep movie."

Over the remainder of our drive, we work out that she—of course—will be my confident supervisor. I'll bumble my way through the interview, and as I do, I'll get a sense of what our dear Bertram Casimir responds to. If he's irritated, I'll dial it back. If he likes the attention, I'll show interest in whatever he has to say. Improv is where I really shine, but I can tell that Elodie does best with structure. As soon as the car is parked, she's whipping out her phone to punch in some notes in her memo app.

"Wait," she says as I open the door to get out. I turn to face her, surprised that she's extended a manicured hand out to me. She gives me a firm handshake. "I have to say, Margaux, it's a pleasure doing business with you."

The house is dark when I tiptoe through the front door. From the foyer I can see into the kitchen, where Waylen has left a plate of food for me, wrapped up in foil. His way of reminding me that I missed dinner.

He's still awake. I hear him tapping away at his computer, the floorboards groaning as he rolls his desk chair across them.

In the kitchen, I make as little noise as possible and heat up the plate of seared tuna and stir-fried vegetables. The clock on the microwave reads 11:59. At least I kept my promise to be home before midnight.

Waylen is still mad at me. I can feel it lingering in the air like a thick and pungent perfume. When he's upset, he makes himself practically invisible. The kitchen is spotless—all the dishes washed and put away, the sink empty, the counters wiped clean. He's purged any trace of his presence while I was away.

He's been pushing me to retire ever since he got out of the game. I suppose he thought that Collette would be enough to change me. He views my job as a torrid affair, like it's a lover that I can't seem to leave. He despises Mr. X for the role he plays in this as well.

It doesn't matter how much time I give him or that I spend my days fully dedicated to our daughter's student career—even tonight with Elodie, I secured a plan to keep her in good social standing by offering her up as a tutor. It wouldn't matter even if I only snuck out of the house long after he was asleep and returned before he woke up. He won't be satisfied until I give it up; we've had enough fights on the topic. But he's run out of ideas to try to wear me down. Maybe that scares him.

I look up when I hear footsteps coming down the stairs. That will be him, with a disappointed, weary expression and greeting me with a sigh. Maybe he'll apologize for being upset with me earlier, or maybe he'll just ask for my opinion on how well he seasoned the fish.

But the figure that emerges from the darkness of the hallway is Collette, her hair tousled with sleep. "Mom?" she says softly. "Did you just get home?" She climbs into a chair across from me.

"I was working on some PTA things and it ran a little late," I lie. I have worked hard not to shatter the perfect image that Collette has of her life. She doesn't even know that Waylen and I argue. She's smart, though, and she's getting older. She's bound to pick up on it eventually—and when that day comes, she'll want to know just what we're fighting about. "Actually, I spent the evening with Mrs. Blevins—you know, Finnegan's mom. She's not so bad when she's not wearing a whistle around her neck and directing traffic."

Collette wrinkles her nose, but whatever she's thinking, she's too tactful to say. My daughter isn't the sort to make waves. She's quiet, polite, and so reserved that she intrigues her classmates. Rather than a shy little girl who's easy to bully, they see a pretty, well-dressed, well-groomed peer whose social fate depends on what she chooses to say—only she never says anything at all. Nobody knows what to make of her, and there's power in that. Even I don't know what to make of her half the time.

But she is observant. I know that much.

"We thought it would be nice if you girls got to know each other a little better," I say, cautiously broaching the subject. "So, you're going to tutor her in math after school one day next week. She's struggling, and it's your best subject."

Collette raises her head. "I can't stand Finnegan." There's only the barest whine to her words. "She's the worst."

"How is she 'the worst'?"

"Mom, you don't know what it's like at school," Collette says. "It's like a vat of boiling lobsters meets *The Hunger Games.*"

"You know," I say, "sometimes when people are mean, they're just criticizing the things they don't like about themselves."

Collette huffs. "She must *really* hate herself, then," she mumbles.

"Try to make the best of it," I say.

Collette crosses her arms and leans back in her seat. I wish that she'd say whatever she's thinking. I wish that she'd argue, that she'd insult me—anything.

"I'm doing this for you," I tell her. "Mrs. Blevins has a lot of pull with the PTA. She's going to handle a lot of casting for the upcoming Christmas play. Maybe she can help you get a good role as a way of saying thank-you."

This does nothing to soften the sudden edge to Collette's expression.

"You want to get into a good college, don't you?" I say. "Prep work doesn't start in high school. They're going to look back at your entire student transcript. Tutoring, starring in plays—all of that will look great, especially if you still have your eye on a theater major."

Collette's voice is so soft that I almost don't hear it. "Stop."

"What?"

"Stop it," she says, a little louder now. "You know Finnegan sucks, and Mrs. Blevins sucks. You're lying about wanting us to be friends. You lie all the time."

"No, I—"

"You even lie to Dad," she fires back, before I can argue. "You didn't want him to know that I went to the trial today. You wanted me to tell him we went to the dentist. Why wouldn't we just tell him the truth?"

My eyes dart to the doorway. I'm almost expecting Waylen to be standing there, waiting for an answer, as though they've formed an alliance against me and planned to strike. But it's just Collette, the living evidence of the one time in my life I was foolish enough to fall in love.

I want—not for the first time—to tell her everything. I want to tell her about Mr. X in particular, who asks about her when he's brazen enough to be vulnerable with me. I want to tell her that the world is rife with injustices just like the one we learned about in the courtroom today, and that life is nothing like the fantasy books she reads: Sometimes the good guy doesn't win. Sometimes good doesn't prevail. Sometimes the world is cruel and ugly and filled with villains who get off scot-free.

I want to tell her that I can't fix all of it but that I do whatever small bit I can to right the wrongs that are out there. I want to tell her that motherhood didn't make me soft the way that Waylen hoped. It made me hard. It filled me with rage and defiance and a passion that scares me even now, because it hasn't dulled, it hasn't faded, and I know that it never will.

But all I say is, "Your father doesn't understand." I hate how patronizing I sound. So I add, "He doesn't want you to know about crimes like that, but I disagree. I think you should. I think knowing what's out there will keep you safe."

Collette frowns pensively. It's quiet for a long time after that. She watches as I eat what's left on the plate, even though my appetite is gone, and I want to go online and do a bit more research on Bertram before going to bed.

"Can I go to another one?" Collette asks.

I look up at her.

"Trials," she presses. "I had fun."

After dinner, I brush her hair, braid it, and spray it with a water-and-conditioner solution she found the recipe for online. It promises to add volume, and who am I to argue? I smile at her. It is nice, I think, when things are normal.

By the time she's settled in, the house is quiet. Waylen has left his office and climbed into bed, though I don't believe he's asleep.

I sit on my side of the bed and watch the rise and fall of

his chest. It's only in the still, late, dark quiet of the night that I can't hide from myself. That's when I love him the most, in a way that cuts through all the layers I wear like armor. I love that he cares about Collette and me—really cares about us. I even love that he's jealous of my job, because it means he wants me to be safe. I love that this life we've built makes me feel normal, like the fire never happened. When I'm with him, it's a preview of who I might have been if things had gone differently.

When we got married, he and I stood at the altar envisioning different things, surrounded on all sides by lilies and violets. He wanted domestic bliss, and I anticipated something more like Mr. and Mrs. Smith.

A long time ago, before all of this, I could have settled for an easy life like the one I pretend to lead, one where the biggest problem is whether we can afford a new water heater, or how to survive a holiday with my in-laws.

Waylen doesn't know about what happened to me between then and now. He doesn't know about the trial, the accusations, and all the work it took for me to reinvent myself.

Tell him, something within me whispers, the way it often does. But I push the thought away. Even if I'm living a lie, I don't want to lose it. I don't want to lose him.

FIVE

When the drop-off line is finally empty, and the last child is safely through the double doors of the school, I wait for Elodie. Her domineering personality may not have earned her a lot of heartfelt friendships, but it has gifted her with social connections. The other parking police volunteers flock around her like crows on carrion, all trying to maintain her favor.

It turns out she's especially close to Principal Wheeler, though she's vague on the specifics. And her husband is coaching the middle school soccer team and has a lot of say in which teams will receive funding for new equipment in the spring. Where did she come from? This magnet capable of making us all orbit around her like planets around a burning new sun.

I'm still deciding whether I like her, or how much of a fool I'd be to trust her.

This morning we texted back and forth about our cover

story. Turns out she has an interest in interior design and she wants to come along with me as I consult with a client about new ceiling fixtures. At least, that's the story she's telling the clucking hens as she says her goodbyes and then makes her way to my car. She's still smiling and waving as she climbs into the passenger seat and pulls the door shut.

"God, they're boring," she says. "But at least they're not catty like the ones in LA."

"They're still catty," I assure her. "Just wait until Girl Scout cookie season, and try to dodge any flying foldout tables."

She snorts. "I still like Connecticut, even if it's cold," she says, prying off her gloves so she can warm her fingers by the heating vent on the dash. "The beach sort of sucks, but you can't beat the lobster rolls."

"I used to live on the West Coast," I say.

"Oh yeah?"

"Well, Oregon," I say. "Some small town nobody's ever heard of. It's where I was born."

"Never been," Elodie admits. "I hear Portland is—weird."

I laugh. "It was nowhere near Portland, so I couldn't tell you."

"So, is your family still out there?"

The inevitable question, and one that I was anticipating. Over the years, I've learned that lying outright is more trouble than it's worth. The best approach—depending on what the situation calls for—is to only share the information that accomplishes your goals. Right now, I want Elodie to trust me. I want her to see me as something other than a catty PTA mom like the ones who are kissing her ass in the drop-off line. I want to be just vulnerable enough that she doesn't pity me, but begins to contemplate sharing her own secrets. If I do it right, I won't have to ask her a thing. She'll start to talk.

"My family's dead," I say. "My parents, at least. I have a brother, but we don't keep in touch the way that we used to."

Elodie blinks, startled. But before she can offer up any uncomfortable condolences, I go on. "It happened when I was little. I barely remember them." I'm bordering on lying, so I deflect. "I was raised by grandparents. That's how I ended up on the East Coast, but really, I stay for the frozen sidewalks and all those festive construction cones."

I feel an odd satisfaction that I've rendered her speechless. Or maybe it's just that she doesn't want to be rude by saying the wrong thing. Either way, it's a victory. I'm merciful, though, and I go on to explain how my upbringing brought me to this point. I paint the picture of a troubled youth turned teenage delinquent. The petty crimes, the drugs, the brief stints in jail, and Mr. X offering to bail me out if I agreed to do things on his terms.

It's more than most people get to know about me. Even Collette has been spared the details, though I imagine I'll tell her one day. Right now, she's young enough not to realize that I was somebody before I was her mother.

"I had you all wrong," Elodie says.

"Yeah?" I ask. "What did you think when you met me?"

"New money," she says. "Rich husband. Your day job is interior decorating, which—let's face it—is a hobby someone does when they don't really need the money."

"Interior decorating may just be a front, but you'd be surprised. Especially weddings and events. You can make a killing."

"Oh, when I tell people about today, I'll say we made a fortune," Elodie says with a flourish. She is comfortable wearing masks and slips into them so easily. I can see why Mr. X likes her so much. Even I had underestimated her for a shallow suburbanite.

To pass the time as we drive through the richest area in the state, we make a game out of counting women in wool coats walking golden retrievers and poodle mixes. I win with three labradoodles on my side of the street.

When we arrive at the Atlantic Bay Towers, I don't even need the GPS to confirm that we're in the right place. The building is a garish new construction made of gleaming white brick. It's meant to look antiquated so that it fits in with the rest of the city, but its newness is as apparent as a throbbing sore thumb.

Elodie shrugs out of her coat and tosses it into the back seat. Underneath, she's hidden from the PTA moms a decidedly un-Elodie outfit: a houndstooth pencil skirt and white blouse with ruffles running down the seam of the buttons. She winds her hair into a bun and uses the visor mirror to apply a shade of deep red lipstick. "I'm your boss, right?" she says. "So I should look like I take myself too seriously." She glances at me. "I draw the line at coffee breath, though."

"Every bad supervisor I ever had seemed to bathe in Calvin Klein Eternity," I say. My own costume is a bit more subtle. I'm wearing a green tweed dress from Tuckernuck, costume pearls around my neck. While Elodie winds her hair into a bun, I let mine down. It is the hair of a chimera, changing me into someone new with little effort. It is long, red, and filled with curls and waves of different sizes and shapes, as though a dozen different dollmakers couldn't agree on how to weave it.

It's important to be aware of your assets—to let every feature work for you, and to work with them, not against them. I can never be sexy or upper-crust like Elodie. But I can be—as she put it—new money. Doe-eyed, baby-faced, unaware of my own sexuality. I suspect it's the kind of girl Bertram Casimir would find endearing—someone he can overpower and impress, promise to take care of and then hold captive. His own personal Rapunzel.

When I take off my wedding band, Elodie whistles. "Your character isn't married?" she asks. "Who knew you could be so . . . bad."

"No." I hold up my naked hand, giving my best virginal expression. "I'm very, very good."

Plenty of jobs would require one to remove a wedding band. A pastry chef. A surgeon. Someone who tests metal detectors. It can feel weird to remove something that's meant to symbolize eternity. But the baffling part for me is always putting it back on, like I'm agreeing to my vows all over again each time.

"I did some more research," I say. "I think I should talk to him while you rifle through his laptop."

She shows me the thumb drive she's been carrying in her pocket. "I was able to download a software that will allow me to copy the documents on his laptop even if it's password protected. It's some kind of fail-safe in case you get locked out of your computer."

"That's smart," I say. "I was thinking we'd have to replace the laptop itself with a lookalike."

"Nah, it's a piece of cake," Elodie says. "It's how I was able to access all the records and take down that pyramid scheme I was working for in California. Bastards convinced me to invest five grand in their snake oil."

I can't help laughing. "That's *beyond* petty. That's—"

"Beating the one percent at their own game," she says, rubbing her fingers together in a money-counting gesture.

We make our way into the lobby. It's gaudy, with marble tiles and a trickling fountain of a spitting, naked cherub. Elodie confidently takes the lead, striding ahead of me on stilettos that echo in the cavernous space.

"We're here for Mr. Casimir," she tells the man at the front desk. He's young, possibly a recent college grad. "We're his nine o'clock."

The man flips through a paper ledger, and after a beat he narrows his eyes thoughtfully. "I don't see anything for today."

"Really?" Elodie tries to peer over the desk, and the man is visibly uncomfortable as he tilts the ledger away from us. "Check tomorrow. Maybe something got messed up." She turns to me. "You booked it, right?" she says, waggling her brows at me.

"Of course," I say, and my nervous stammer isn't entirely an act. Oh, she's good.

"Um." The man, who is in no way employed by Elodie, is as unnerved as if she held his job on the line. "I am terribly sorry, but there's nothing here."

Elodie turns to me and holds out her hand expectantly.

"Show me the appointment confirmation email on your phone," she says.

I make a show of scrolling through my phone, looking flustered.

"You didn't get a confirmation," Elodie says flatly. "What did I tell you? *Always* get a written confirmation."

"I'm sorry, I—"

"That's just great!" Elodie cries. "You know, I took a chance hiring you for my assistant, and in case you haven't noticed, the economy is in the toilet. You're damn lucky to get a salaried job with nothing but your useless business degree. And you can't even get a simple confirmation?"

I lean against the counter like it's the only raft in a choppy sea, and I give the man my biggest puppy-dog eyes. "Help," I mouth to him, as Elodie stomps away on those heels to pace the lobby.

He takes pity and nods at me. "What were you here to see him about?"

"We're press," I say. "The *New Haven Register*." I raise my shoulders sheepishly. "A small thing, you've probably never heard of. That's why this interview was such a huge get for me." I sniffle. "I, like, really need this job."

He raises his voice loud enough for Elodie to hear. "Let me see if there's something I can do."

Elodie is burning with enraged Karen energy that manages to terrify even me. It's no wonder the drop-off line at the school has gotten so much more efficient since she took over.

The man murmurs softly into the receiver, turning his back to us. Elodie winks at me, and I can't hide my smile. This is more fun than I thought it would be.

I nudge her with my shoulder and nod to the security camera watching us from a far corner of the room. Mr. X has no doubt found a way to hack into it and watch us.

The man at the desk hangs up the phone, and I go back to looking like I'm on the verge of tears. Elodie has not dropped her act for even a second.

"Mr. Casimir says he'll speak with you."

I clasp my hands together gratefully. "Thank you. Thank you so much."

Mr. X has been able to surveil the building. He tells me that Bertram doesn't get any visitors besides grocery delivery, and he almost never leaves. Even if he's a total recluse, it's possible he's just lonely enough to entertain the occasional stranger.

"You're damn lucky, Margaux." Elodie is enjoying her character a little *too* much.

When the elevator doors open, the button for the penthouse is already lit up, preprogrammed by the man at the desk. Security at this place is tight. I've been in luxury buildings before, but nothing like this. I wonder what other sorts of millionaires live here, or if Bertram is the only billionaire. Likely so. It's odd that he would end up in a place as remote as southern Connecticut just to watch the seasons change. He could have picked one of those dystopian marble-slab high-rises in NYC, just ninety minutes west of here.

The elevator slows to a stop, and just before the doors open, I tell her, "While you're doing that, I'll finesse him."

"Good idea," she agrees. "I would probably just scare him. Men always think I'm going to bite their heads off for some reason."

"Some mysteries will never be solved."

Elodie bursts into laughter but shuts her mouth abruptly when the doors slide open. She's back in character.

We're standing in a marble foyer now, with nothing but the door to Bertram's penthouse. Another camera stares at us from the ceiling with its unblinking eye. There's yet another camera beside the door—for Bertram's own private viewing. I step forward and knock.

It takes a minute for him to come to the door. Although it's late morning, billionaires don't keep the same schedule as the rest of us. He could have been napping, or playing golf, or rolling around in a hot tub full of gold coins while models poured champagne directly into his mouth.

My first thought when I lay eyes upon the famed Bertram Casimir is how—ordinary he looks. Handsome, to be sure, with glittering green eyes and a manicured beard, dark hair and a solid build. But for all the hype in the media, I'd expected him to be shrouded in beams of holy light.

He looks at me and then at Elodie with the smooth demeanor of someone who is used to the press, and simultaneously the wariness of someone who keeps his cards close to the vest.

I extend a hand. "Margaux Green," I say, giving a fake last name. "*New Haven Register.* Thank you so much for speaking with us; I'm so sorry for the mix-up."

His hand is cool and soft. His smile is guarded but charming.

Where is your girlfriend, Bertram? I think, as he and Elodie exchange pleasantries and he invites us inside. *Did you use these hands to kill her?*

There wasn't much on the internet about his girlfriend, a thirty-year-old Londoner named Annie Clarke. I could find only one photo of her, taken at a distance by a paparazzo as she and Bertram crossed the street in downtown Westport. They were holding hands. She was wearing large sunglasses and a beige trench coat. When I looked at the image, I tried to read her body language. Was she happy? Scared? Had they argued before leaving the house, or had he professed his undying love to her as he served her breakfast in bed in their penthouse apartment? But there was nothing to interpret, like all things in his life, another mystery.

Besides, I haven't written Annie off as dead, like Erin fears she is. It could have been a private breakup. He could have paid her off so that she didn't run to the press with the intimate details of his very private life.

And it *is* a very private life. Bertram's apartment is as sterile as a furniture showroom. The furniture is unrumpled, a gas fire burning neatly in the hearth. There's not a single book or errant coffee mug, not a photo on the walls to give any indication of who he is.

Elodie loves the place and tells him as much. But he doesn't acknowledge the compliment. Instead, he guides us to the white faux-leather couch and offers us a drink.

"What are you having?" I ask him.

"Espresso," he says. "Best source of caffeine. I don't buy into energy drinks."

"That sounds wonderful," Elodie says, speaking for both of us. "We'll have the same."

He moves for the kitchen, and I catch a glimpse of it

through the doorway. Equally sterile, with small, sleek appliances designed to fit compactly on the open shelving.

I pull out my notebook.

"Where do you think his computer would be?" I whisper.

Elodie nods to the hallway. "One of those rooms. Maybe a home office? Bedroom? I'll need some time to check. Can you distract him?"

Bertram returns to us with a silver tray containing three neatly presented one-ounce cups of espresso. A lemon rind sits on each of the saucers. Of course, I'd bet he has some pretentious story about how he learned to appreciate espresso in Italy. I'd bet he's filled with boring stories about where he's been and what he's seen, all of which conveniently leave out any shred of his own personality.

As he's setting the tray before us, I stand, and just as I'm raving about how frothy the crema looks, as though I've never seen coffee before, I bump the tray and send the little ceramic cups flying into the air. One splashes him in the chest, instantly staining his gray polo.

"Margaux!" Elodie hisses. She stands immediately and begins scooping up the mugs, which miraculously haven't shattered. They're probably made of some new innovative eco-friendly material that's pitched as containing zero plastic and being highly sustainable. These tech gurus are always on that trend.

"I'm so sorry!" I clasp a hand over my mouth. "Please, let me clean it. I used to work for a dry cleaner. I can get the stain out before it sets."

"It's okay," Bertram starts to say. "Really, I—"

"If you don't get that stain out, you're fired, Margaux,"

Elodie says, her voice practically a growl. She speaks quietly but still makes sure Bertram can hear her. "You're already on thin ice." Then, she flashes Bertram that winning smile. "I am so sorry about this. Nepotism hires, am I right?" She holds up the mugs. "I'll get this cleaned up in here. Margaux will help with your shirt."

Bertram doesn't protest as I drag him toward the hallway and into the bathroom. Maybe it's because he pities me. I close the door behind us and sag my weight against it, doing my best to summon up some tears. I took an acting class in high school, and the drama teacher taught us that the best way to conjure up some tears on cue is to let your eyes dry out by not blinking. When I cover my face with my hands, it's a good opportunity to sob. By the time I lower them again, Bertram is standing before me, looking startled.

"She's going to fire me," I say. "She already hates me."

"Hey," Bertram says, with surprising sincerity. He reaches for the hand towel and dabs at my cheeks, though they're barely damp. The crying on cue was never my strength. This pathetic act in general isn't my favorite tactic—I used it once before, on one of my early jobs with Waylen, and he absolutely hated it. *"You're too confident,"* he'd said. *"I don't buy it."* I didn't cry in front of him again until Collette was born.

The towel Bertram brings me is heavenly soft, and white as a summer cloud. "She won't fire you," he assures me. "I'll tell her you're doing a great job."

I sniff miserably. "Yeah, so far everything is going really well."

He smiles and gives me a small laugh. "All right, then, I'll let you work for it. You can start with getting the stain out of this shirt." He tugs at the fabric, offering the coffee-splattered bit to me.

"It'll be easier if you can take it off," I say, wincing apologetically.

He shrugs out of the shirt with smooth confidence, revealing a gray sleeveless shirt and a subtle ripple of muscles. He isn't at all embarrassed, though he seems to catch on that he's taken me aback. I shake it off, gather his shirt in my hands, and make my way to the sink.

Everything about his apartment is sterile; if it's not white, it's gray or stainless steel. The bar of soap fits this theme as well. It smells like lemongrass and ginger.

Before I can stop myself, I begin to think of my childhood. We'd lived in rural Oregon, in a little farmhouse surrounded by tall grass where I would catch insects with my brother on summer nights. Without the light pollution of the city streetlamps, the sky was pitch black with dots of glowing white stars, and the air smelled just like this bar of soap.

I hate what it reminds me of, and that I still miss it, despite the awful way it came crashing to a halt forever. I hate that my mind still goes back to that place when everyone was still alive, everything tainted now by the tragedy that took it all away. It's not a place I want to revisit. Even my husband doesn't know the half of it.

I must have been taking my frustrations out on the shirt, because the stain lifts easily. I wring it out and then hold it up for Bertram's approval. It's a Ralph Lauren, retailing for two hundred dollars tops. It's pennies for someone like him. He was probably just going to throw it in the trash, but he humors me.

"There, see?" he says, gently taking it from my hands and draping it over the glass shower door to dry. "It's as good as new." When he turns to me again, he tilts my chin with his finger, smiling in an infectious way that causes me to do the same.

Oh, his charm is dangerous. The smooth London accent doesn't help at all.

I force myself to think of Erin Casimir, so distraught in her dumpy apartment, lamenting all this man had cost her. And poor Annie, who could be hiding out somewhere, or worse, buried in the Long Island Sound, getting feasted upon by the sea life.

The perspective helps me, and I slip back into character. We've been in here long enough for Elodie to have found his laptop and used the thumb drive by now.

"Thank you," I tell him. "For being so understanding."

"I've worked for my share of assholes," he says, nodding to the closed door as though it's Elodie herself. "Chin up. If you can take what she dishes out, you'll go far. Just don't make the mistake of thinking you're only as good as how she treats you."

Solid career advice from a man who may be a murderer and a high-end thief.

Even though our interview today is just a front to gain access to his files, I'm looking forward to picking his brain. I want to know just how much of a fraud he is, and if he knows anything about the software he stole from his sister. I want to know what he'll do when he's actually challenged by a reporter, as opposed to getting his ass kissed because he's rich and powerful.

By the time he's changed into a fresh shirt—sky blue this time, same cut and style—Elodie is waiting for us in the living room. She's cleaned up the espresso with the meticulousness of a talented perfectionist.

She flashes me a wicked grin when our eyes meet, and she pats her pocket, where I can see the slightest outline of the thumb drive. Got him.

The rest of the interview goes smoothly. I ask the standard questions about how he got started, where his passion for tech began. I pretend not to notice the way he's smiling at me as I twirl my hair around my pen. He remarks that most interviewers these days use tablets, and I tell him I'm old-fashioned. "I don't know how computers really work," I admit sheepishly. "The IT department in our office hates me. I'm always causing some kind of issue just trying to get into the company portal."

"Ah," he says, leaning back against the couch. The faux-leather cushions squeak against the fabric of his belt. "So, you want to learn all of my secrets."

I let him think his charm is working, though in truth, I can see the appeal. If I were a young, naïve woman looking for Mr. Right, he would tick all the boxes.

I lean forward, covering my notebook with my arms so that he'll forget it's the reason I'm here. "Mr. Casimir—"

"Bertram," he corrects me.

"Bertram," I say, slowly, like I'm tasting the word. "Can I ask why you'd be in a place like this? It's a beautiful apartment, I like it here myself, but isn't all the techy stuff out in Silicon Valley?"

Elodie raises a brow at me, but she doesn't comment. She's already satisfied her role as the irritated boss. Too much more and it will come across like she's bullying me.

But Bertram hasn't forgotten my notebook, and he glances at it, wedged between my elbows and thighs. "Off the record?" he asks.

"Off the record."

"It's inefficient," he says. "Unsustainable, I mean. Everyone is trying to out-innovate each other. Most of the companies, the really big behemoths, aren't profitable. They're just waiting for the others to fail so they can dominate the market. Then, inevitably, they'll pepper their software with ads, use algorithms to manipulate their users, and forget that they were designed to help people, not profit off of them. Take AI, for example. It's designed to line pockets, not improve the user experience."

"That opinion must make you a bit of an outlier," I say.

He taps his temple with a perfectly manicured finger. "Not if it stays in here," he says. "Not if I ignore the noise out there, keep my head down, and focus on my goals. And, Margaux, I always achieve my goals."

I study him the way I would reread an unclear passage in a book until I start to comprehend it. Only, with Bertram, there's something preventing me from understanding him. Maybe this would discourage some, but it only heightens my interest. It isn't every day you meet a self-made billionaire who could be a murderer, too.

I don't do any of this for money. My relentless need to right wrongs is what keeps me going. I'll never get enough. That's why Waylen's impatience waiting for me to burn out will only continue, because it doesn't matter how much we squirrel away in our savings account, or how many hours I clock. There's something else keeping me going, and he doesn't understand what it is because I won't tell him. Because if I told him about the fire, I'd also have to tell him that it was my fault.

I focus on Bertram, and the past slips away. He says he always achieves his goals. So do I.

SIX

Elodie is still shuddering when we step into the coffeehouse. "He made my skin crawl," she says, after we've ordered our drinks and settled into a table by the window.

It's midday, and the place is practically empty. Mr. X was able to tap into the security cameras and tell us precisely where to sit so that our screens won't be recorded. Public places aren't always ideal, but home isn't an option. Waylen is there, and any reminder of this particular line of work is best avoided. Elodie says that her own house is chaos while her husband is taking care of the twins, both of whom have ear infections that have banned them from day care.

Elodie sets up her laptop and fits the thumb drive into place. "How will we know what to look for?" she asks. "We can get into his files, sure, but I doubt there's a folder that says 'ideas I stole from my sister.'"

I watch as a list of folders appears on the screen. "A thief doesn't always go into a house knowing where the jewelry is," I say. "It takes a little bit of creative snooping."

"So we're jewel thieves now," Elodie says. "I like it."

"I'm less interested in Erin's software," I tell her. "We'll sort that out for her, of course. But I'm more intrigued by this missing Annie."

"Right?" Elodie whispers, her eyes going wide. "All I could think about while we were in his apartment is, 'Is this where he did it?' and 'Who helped him get rid of the body?'"

We don't know that there even *is* a body, to be fair. But Elodie is right. While Bertram was charming the pants off of us in there, I was putting myself into the shoes of some unsuspecting young woman bewitched by his billionaire playboy charm. Even now, some part of me screams that he's innocent, that he really is who he claims to be. He was soft-spoken, not cocky like the narcissists I've hunted down before.

He's good at what he does. Really, really good. But I'm better.

After we've clicked on the dozenth folder and browsed through the hundredth page of programming, Elodie is going cross-eyed with boredom. Bertram categorizes every aspect of his life, right down to the sales invoices for his online purchases. For a billionaire, he lives modestly, but he spends a lot on delivery. Typical of a reclusive genius.

When we open a folder unceremoniously titled "old data" I'm expecting to find something useful. A draft of Erin's original coding, or some alterations he made to reconfigure his forged work into something he could plagiarize.

I am *not* expecting to see a photo of a woman standing on a beach in a blue and gold bikini, with a smiley face emoji covering her face.

All of the files are images. In all of them, the woman's face is covered by that same emoji. In the ocean. Holding a cocktail against the sunset at a seaside resort. A smile emoji and Bertram together on a crisp down comforter, as Bertram holds the phone over their heads to take a picture.

"Jesus," Elodie says. "He really hates her."

"I don't get it," I say. "Why would he edit the pictures like this?"

Elodie flashes me a wicked grin. "You've never been through a bad breakup, huh?" she asks. "I've been there. You want to keep the pictures, but you don't want to see that person's face ever again."

"Doesn't it seem a little . . . serial killer?" I say.

Elodie shrugs. "A bad breakup will make anyone a little unhinged."

Elodie is starting to grow on me, but she's still—well, Elodie, and I suspect that will always be an acquired taste.

"They're dated this past August," Elodie goes on. "Only a couple of months ago." All of the photos are dated within a week of one another, suggesting this was some romantic couple's getaway. The last photo is of Bertram glancing down at his phone while seated at an outdoor dining table. I can see why Annie must have snapped it. Even in this candid shot, he's beautiful, his chiseled jaw shadowed by the rising sun, a sly quirk to his lips. His hair is wet, like they've just gone for a morning swim, and his damp shirt clings to his chest.

Elodie whistles at the previous photo, of the woman's

hand entangled in Bertram's, with an engagement ring shining on her finger. "That looks expensive."

Annie was a woman in love. Maybe it didn't matter to her that Bertram had more money than God. Whatever she hoped their future life would be together, he'd promised it to her. Life, for a brief moment in time, was too good to be true.

Elodie points to the glittering sea behind him. "Maybe that's where he dumped the body. The real question is why."

Why, indeed.

"Okay, you haven't said anything for a long time, and it's starting to worry me," Elodie says. "What's going on? What are you thinking?"

"It just doesn't add up," I say. "Even if he had no intention of marrying Annie, even if everything he told her was a lie, what would be the point in killing her and risking his fortune to spend life in prison? Unless he knew he could hire someone to make it go away, or someone who did the dirty work for him."

"Um, because he's a psycho," Elodie says. "Look at any of these tech billionaires and tell me you'd be surprised if they had a *Kiss the Girls* situation in the basement of one of their mansions."

"Maybe," I say, my voice trailing as I consider. But it doesn't add up. If Bertram has it in him to kill someone for the pleasure of it, why not kill his sister? He could have stolen her software and made off with it, never having to worry about her going to the press.

"Did Erin mention if she'd ever gone to the media to dispute the real ownership of her brother's app?" I ask.

"Not that I'm aware," Elodie says.

"Maybe he threatened her," I speculate.

"Seems more like a family dispute," Elodie says. "Her parents already disowned her for simply accusing him, and that's without her taking any kind of legal action or going public. Maybe she keeps her mouth shut publicly because she wants to mend a bridge with them someday."

I zoom in on the photo we were just looking at, where I can see the corner of the restaurant just at the edge of the frame. The shingles are aged, painted white, distinctly New England. An old house that's been converted. "I think I know where this is," I say. "Foreshore Lobster Co. Waylen and I thought about using it for our wedding venue, but we ended up at some other place his mom and sister picked out for us."

"You're thinking we should go." Elodie catches on. "Do a little snooping. But it's been months—what evidence could there be?"

I down the last of my iced coffee, gather my things, and stand. "Won't know until we get there. That's the fun of it."

On the way to the restaurant, I text Mr. X a quick update: **Possibly a lead on the urder-may. Nothing on the oftware-say.**

He hates when I use pig latin. Says it's not at all cryptic, and it makes me sound like I'm a kid. But annoying him is one of the job perks. I risked my neck spending the morning in the apartment of a possible murderer, why not poke the bear a little bit?

It's a frigid October afternoon, so it's not a surprise to see that the parking lot of Foreshore Lobster Co. is mostly empty. It's a small restaurant, and the outdoor seating arrangement is covered in tarps on the patio, but the indoor portion has its OPEN sign facing outward. Beyond it, a modest three-story hotel advertises its vacancies.

Elodie grouses about the cold like a true Californian as we step out of the car and make our way into the restaurant.

My phone buzzes and I check it, expecting a snide comment from Mr. X about my goading, but it's from Collette: **Mom, please don't make me tutor Finnegan. She's awful**

I type back a quick reply: **We'll discuss later**

She responds with a row of eye-roll emojis. It's about lunchtime, and the only time she can use her phone at school without it being confiscated by a teacher. I wonder what must have happened at the social hub of the school cafeteria to upset her, though it isn't hard to imagine. That's where most of the bullying took place when I was a kid, at least.

I've been lucky with Collette. She's a diplomat and averse to the drama that often comes with being on the cusp of middle school. Sure, I worry that she doesn't socialize nearly enough, but she has never been an active participant in bullying, nor, mercifully, has she been a target.

I knew it couldn't last forever, though. It was inevitable that her path would collide with someone who would break her winning streak. May as well be the new popular girl who wears Sephora lashes and brings a forty-five-dollar Stanley cup to the sixth grade.

We're greeted by the hostess at the podium, a sun-freckled brunette who smiles cheerily at us. "Table for two?" she asks.

Elodie opens her mouth to answer. She's starving and spent the ride over here talking about how we can at least get a delicious lobster lunch as our reward for venturing all over the state in the freezing cold. But I speak up before she has a chance. "Actually, we'd like to speak to the event coordinator about the wedding venue." I wrap my arm around Elodie, whose body stiffens in confusion. "We're getting married."

SEVEN

Once I see the hotel's wedding venue, I remember why Waylen and I rejected it more than a decade ago. It's funeral-parlor chic, with cloth-draped chairs and a peach carpet. The view of the ocean is pretty, at least. Elodie and I pretend to be interested as the chatty event planner leads us from room to room, detailing the catering options and how many people can be seated in the dining room. Live music optional for a fee, of course, or we're welcome to hire our own entertainment. The sweethearts package comes with a wedding cake, baked and decorated by their own personal chef.

Elodie has recovered from the plot twist I threw at her earlier, and she's fully embraced her fictional role as my spouse-to-be. If she finds this building half as gaudy as I do, she doesn't let on, chattering and asking questions about floral arrangements.

"To be honest, we don't get many winter weddings

here," the event coordinator says. She's in her sixties at least, with silver hair swept into a classy beehive, and her blue eyes are heavily done in matching eyeshadow. "Most couples prefer the summer, so they can be out on the beach."

"We're a couple of snowbirds," I say. "We usually spend our winters down in Florida, but this year, we thought it would be fun to see the snow."

"Oh, that's nice," the woman says, her bracelets and rings clattering as she presses a hand to her chest. "When's the big day?"

"The first week of December," Elodie says. "Call me superstitious, but I think winter weddings are good luck." She points to me and then back to herself. "Her parents and mine both had summer weddings, and it ended in divorce."

"She thinks it's a curse," I say, feigning playful annoyance.

"She thinks I'm being silly," Elodie goes on. She leans toward the event coordinator conspiratorially. "But you must see a lot of weddings here. You tell me. How many summer weddings have ended with some sort of tragedy?"

I can't help my wicked smile. She's great at improv. Elodie is a chameleon, able to adapt to her surroundings, and when she ditches the snooty, uptight thing she does, she can be quite likable.

The event coordinator winks. "Most weddings go beautifully, especially here. There's nothing for you to worry about."

"Oh, come on," I say playfully. "There must be something."

"Give us the tea," Elodie adds. "I'm right, aren't I? Summer weddings *are* cursed."

"No, no, summer weddings are not cursed." The woman's eyes dart back and forth, making sure we're alone on the tiny dance floor surrounded by empty tables and chairs. "We've had nothing but happy couples! Well . . . except for one."

Elodie sits at the edge of a nearby chair, leaning forward excitedly. "Really?"

The woman looks nervous now. "I shouldn't—"

"Please?" I take a less pushy approach, sitting across the table from Elodie. "We've bickered so much about when to have the wedding. Maybe I'll feel better if you tell me that the summer is a bad idea."

"They never actually booked the wedding," the woman says, holding her palms up as though warding off an attack. Her voice lowers to a hush as she joins us at the table, and there we perch like a trio of gossiping schoolchildren. The exact sort of clique my daughter abhors.

"But they asked for a tour of the place when they stayed here. They were from England, and apparently the young lady had her heart set on the beach. The man was a real charmer. I don't know what they did for a living—something with computers maybe. I got the impression they had a lot of cash." She swipes one hand over the other, miming a stack of bills.

"What happened?" Elodie asks, truly rapt. Elodie is wearing a lot of jewelry, and none of it looks like the costume stuff I have on my dresser. I can tell she's still thinking about the engagement ring she saw on Bertram's hard drive.

"Well, they stayed for a few days, and they were all lovey-dovey holding hands on the beach and ordering our couple's dinners—that's lobster for two. And then one night, I was closing up late after showing the dining hall to some CEO looking to host his retirement luncheon here. I heard this awful shouting coming from one of the rooms. The young woman stormed out of here in tears. Nearly knocked me off my feet when she bowled into me. The next day, both of them had checked out."

Elodie's face falls. "That's it?" she asks. There's more tension than that at a PTA meeting.

But the coordinator's nervous yet pointed silence tells us that is not, in fact, everything.

I reach out and put my hand over hers. She flinches. "What is it?" I ask.

She frowns. "A week later, I'd forgotten all about it. Lovers' spats aren't the only things going on around here, and it was an especially busy time for me. But then the police showed up. Apparently, the young lady's family had reported her missing when she stopped returning their calls."

Elodie is already glancing at her phone, no doubt looking for a hit on any news articles now that we have this new information. She moves faster than the speed of gossip.

"Oh no," I say. My tone doesn't express the rush that goes through me. It's the satisfying thrill I feel when I've just had a breakthrough. I'm amazed by Elodie's easy ability to pry gossip out of a stranger. This is going to be more fun than I thought. "But surely it was just a misunderstanding. They found her eventually?"

"Don't know," the coordinator says. "The police never

followed up." She stands, clearly flustered. "If you'll excuse me, I—I've already said too much. Please, you ladies help yourselves to looking through the venue again. Here's my card if you'd like to book your event. We'd be glad to host your reception."

She's out of there as fast as if she'd seen a ghost. I scoot my chair closer to Elodie's and look at her phone. "Anything?" I ask.

"I'm using my VPN to search British headlines, since nothing is coming up here," Elodie says. I'm annoyed with myself for not thinking to do this when I was doing my own research last night. But still, there's nothing. Not a police report. Not a "Have you seen me?" Facebook post. There is nothing at all besides the same blurry paparazzi photo we've both already seen.

I think back on Bertram's irritating charm. The way he made me want to believe his softhearted lonely genius act. His kindness when he thought I was just a bumbling new journalist on the brink of getting fired.

But the evidence is there. Or rather, the evidence is *not* there.

"He made it go away," I say. "With all his money, he must have some resources. Someone who made this all disappear for him."

"'Old data,'" Elodie says, shuddering as she recalls the name of the file with Annie's photos. "That's all people are to him."

"We'll have to go back there," I say. "I can say I misplaced something."

"Are you crazy?" Elodie hisses. "He's dangerous."

This isn't a conversation to have in a place where the

walls have ears, so I drag her to her feet and we make our way back to the car.

"I've worked with murderers before," I say, warming my hands as the heat blasts through the vents in the dashboard. "I just put a woman away for murdering her husband back in the eighties."

"That was you?" Elodie says. "I followed that case. There was a whole podcast about it."

"Granted, she was sloppy," I say. "It wasn't hard to prove. The police at the time just didn't think a PTA mom would be capable of such a thing, so they never really investigated it."

"But you weren't alone with her, in her apartment, with nobody to hear you scream," Elodie presses. "And she wasn't a billionaire with cronies to bury your body for her."

I bat my eyelashes adoringly at her. "Aw, El. I didn't know you cared."

"I don't," she says as I throw the car into drive. "But if you end up buried in pieces in the Long Island Sound, it's going to fall back on me. Mr. X seems to really like you."

I smirk. "He seems really invested in this case," I say. "He hates billionaires."

"Who doesn't?" Elodie says. "Look at what they're all doing."

I nod. "But we have to stay objective. At least professionally. If we let our own feelings get into the mix, we'll make mistakes."

Elodie clenches her jaw, but she nods. "Let's fry this bastard," she says. "And then get manicures."

"Bloodred nail polish," I add, making her laugh.

At Elodie's insistence, we stop somewhere for a late

lunch. By the time we're done, it's nearly time to pick the girls up from school. She's regaled me with her own plan to do some deeper research. Pull security camera footage from neighboring buildings, do a deeper dive into Bertram's files. I nod along, admiring her tenacity. But what I don't say is that she's being far too cautious, that a great reward requires greater risks.

I've decided here is where we'll diverge. While Elodie investigates this digitally, I'll take a more direct approach. Maybe she'll stumble upon something we missed the first time, but, just maybe, this will require more of a risk than Elodie is willing to take.

After I drop Elodie back at her car, I call the front desk at Bertram's apartment building. I know the odds of getting his phone number are exactly zero, but all I need to do is get close to him. I recognize the voice of the man at the front desk when he answers—the one who helped Elodie and me get through to Bertram.

"Hi," I say, disguising my voice. Years of reading bedtime stories to my daughter have made me a pro at this. I can sound like anything from an enchanted princess to an evil sea witch. A harried delivery courier is somewhere between those two things. "I'm calling from UPS. A resident of your building has a delivery scheduled, and it's going to require a forklift. Does your building have a service elevator?"

"Oh my goodness," the man says. "How big is the delivery, exactly?"

I pretend to be checking a document. "It says the dimensions are ten by twelve feet, six feet deep. Should be arriving tomorrow. Can I confirm someone will be there to sign for it, and that there's a freight elevator?"

"We do have an industrial elevator, but it's usually for furniture deliveries and residents who are just moving in. Who is it for?"

"Bertram Casimir." I pretend to have difficulty pronouncing the name. "The penthouse. Arrival will be around four p.m."

This will give me enough time to pick Collette up from school, check in with Waylen, jet out of the house to run my little errand, and be back before dinner.

"Someone will be there," the man assures me, and we hang up.

A recluse like Bertram relies on things being safe and predictable. He is surrounded at all times by cameras and security guards. So if he's expecting a package and doesn't know what it is, that will already rattle him. And when I happen to show up instead, under the guise of wanting to ask about his charitable donations, he's going to be downright confused. He's going to get that nettling, impossible-to-prove sense that something is amiss.

That's what I want. To keep him off his game so that he makes a mistake.

I have a new text from Mr. X asking how today went. I type back that we may have a few leads, but I leave out my latest plan, just in case he tells Elodie about it and she tries to stop me. Working with a partner always has its flaws, and while I've come to admit that Elodie is brilliant, her flaw is that she's too cautious. I can't blame her for that—she's coming from small-time white-collar investment fraud. I won't involve her in the dirty work. I'll handle it myself.

EIGHT

When I wake up at six o'clock and Waylen's side of the bed is empty, somehow, I know. We're overdue for a Talk with a capital *T*.

My husband is a man who thrives on routine. Working from home leaves too much room for potential disarray, so he holds himself to the rigor of a true office job. Awake at seven, out of the shower by seven thirty, coffee and breakfast done and dishes washed before eight. It's enough to stress me out, but Collette is just like him. I see it the older she gets, how panicked she is if I'm five minutes late to pick her up from school, begging me to drive her back to a friend's house if she accidentally forgot to pick up a book she loaned them.

If either of them does something out of character, I know it's because something more pressing is occupying their mind.

I don't get up right away, though. I lie staring at the

ceiling, listening to the sound of the Keurig pouring coffee into Waylen's mug, reluctant to enter into the same argument again. To distract myself, I wonder about how I'll approach Bertram when I head to his apartment to talk about his charity donations. He gives millions per year to various STEM programs for youth, domestic violence shelters, and environmental efforts to combat climate change. As far as I can tell, he's never made his donations public. I had to do a lot of digging to find the records online. It'll be tricky to walk the line between being a serious reporter and being a fledgling buffoon who can't tie her own shoes without falling over.

I find myself wondering if he's as orderly as my husband. Somewhere across the miles between us, while the shoreline is slowly waking, is he already up and doing some bougie version of hot yoga? Is there a masseuse laying burning stones on his spine to cleanse his spirit? Is he blending a lean green juice with wheatgrass and some miracle seed he's imported from a small village in Senegal?

Eventually, I drag myself up and make my way downstairs, still in my pajamas.

Waylen, as expected, is sitting at the counter with his coffee. He's wearing the same fitted T-shirt and boxers he wore to bed, but it's only now that I notice the way they fit him, how much broader his shoulders have gotten since he renewed his gym membership.

In more than a decade of marriage, his brown hair has turned prematurely gray, and it suits him. A young silver fox that any of the women I know would be happy to lay claim to. He's a good man, a doting father, attentive partner. If I had made a list of attributes for the perfect husband back when I was a little girl—the kind of prince I wanted to sweep me off my feet—he would have ticked all the boxes.

I remind myself of this often, because it's been many years since I dreamed of a Prince Charming.

Now he gives me a wan smile. "Would you like some tea?"

I would like to skip the formalities, so I shake my head and sit across from him. "What's on your mind?"

"You're on a mission," he says. "I can tell it's a big one from the way you've been acting."

He's trying to bait me into asking how, exactly, I've been acting. But I just want to get this interrogation over with, so I don't take it.

"It should be straightforward," I say. "A month tops. Some sibling rivalry over a phone app called Budgie."

Waylen's expression is unreadable. He grabs his phone, scrolls through something on the screen, and then slides it to me. It's a Reddit post titled **Men who got away with murder? Help! Trying to research for a college paper.**

I glance at Waylen, who scrolls down to the third reply. It's about Bertram Casimir, and it's a vague accusation. Some anonymous poster claims to have worked for a small copy and print center outside of London, and the parents of a young woman named Annie came in and printed up a hundred missing person posters. One of the posters hung outside of the copy center for a week before it was torn down. It promised a ten-thousand-pound reward for information leading to her safe return. She was last seen leaving the UK with her boyfriend, tech mogul Bertram Casimir.

"Seems like it's not that straightforward," Waylen says.

"How did you get his name?" I ask.

Wrong question to ask. His neutral expression betrays his frustration. "You forget I used to be in this life too, Margaux," he says, taking on the tone he uses when he's being stern with our child, like he thinks every word he's about to say is dire. "I have my ways of finding out."

"You could have asked me," I say. "It's never been a secret I've kept from you."

"Don't talk to me about secrets," he says, and sighs. "I think you know what I mean. It's been weeks since we've talked about anything besides what to make for dinner."

"I didn't think we *had* to talk about everything," I say. "I thought we just knew."

"We used to," he says, and the words hit me harder than they have any right to.

Waylen isn't confrontational. And according to the court-ordered therapist I had when I was twelve after my parents died, I am a classic avoider. To me, this feels like a match made in heaven. We never have to talk about anything. If we ignore it, maybe the problems will pack up their bags and leave.

But Waylen has been stewing on this one for a while. I can see it in the way he fidgets with his coffee mug and avoids my eyes. "How long is this going to last?" he asks me. "How long until Collette and I are enough?"

"Don't do that," I snap. "Don't bring Collette into this."

"She's never *not* been in this," he counters. "She's the reason for everything."

He's right, but I try not to think about that. The morning I paced back and forth in the bathroom of my tiny apartment, waiting to see if two pink lines were going to show up on the stick, my heart was beating out of my chest. I buried the positive test in the wastebasket under wads of tissues and didn't tell Waylen until a doctor had confirmed. I wasn't ready to be a mother. I didn't think I'd ever be ready.

But my fears about motherhood were washed away in the tsunami of Waylen's excitement. I told him over dinner, nervously pushing around my penne alla vodka with my fork. He threw back his chair, lifted me from mine, and spun me around, laughing a madman's laugh of pure glee. He'd always wanted a family.

When I think about my life since Collette was born, there's no regret about keeping her now. But the rest of it—the wedding, Waylen's sister doing my hair and makeup before I went to the altar, the mortgage and the suburbs, Waylen trading his vigilantism for a stable career in publishing—I've been waiting to love as much as I love my daughter. One of these days I'll have to admit that I don't. I just don't.

As if Waylen can read my thoughts, he softens. "Of course I worry every time you walk out that door. I know the risks of what you do. I used to do it too. And I can't just call the police if you disappear on me."

I stare at the granite countertop. Silver swirls with glittering flecks. Waylen's mother hired an interior decorator as her wedding gift to us, and I let her have carte blanche over all the decisions. *"You're so agreeable, dear,"* she'd said. But my head was spinning. When the walls are closing in on you, you aren't concerned with which paint swatch looks best on them or whether to choose a ceramic sink or a steel one.

"I look at the parents at Collette's school," I finally say. Waylen leans in, eager for my words. "And I think they're so lucky to be worried about such little things. They never think about what's happening out there." I nod to the window, gesturing to the greater world. But even from here, things look peaceful. Flurries of snow melt on the pavement.

The world looks safe from here. When something terrible happens on the news, we press for details. We try to think about the ways it could never happen to us, but the truth is that nowhere is truly safe. Darkness moves like a winter breeze.

By the time Collette arrived, Waylen was eager to prove that we could have what he called a normal life and was already trying to convince me to ditch the vigilantism. He had worked his way up to an editorial position at his publisher. And because we lived in a Connecticut suburb ninety minutes outside of Manhattan, he was making New York money without having to pay New York expenses. "You don't have to work," Waylen told me. "Take up painting. Learn how to fix cars. Whatever makes you happy." With one little caveat that he didn't say out loud, of course: *Stop trying to fix the world.*

I tried for a few months. I avoided the news. I tried journaling. I watched videos on meditative breathing. Collette was a low-maintenance infant. Try as I might, I couldn't connect with the other parents at the revolving "mommy and me" classes I signed up for. I became an insomniac. When I put Collette down in the afternoon, I napped between her feedings.

Until the day I heard strange footsteps coming up the stairs. Groggily, I'd awoken in the rocking chair in the nursery and looked out the window. It was late afternoon, that time when the sky feels too bright and yet dark at the same time. Waylen's car wasn't in the driveway, and I knew something wasn't right.

Paralyzed by fear, I watched as a stranger's shoes walked past the crack below the nursery door. Collette was awake and staring too. I slid my hand between the slats in the crib and pressed one finger to her puckered mouth, willing her not to cry, not to make a sound.

I still don't know how long we stayed like that. Her warm little breaths against my skin, both of us listening as someone rummaged through our lives. I could hear him shuffling through my jewelry box in the bedroom. He would take my mother's engagement ring, the ruby earrings that had been in my family for three generations. He wouldn't bother trying to crack the safe in the closet—he took the whole thing, containing ten thousand dollars cash, among which, the pickle jar of my old waitressing tips that Waylen and I kept for sentimental value.

My cell phone rang from where I'd left it on my bedside table. Waylen would be calling to check on me, to ask if the rash on Collette's cheek was clearing up, and if I wanted him to bring home something for dinner. The phone rang until it went to voicemail, and then he tried again. The strange footsteps stopped moving. I squeezed my eyes shut.

I think our intruder realized that someone was home. Nobody leaves their cell phone behind. He would be looking at the photo that came up when Waylen called me: us on New Year's Eve, his hand under my chin before he pulled me in for a kiss.

If he came into the nursery, I knew how to defend myself. But it was Collette I feared for. She was a vulnerability I wore on my sleeve.

I tiptoed to the closet and I unscrewed the doorknob very slowly. I clutched the teddy bear handle in my palm so that the long screw stuck out between my fingers like a little knife. It was blunted, but it could take out an eye. I pressed myself to the wall, beside the door, and I waited for him. If he entered that room, I would kill him.

But his footsteps moved farther away. Down the steps and out the door. I felt it when his presence left. Collette felt it, too, because she started to cry. A keening scream that turned her all red like I'd never seen her. And in the bedroom, Waylen was calling me for what felt like the hundredth time.

"That's it, that's fucking it. We're getting out of this hellhole," Waylen had said. It was one of four break-ins on our street that day, and after a while, police gave up trying to find whoever had done it.

We moved out of our rental house and into a gated apartment we could barely afford, which was enough for Waylen. There was round-the-clock security, he told me. Nothing bad was going to happen.

But I was restless. The police never found the intruder; he was still out there, and he had seen our pictures all over the house. Some crystal-clear portrait of our family lived in his head, but to us, he was just a shadow. A nightmare. I didn't sleep. I stalked neighborhood watch websites. I read about every break-in that had happened in my town, which led me to break-ins happening in other towns, which led me to murders, rapes, arson, shootings. Things that had always existed, that I had always known existed. But suddenly I couldn't bear it.

I don't have to say any of this now, because Waylen remembers. The very next day, I called Mr. X and told him I was back in. Waylen doesn't say anything more now, because he knows that if he pushes me too hard, I'll leave. I've done it before. For a few hours, or to spend a night alone at a hotel. He worries that one of these days, I won't come back.

Mom?" Collette squeaks as I breeze past her. She's standing in her pink nightgown, her golden hair rumpled on one side. She will never know what it feels like to be unsafe, not if I have any say about it. She'll never know what it's like to watch her whole life burn away to nothing, to be thrown out into the world where everyone is suddenly a stranger.

I kiss her forehead and tell her I'll meet her in the kitchen in a few minutes. Then I take a hot shower, scouring the peach blossom body wash into my skin.

"Come on," I tell Collette, who's scrolling through her iPad at the breakfast table, neglecting the eggs Benedict Waylen has made her. "I'm taking you to school."

"Now?" she asks. "It's super early."

"I've got a design consultation with a client," I tell her. The way her jaw clenches tells me that she knows this isn't the truth, but she hasn't figured out the rest of it yet. But she takes a bite of her breakfast to appease Waylen, then she slides out of her chair and grabs her backpack.

I back out of the driveway without giving the car a chance to warm up in the cold November air, and we're halfway down the street when Collette asks me if her father and I have had a fight, if it's something she did wrong.

"No," I tell her, and give her my best smile in the rearview mirror. "Everything is fine. I'm just in a hurry today."

We're almost to the school when I notice the car that's following us. It isn't exactly subtle—a black BMW with tinted windows. It maintains a distance but trails along with every turn through the suburban back roads that lead to the school, even when I don't signal.

I glance at Collette, who is staring at her iPad. She knows she can't bring it to school, and it isn't allowed until her homework is completed in the evening, so she absorbs all the screen time she can get without a lecture in the mornings. For once, I'm glad she's distracted, because she doesn't pick up on my nervousness.

Not with my kid in the car, is all I'm thinking. *Any other time.*

It could be anyone. In my line of work, I don't always make friends wherever I go. The relative of someone I put away years ago, or a supposedly reformed criminal who has changed his mind and decided to pay me back for the ordeal I put him through.

When we come up to the school, I hit the gas and speed past it. Collette raises her head. "Mom?" she says. "You missed the turn."

"Did I?" I laugh, and it sounds a little too manic. "I must

have been distracted. I'll go around. Don't worry, we're still early."

"But you said you had to be at work." She sets her tablet down now, her brow knitted in concern. God, she's so much like me that it frightens me sometimes. A budding little investigator. Why can't she be like the other kids in her class who turn into zombies when you put a glowing screen a few inches from their faces?

"Collette," I say, more sternly. "It's fine."

I zip around a corner that leads to a narrow one-way street and turn down the first alleyway I see. But it's a dead end, and I slam the brakes so I don't crash into the dumpster ahead of us.

I glance again in the mirror and watch as the car with the tinted windows speeds past the alley, the driver thinking I'm still on the loose. I wait a few more seconds, but they don't return, and I let out a breath.

"Mom?" Collette's voice is trembling. "What's going on?" I open my mouth to speak, but she says, "Don't lie to me!" Tears fill her eyes. "Whose car was that? Are we going to get murdered?"

"Nobody is going to murder us," I say. "Why would you think that?"

"Because when someone wants to murder you, they follow you home. There was this case on a podcast Finnegan told the class about."

Great. Thanks for that, Finnegan. I can hardly judge Elodie for letting her daughter have access to true-crime podcasts when I'm taking Collette to courtrooms.

I back out of the alley at full speed and turn the wrong

way down the one-way street, running the stop and ignoring the horn that blares at me in protest. Within seconds, I'm on the highway, and I realize that I must have run several lights to have accomplished this, but my adrenaline won't let me stop. Collette is whimpering, but she says nothing now.

"There's no school today," I tell her. "It's fine. Everything is fine. But I'm taking you to Auntie Ellen's house."

Waylen's sister lives forty-five minutes from us, in the middle of farm country where it's impossible to get a cell signal, never mind getting your GPS tracking to work. Collette will be safe there. "You're sick," I tell her. "You've had a stomach bug since last night, okay?"

Collette doesn't answer me. She arches upward and tries to turn around in her seat to make sure nobody is following us.

Ellen won't mind. She's always saying we should visit more anyway. She homeschools her two boys and spends most of her afternoons tending to the horses on her sprawling property. Whenever Collette does visit, Ellen relishes the opportunity to teach her about how to apply makeup and French braid her hair.

"And, Collette," I begin, but she already knows what I'm about to say.

"Don't tell Dad." She takes the tissue I hand her and begins cleaning up the tears. All at once she has composed herself. She's good at burying whatever she's feeling. She's learned how to do that from the best.

"Mom," she says, with an authoritative tone that no eleven-year-old should have. She's always been mature for her age, my Collette, and so serious when the situation takes a sudden turn for it. "I was listening to this podcast about this mom whose husband just got out of prison—"

"Collette, really."

"Just listen," she says, still dabbing at her tears, even as she sobers up from her initial fear. "The mom took her kids and moved far away, but she had a code word, so anyone who tried to pick her kids up from school needed to know what it was, and then the kids would know that person was safe."

"There's nobody from my past who's getting out of prison," I tell her. "You don't have to worry about anything like that." And my current case . . . I doubt Bertram has any reason to suspect me yet, but if I play my cards right, he'll be behind bars for a long time. That is, if he's guilty. Even though he appears squeaky clean, he must have slipped up somewhere. Mr. X has never led me down a dead end.

If Bertram is the one following me, it must be because he wants to know as much as he can about me. Because he suspects I'm sniffing him out? No, I didn't give him any indication that I'd be doing that. Because he wants to learn all he can about me, so he can use me in some way? He's a billionaire, which means he has the resources to stalk anyone who comes into his life. Maybe he's paranoid. Maybe he has some way of knowing we copied the contents of his laptop. He is a tech genius—supposedly—after all.

"We can use a code," she insists. "If we need help, we say—" She looks around the car, contemplating. "Nail polish." Her eyes have landed on my manicure.

I'm proud of her for coming up with something so clever. I smile at her in the mirror, trying not to let on that

I'm checking for cars behind us. Nobody is there, thankfully.

"I'm so proud of you," I say. She doesn't seem to mind that she's just like me at times.

She understands this small conspiracy between us, and that something is happening beyond what I'm going to explain to her—so she doesn't press. She is adding up all of the little white lies I've asked her to tell her father.

But she doesn't know about the bigger betrayal. Even though I'm taking Collette to his sister, I'm breaking an agreement we've had for years.

During our first mission, when we were still trepidatious around each other, we skirted the parameters of our relationship like spies around security lasers in a mansion with a million-dollar crystal vase. While neither of us would have called it love, there was a lust factor. We were in our early twenties. I was trying to outrun a past that I never spoke about—not even to him. Waylen's petty fraud was no match for the secrets I keep, but even so, we found a way to connect with each other.

The first night we made love, it wasn't planned. I could feel Waylen falling in love with me, as though he were succumbing to a poisonous mist that had infiltrated the oxygen in the room. We dozed on his bed, and while I was still half asleep, it started to rain. Thunder shook the walls of his tiny apartment, and lightning flashed.

He got up to close the window. I watched him move, the taut muscles of his naked body catching the shadows of the next bolt of lightning. He wrapped his arms around my chest when he returned to bed.

"When I was a kid, I got caught in a rainstorm like this

while my parents were driving us home," he said. "We saw a tree go up in flames when a power line hit it."

I'd turned to face him, curious that he was starting to be vulnerable with me. "There was a tornado, a totally freak thing that even the meteorologists hadn't predicted. The only thing around us was this huge furniture store. It was closed, but my dad smashed in the glass door so we could all get inside. He said the safest place to be in a storm like that was a building with lots of plumbing and electrical wires. That's why I picked this apartment."

He lived in a small unit of a massive building, on the fourteenth floor. I'd assumed his reasons were budgetary. But it fascinated me to know how deliberate he was. Not just in the way he spoke, the way he dressed to match the mission, the way he kissed me as though we were the only two people in the world—but even something as mundane as choosing an apartment.

In his arms that night, I felt the safest I had ever been. Like I'd found someone who knew how to keep us safe. Someone who saw the details that even I—with my constant catastrophizing—would miss.

A lot of people think that the safest place to weather a threat is in the trenches, behind a tree or under a porch. But really, it's a place with large crowds where you can hide, and with towering walls and wires to absorb the electric shock.

Bertram Casimir is not a literal tornado, but he does pose a similar threat. Waylen would hate that I'm taking Collette to his sister out in the country. We agreed that no matter what, when something was wrong, we would meet at the only shopping mall still left after the pandemic shut down the surrounding businesses. We agreed that we would meet in the parking garage underground, and if we couldn't call the other for help, we would wait.

I should be doing that, my logical brain is telling me. But something else—something I can't seem to place my finger on—tells me that Waylen should never hear about this. And that voice, duplicitous as it might be, is loudest.

NINE

After I've dropped my daughter off, I call the school to let them know she'll be out sick today. Then I speed like hell toward Bertram's apartment.

Elodie calls, predictably right when school is supposed to start, to ask me where I am. "I wanted to tell you what I was able to find online," she says.

"Collette has a bug," I say. "Sorry. I was going to call you and check in this afternoon."

"Lots of stuff going around at the twins' daycare, too," she says. "It should only last forty-eight hours. Anyway, when can you meet up? We shouldn't say too much on the phone."

As I take the off-ramp, I'm glancing at all my mirrors. There's no sign of whoever was tailing me earlier, but I'm sure they won't give up that easily. If they find me again, I can't risk leading them back to the house.

"Margaux?" Elodie's voice comes through the Bluetooth. "You still there?"

"Yes, sorry," I tell her. "Um—today is going to be difficult." As I'm stopping at a red light, I spot my friend in the black BMW at a parking lot across from the intersection. They were waiting for me. "Shit."

"Everything okay?"

"Yes," I blurt. "I have to go." I'm not sure if Elodie hears the string of expletives I mutter as I disconnect the call.

There's a gun locked in my glove box. Mr. X adapted the door so that it only opens with my thumbprint, ensuring Collette will never find it there. But a lot of good that will do me now if this car decides to run me off the road, or if they shoot through my rear window.

The light turns green. Whoever it is, they didn't place a hidden tracker on my car, because they would have followed me on the highway if that was the case, and they didn't realize until too late when they'd lost me in that alleyway.

But they're determined nonetheless, and they knew I'd be headed this way.

I turn left, away from the school and away from my neighborhood. They're going to catch up to me. It's inevitable. And suddenly I'm thinking of Waylen, whose angry silence filled the house when I left this morning. No doubt he's still stewing on it, wondering why I can't be his perfect wife, wondering why he still loves me despite his better judgment.

And of Collette, who threw her arms around me when I dropped her off, hugging me in a way she rarely does anymore. She's getting older now, and she doesn't say, "I love you."

She used to say it all the time when she was a toddler, blowing kisses, her chubby fingers wiggling like starfish as she waited to be held. I never thought to notice when she stopped saying it, when she stopped crawling into my lap and nuzzling me like a sleepy cat. I can't remember the last time I read her a bedtime story, or carried her from her car seat to the bed.

I try to imagine how she'll look in a few years, when I'm dropping her off for college. I can almost see her, tall with long wavy hair, lugging a suitcase up the steps. I wait for her to turn around so I can get a look at her face, to see the angles of the budding young woman she's becoming. But she doesn't turn. She doesn't hear me calling for her.

All I see is that BMW in my mirror, gaining on me. I speed up, the shoreline blurring beside me, the water cold and glittering, flanked by jagged rocks. It's not the ideal place to hide a body, what with the water chopping up against them. But maybe they mean for me to be found, to send a message to Mr. X, to my family.

I grab my phone and dial Mr. X's number. He always answers on the first ring, but this time he doesn't. It goes to voicemail, something that has never happened. "Goddamn it," I shout at my phone. "The one time I need you to be stalking me, and you're taking a break." I hang up. Briefly, I wonder if someone has gotten to him, too. If he's even alive.

I swerve off of the road and onto a patch of dirt. There's a row of Cape Cod houses across the street, and maybe if I'm lucky, somebody is home. If this is the end for me, they'll call the police to report what they've seen. Waylen and Collette won't spend months wondering what happened to me, appealing to the news, making sappy Facebook posts about how much they want me to come home. It'll be clean, quick. They can have the funeral and know better than to look for me in crowds.

But if today is the day I die, I won't make it easy for them.

I retrieve my gun from the glove box and tuck it into my waistband before opening the car door. The gravel crunches as the car pulls up behind mine. *"I can't just call the police if you disappear on me."* Was it only this morning that Waylen said those words? It feels like ages ago. He won't be able to do this without me. He's too sensitive, too caring and sweet. He'll fall to pieces, and Collette will be tasked with holding him together. That will be her burden in life because she's twice cursed. Cursed with my strength, and cursed with having me for a mother.

It's a quiet suburb, not a single car passing us on the road now. But there are cars in the driveways of the adjacent houses. Wealthy retirees line the coast, and families that hire someone to clean their houses or nanny their kids. My heart has stopped pounding and I'm eerily calm. I have no idea why.

I'm expecting a driver to get out and accost me, but the back passenger door is the one that opens. In my mind there's a revolving door of every "client" I've ever put in jail or made to atone for their crimes. I do try to give them all a fair chance, and it's not my fault if they pick the option that lands them life in prison. If they play fair, if they do as I ask, they're free forever and I will never darken their doorway again. It's a promise I've always kept. So who is it? What loose end did I not properly tie?

A brown faux leather oxford shoe steps out. Bertram Casimir. His green eyes catch the light, which gives the illusion of a playful wink, but his expression is stony. His jaw is tight and his lips are set into a grim line, like a disappointed parent.

Is this the last thing Annie saw, before the end?

My mouth opens, but for all the questions spinning around in my head, I can't seem to form words. I end up gaping like a fish.

"What do you want, Margaux?" he asks. "Why are you snooping around my life?"

"Me?" I manage, and to my surprise my voice sounds firm. "You're the one chasing me all over town."

He takes one step toward me, and then another. My palms go cold, but I don't back away.

"Pretending to be a reporter," he says, so close now that I can smell his cologne. "Pretending to be a delivery person." I glance at his hands, at his pockets and waist. I don't see a weapon. But then, I can't see the driver of his car. For all I know, there's a gun trained on me right now. "Did you think I wouldn't look into you and your little friend from the supposed 'newspaper'?"

His voice is so calm and flat that it frightens me more than if he'd come out shouting, guns blazing like a cowboy in a TV western. It's apparently my turn to speak now. He raises an eyebrow expectantly.

Lying comes so easily to me most days. I've been doing it since I was a child. The day my parents died, all the rules were broken. I was a tightly bundled package, tied up with a little pink bow, and then suddenly it was as though someone pulled the ribbon loose. The box opened up and everything I was taught scattered in a million directions. I didn't chase the pieces because they didn't matter anymore.

But now I struggle to come up with something convincing. I hadn't expected to be caught. In all my years, I've never been found out. And so quickly.

But why had he followed me here? If he knew I was headed to his apartment, why not wait for me there?

The cameras.

He must not want any record of us meeting today.

"I was curious about you," is what comes out. "My friend was doing me a favor, but she isn't a part of it. It's just—I was always interested in tech, but I never had the opportunity to pursue it."

It's a weak lie, but one that will fuel his ego. I can only hope that's enough. But his expression remains unreadable. He nods to the open door. "Get in," he says. "We're going for a ride."

Now I take a step back. "No," I say.

He reaches into his pocket and my hand goes toward my gun, but he's only grabbing his phone. He swipes through something on the screen, then holds it up for me to see. The picture was taken this morning. It's of me climbing into my car, Collette standing behind me in the driveway with her hair neatly braided, wearing her sparkly purple backpack. "Get in the car," he says again.

I don't ask about Mr. X. If Bertram has already gotten to him, if he's still alive, just in case there's a chance that Bertram doesn't know about him. *Please be tracking my fucking phone,* I think. Bertram hasn't tried to take it away from me. But it doesn't matter because he's already found my Achilles' heel, the one person in the world I'd do anything for, including getting into this forsaken BMW that's now taking me God knows where.

There's a glass panel between us and the front seat, and its tint isn't as dark as the outside windows. I can just make out the silhouette of a driver who hasn't said a word to either of us. He seems to already know where he's headed.

"You don't need to be so nervous," Bertram says, looking at the way I'm clenching my skirt in my fists. "I'm not going to hurt you. Just show you something."

I don't say a word. At least, not until I can get a good read on him.

After a few minutes, I no longer recognize where we are, but I make a note of landmarks in case I'm able to run for it. A Little Free Library. An abandoned rustic firehouse with weeds growing through the cracks in the pavement. We turn down an unpaved road that's mostly dirt, until we're on some sort of private beach.

I don't check my phone, but nobody has tried to get ahold of me since Elodie's call. It will be hours before anyone expects to hear from me. It will get dark out. Ellen will call Waylen to ask when we're picking Collette up. He'll know, then, that something has happened.

The car stops in the middle of the beach, right where the dirt road turns into sand. The sun has broken through the clouds now, giving light and color to the dreary autumn morning. But a cold wind blows through when Bertram opens the door.

I could shoot him now, as he turns his back to me to

exit the vehicle. But then there's the driver to contend with. I won't be able to outrun him. And if the driver doesn't try to kill me, but instead plays it straight and calls the police, that wouldn't end well for me, either.

After weighing the limited, crappy options, I follow Bertram outside. We take a few steps toward the water, and then I see the strangest thing up ahead: There's a blanket laid out in the sand, weighted down on all four corners with rocks, and what looks like a—is that a *picnic basket*, of all things?

"Sit," he tells me, and the menacing deadpan voice has changed. He sounds more human now. As curious as I am confused, I do as he asks, and I watch him retrieve two glasses and a bottle of wine. Then a charcuterie board of fruit, cheeses, and crackers, wrapped carefully in layers of plastic.

"What is this?" I ask.

"There are no good beaches where I grew up," he says. "At least, not like the ones here." I watch as he undoes the plastic, revealing an array of fruit so colorful and fresh it's almost cinematic. "Even on a cold day, it's pretty, don't you think?"

I take the glass of wine he hands me, warily. It's a relatively cheap Bordeaux from the package store. I would expect something off-label and pretentious from a billionaire. Either way, I don't drink, not even after he takes a sip from his own glass. "There are a lot of people who have found their way to me recently," he says. "They use various aliases, under many guises." He smiles, boyish and charming. There's a dimple on his left cheek. "They want to cozy up to me for some favor, or—more often—someone has sent them."

"And that's what you think I'm doing," I say. "Cozying up for a favor."

"You tell me."

"I already did."

"Yes, but you were lying." He eats a grape, then nudges the plate toward me. "I did a little digging, and you don't have any background in technology. Went to school for fashion, dropped out your first year, got married, moved to a suburb, and now decorate living rooms and wedding venues for a living."

Where the hell are you? I will my thoughts to Mr. X, who still hasn't texted me back. Every day of my life, I can count on the fact that he's following me, maintaining a protective perimeter. I imagine him dead and bleeding from a series of bullet wounds in an alley somewhere. Tied up and anchored at the bottom of the Long Island Sound. He has never given me cause to worry about him—it's always the opposite, him worrying if it takes me more than two minutes to respond to his texts, or the GPS on my phone acts glitchy and he loses me for a few seconds too long.

But I betray nothing and meet Bertram with a cool gaze. I eat a piece of cheese from the charcuterie board. Brie, the expensive kind they sell at liquor stores.

"I'm a storyteller." I say this like it's a reluctant confession. "Not a journalist exactly. You're right. I don't work for a paper. But I get to the heart of things and then I write them down."

He raises an eyebrow. "A novelist?"

"This one is nonfiction," I say. I'm ad-libbing. But I'm a good liar, which is a source of contention with my husband, who wears his heart on his sleeve, and my daughter, who is better at it than she cares to admit. "I found out that you were living here and I wanted to learn more about the billionaire life. Elodie—she's a senior editor—has ties to a publishing house. She said that if I could write about your life in a compelling way, she'd offer me a six-figure book deal. That may be small change to you, but it could do a lot for me."

He studies me with such a steely gaze that I can't tell whether he believes me. His eyes are cool and sparkling green against the gray sky behind him. I'm thinking that I've screwed up this one. He's too clever, too guarded. Whether he killed his girlfriend—and where he put her body if he did—is for me to find out, and it won't be easy. However he managed to steal his sister's code and evade any threats of a lawsuit, he covered his tracks well. He doesn't make the usual slipups, like thinking a private web browser will erase his search history.

"I see," he says, after a long pause. He nudges the untouched glass of wine that I've set down toward me, and I take it, because I don't know what will happen if I make him unhappy. I'm out here alone with little in the way of a running start if he decides to lunge for my jugular.

But he doesn't get angry. He has the same quiet thoughtfulness that I see Waylen get sometimes when he's hunched over the computer on a long night, poring over a manuscript that's especially dense.

"I'm going to tell you something I don't tell many people," he goes on. Now he isn't looking at me, but at the water on the horizon, as though it's an old friend. "I was engaged a while back. It ended badly."

Annie Clarke. Oh shit, he's going to give me something

after all. I don't let on that I'm anticipating his next words, that I need to hear what he's going to say. I pretend this is brand-new information. "I'm sorry," I tell him. "A bad breakup?"

So, he's going for the pitiful angle. I try to work out what his plan is—because men in positions of power always have a plan. On the surface, he's talking as though we're on an impromptu date. Maybe this is his way of appearing vulnerable, opening up about his past, coaxing me to let my own guard down. Stalking me and following me like a creeper from a true-crime podcast isn't the best way to go about it, but I remind myself he is a recluse. Maybe he's forgotten how to act normal, if he ever knew.

Today, of all days, Mr. X is unavailable, when I need his advice. *Redirect,* I think. I'm not playing a romance angle with him. I suspect that will only make things messy. But I don't act yet. I want to see where this is going, because he's likely to give me something I can use.

He laughs, but it's a sad laugh, one that brings a bitter sneer to his upper lip. "Worse than bad. It doesn't matter. Anyway, what I'm saying is that I knew you were lying to me when we met, but I let you do it because you reminded me of her, or at least, the girl I thought she was. And I suppose that melted me a bit."

I don't know what Annie looks like because her face was covered in every available photo, but this isn't information I'm supposed to have. So I carry on playing dumb, and I let him do the talking.

"She was tenacious like you. And creative." There's a playful gleam in his eye when he looks at me again. "Bit of a liar like you as well."

Where is Annie, Bertram? I think. Did she run off to a better life, or is she six feet under somewhere?

"I'm not upset that you met me under false pretenses," he says. "But you should know I'm a very private person. I can't allow you to write a book about me. An article for a technology blog, sure, but nothing deeper than that."

I bow my head. "Can't blame me for trying. You're just so fascinating, it was worth a shot."

His smile doesn't quite reach his eyes. "I hope you find a story that's worth telling, Margaux. And I hope you get your publishing deal. But it won't be with me. I hope you understand."

I nod. This is still salvageable, I think. I can confer with Elodie and Mr. X and come up with a new plan. Seduce him, manipulate him, glue prosthetics to my face and try again under a false identity. Something.

But I'm too distracted to think right now. I'm too worried about Mr. X and his silence and what it means. Did Bertram already send someone to kill or subdue him? I don't dare grab my phone. I don't want Bertram to realize I still have it on me. He obviously wanted to meet me somewhere without cameras. Working in tech, he'd know how to get around digital Big Brother.

Instead, I indulge him in this bizarre little picnic, because I don't want to end up in the ocean next to Annie . . . allegedly. And I think about how all these pieces could possibly add up in a way that makes sense. Bertram is strange, to be sure, but he doesn't give off that cool, detached, sociopathic vibe I've seen from so many of my marks. And he doesn't seem like a liar, either—more like he just keeps his cards close to the vest.

Still, the *wrongness* of this situation unsettles me. For the first time, I want to abandon a mission. I can hear Waylen's voice in my head, begging me to do just that. To come home and be the person I pretend to be. I don't hate interior decorating or event planning. I'm good at it, even. In a split second, an alternate life flashes before my eyes. Watching Collette graduate high school. Retiring on a beach somewhere with my husband, sipping piña coladas and checking my stock portfolios from my phone. Never looking over my shoulder. Never receiving one more texted rundown of another criminal who needs to be held accountable for what they've done.

"I support your writing efforts," Bertram tells me. "We need more people who create things. Especially now. Part of why I work solo is because I don't like the way technology is being used. Sometimes I think we'd be better off going back to the nineties again."

It's such an unusual thing for someone like him to say. I can't tell if he's lying. Around him, my ability to detect bullshit always seems to be faulty.

"I really do support what you want to do," he goes on. "But I ask that you don't contact me again."

By the time he's returned me to my car, I'm left with more questions than answers. Elodie rings just as I'm climbing behind the steering wheel. "Have you been able to get ahold of Mr. X?" she asks me, stirring up the feeling of dread in my stomach once again.

"I'm going to check in on him," I say, making the decision as soon as I've said it.

"You know where he is?" she asks, incredulous. "You've seen him?"

Mr. X hasn't shared his real name with anyone. And he certainly hasn't shown his face, though if you're lucky you may catch a vehicle with tinted windows speeding by and suspect it's him, following you to ensure you're safe.

"It's a long story," I sigh. "I've known him since before he did . . . all of this. But I need a favor from you." I glance at the clock and then at my rearview mirror. Bertram's driver pulls out into the street, dutifully obeying the speed limit as he drives away. "I need you to pick up Collette. I'll text you the address. If she's feeling well enough, she has dance class right after school. I'll swing by and get her from there after I'm done."

"Margaux?" Elodie sounds apprehensive. "Are you sure everything's all right?"

"Uh-huh, of course!" I chirp. "See you later, and thanks."

I am full of lies today.

TEN

"Please don't be dead," I mutter.

The pseudonym *Mr. X* implies some sort of villainous lair. A Transylvanian castle set against the backdrop of a haunted gothic town, or some tech lab on a submarine at the bottom of the Atlantic Ocean. But he is, in fact, all human. He wears T-shirts and khakis, and he gets his hair cut twice a month, parted neatly on one side in the same way he's worn it since he was sixteen years old. He has a boyish face but serious eyes, the look of a man who has seen things that haunt him.

And he lives in a small gray house that he bought with inheritance money, market value of three hundred thousand dollars, precisely enough to purchase and fill with appliances without having to go into any debt.

I know these things about him, but I'm the only one who does. He isn't a trusting person, as evidenced by the five security cameras that are aimed at my car when I pull up to his home.

I drive down the long, paved driveway, then onto the grass, where there's already a dirt path made up of old tire treads, and I park behind the shed where my car won't be visible from the street. It's been years since I've visited—years since I've been invited—but I remember that he keeps this little parking spot to maintain privacy from the neighbors.

I don't bother trying the front door. Not only will it be locked, but he keeps a steel bookshelf in front of it. The windows will also be covered by the blackout blinds. Instead, I try the Bilco door that leads down into the basement. Success! It isn't locked. This on its own is concerning, but for now I'm just grateful I don't have to break a window.

The basement is frigid, filled with boxes and damp. I make sure to close the door behind me, but I don't lock it. Something nettles me, beyond the evidence that things aren't as they should be. Mr. X is as reliable as they come. At all hours, he answers his messages within seconds. It makes me wonder if he ever sleeps, and worry that the nightmares keep him up too often.

As I approach the staircase that leads to the kitchen, I can smell that something is starting to burn. By the time I turn the doorknob, I get a whiff of something vaguely sweet, like a batch of cookies—one of the only things he ever eats, though you wouldn't know it based on his slender frame.

Even before I've opened the door all the way, I see his arm, sprawled precariously against the pristine white tiles. Thin smoke is starting to billow out from the oven door, but the smoke detectors will be disabled—he would rather burn to death than allow rescue crews into his home. Which is why he's going to hate what I'm about to do.

My phone is already in my hand as I rush to his side. The first thing I do is make sure he's breathing. Miraculously, he's alive. Cold and pale, but alive. He doesn't respond when I shake him, and I'm startled by how terrible he looks when I roll him onto his back to check him for injuries. But there's nothing, not even a scratch.

The 911 operator is asking me what happened. An overdose? Accidental poisoning? Suicide attempt? Assault by some mystery assailant who's still lurking somewhere in the house? But I don't know. I'm cursing at him under my breath between the useless answers I utter into the phone.

"You can't die," I vaguely remember shouting at him as I turn off the oven. I shove the bookshelf away from the front door to make room for the ambulance crew. The sirens are already wailing in the distance. "Do you hear me?" I tell him. "You better not leave me. You can't leave me all alone."

Now I sit in the cold plastic chair in the waiting room at the hospital. Nobody has come to speak to me and it's been hours since they brought him in.

After they loaded him into the ambulance and carried him away, I stayed behind to replace the bookshelf and try to put things back the way he likes them. I don't want him to come home to the wheel marks on the carpet or the lamp that got knocked over by the paramedic trying to maintain his vitals.

I hold it together long enough to get in my car and follow him to the hospital. He'll be livid when he wakes up. He'll tell me that if he ever goes dark, I should just leave him be. I should let him die before letting anyone into his space. *What if they find out what I do?* he'll demand. *What if they find my files and realize the cases we're behind?* He'll tell me that it isn't just about him—he's protecting me, too. Me and Collette and even Waylen, although Collette has no idea the shit I've exposed her to indirectly.

When the doctor steps into the room, I stand. My hands are shaking—how long have they been shaking?—and I jam them into my pockets.

It's dark outside, the downtown lights twinkling like busy stars. But the thick glass muffles all the sound, and for now, the world is silent, as though it's on pause.

"You're family?" the doctor asks me.

I nod. Mr. X is going to kill me for this. I am breaking the cardinal rule between us, saying out loud the greatest secret he has, the one that I've never even told Waylen.

"I'm his sister."

Maybe this is the only true thing I've said all day.

My phone is buzzing in my purse, and I know Waylen will be worried first and furious second. I can't tell him the truth. *"You're lying."* Collette's voice in my head. *"You lie all the time."*

"He's stable now," the doctor is telling me, and I struggle to pay attention. "His white blood cell count dipped below normal, so we're checking his CBC and looking for anemia."

"I don't understand." I turn my phone off without checking it. Elodie will also be fishing for gossip about my life, no doubt intrigued by what I've been up to all day that I'm not sharing. "So, he just passed out?"

The doctor sits on one of the chairs and nods for me to do the same. Oh God, nothing good ever gets said by a doctor who wants you to sit down in a hospital waiting room. I shouldn't. I should run away, go back to my family, go back to my pretend suburban life, disentangled from whatever I'm about to hear. That's what he would want.

But he's my brother. I'm all he has. So, I stay. And I sit.

"Jeremy"—the doctor says the name so easily, though I haven't associated it with him since I was a child—"has stage three pancreatic cancer. It's metastasized to his kidneys. He was made aware of this several months ago but has been declining treatment."

The doctor is still going, saying more words even though I want to scream at him to stop. I stare just past him and the muted world on the other side of the window. Only, it's not entirely muted. There's a shrill whining in my ears. A screaming that won't stop. That will never stop.

"I want to see him," I blurt, interrupting something that was probably very important. "Where is he?"

"He isn't taking visitors—"

"I don't care," I say. "I'm here. He's here. Which button do I have to push in the elevator to make us be in the same place?"

The doctor sighs. Maybe he pities me. Maybe he sees fucked-up family dynamics every day when he comes to this room to update people about their loved ones. But he can't possibly know about us.

In any case, the doctor doesn't relent. He tells me that if Jeremy has a phone on him, I can call, but that he was told I was here and refused to see me. Refused. He's too proud to let me see him in a vulnerable state. Ever since we were kids, he's needed to take up the role as my protector.

I wait until the doctor is gone and then I start up my phone, ignoring the red icon alerting me to several missed calls and voicemails from Waylen. I pull up my text exchange with Mr. X, a one-sided conversation of me asking him to call me and if he's all right. Now I compose a new one:

Let me in to see you or I will go back to the house and take a lighter to everything.

He'll know what I mean. All his research, the records he keeps of the work we've done, the prospective new "clients."

Five minutes later, he texts back with his room number.

He's wide awake when I go to him, his bed propped all the way up.

"You look exactly the same," he tells me, at the same time I say, "You look like hell."

For a few seconds we just stare at each other. The last time I saw him in person we were also in a hospital. Collette had just been born, and Waylen, who had been at my side the whole time, finally went home to shower and bring me clean clothes. Mr. X—my brother—stayed only long enough to hold her, and to say, "It's better if she doesn't know." I knew what he was really saying—that he wanted to protect her from our past. The ugly truth about what happened to our parents. What we did. It was better for her to think that everything burned in the fire that night, and that I was the only survivor. My brother wants to protect me so I can have a clean future that isn't marked by my past. So I can be "normal" and not "the one that awful thing happened to."

"So, when were you going to tell me?" I fall into a chair by the bed. "That you're dying?"

"I'm not dying," he says flatly.

"If you thought that, you would have told me sooner," I reply.

He looks at one of the IV bags dripping medicine into his veins, slow and ominously like the final drops of rain on an old roof about to cave in.

"I'm handling my affairs, Margaux," he tells me soberly. "This is the last case I'm working. And then, when it was all over, I was going to make sure you received an envelope with all my passwords. The title to my house. Everything. I'm leaving it all to you, and if you want to carry on, you'll have what you need. But if you want to be done with it, it's yours to demolish if you want to."

This is so unlike him that at first, I don't know how to respond. "Demolish? You've made such a thing out of keeping our little business afloat. Aren't you the one who told me I'd be wasting my potential to give it all up and be a soccer mom?"

"I wanted to believe that because it made me feel better about doing all this," he admits. "But I wonder sometimes—if things hadn't happened the way they did when we were kids—if we would be out there living normal lives. Time cards, day care, morning commutes, playdates—"

"It doesn't matter." I cut him off. "It happened, and this is who we are."

But even as I say it, a part of me is terrified at the thought of losing him. I don't know who I am without my brother. I don't know what I'd do if he wasn't always around to tell me where to go, what to say, to assure me that I'm always safe. I try to imagine being alone with Waylen and Collette, and it feels like I'm drowning in a black hole in deep space with nothing to cling to no matter how I flail.

"We're going to get you into treatment," I say.

"Margaux—"

"Stop it. I've listened to you for years, now you listen to me. I'm going to go out there and talk to the doctor. We're going to get you chemo or—or whatever it is you need. If it can't be cured, we can nuke enough of it to keep you going for as long as possible."

I don't let him argue. I'm on my feet and headed for the door before he can open his mouth.

It's after midnight when I check my phone, already knowing Waylen will be steaming out his ears.

"I'm on my way home now," I tell him. "I'll explain everything." I'm already coming up with a plausible story, something that doesn't give away the truth. As Mr. X enters his treatments, he'll need me to do more for him. I'll have to follow up with doctors, make sure he's actually going to his appointments. Whatever I come up with will have to be believable.

But Waylen doesn't ask where I've been. He's too angry for that. "If you're going to explain anything, explain why you left Collette at her dance class."

Oh shit. Collette. As though I'm looking at scenes from someone else's life, I remember dropping her at her aunt's. Bertram chasing me. Calling Elodie and telling her I'll pick Collette up after her class.

Waylen doesn't let me sit in my guilt. "She thought you must have gotten into an accident. I thought that you were dead on the side of the road. Collette called me in hysterics. Her panic attack was so bad I almost drove her to the ER."

"I'm sorry," I blurt. "I'll be there soon. I'm coming right home."

"Coming from where?" he demands. "She said you dropped her off at my sister's and that Elodie Blevins picked her up? Why wasn't she in school today? Why was your phone off?"

I hang up. I have to, because tears are starting to fill my eyes and that's not acceptable. I can't cry. Not when Collette needs me, and there are alibis to come up with, and murderers to blackmail, and brothers to keep alive. I can't have emotion. I can't be weak. There's simply too much to do.

ELEVEN

So many times when Waylen and I have fought over my night job, the scene has been the same. We argue. Sometimes we yell, and sometimes we don't, but I'm always the one to come home late. There's the fading aroma of dinner, and the gentle hush of Collette's white noise machine as she sleeps. There's one light on, in the kitchen, where he's waiting for me to come and talk it out. Always talking. I've told so many lies at that kitchen table. I've said whatever will get us back to normal. And Waylen, whether or not he believes me, accepts my words because he wants the same thing.

But tonight, when I come home, there are no lights. There's no evidence that there's been dinner. Collette bull-rushes me so hard that I almost fall over. Her gold hair is a flash of lightning in the darkness. Her tears soak into my shirt.

I can't see Waylen in the living room, but I know he's there. I know that they both sat up for hours waiting for me.

I kiss the top of Collette's head. "Go get into bed, and I'll come see you after I talk to Dad."

"Will you promise to wake me up if I fall asleep?"

"I promise," I say.

She gives me one more squeeze, and she nods. "Will you tell me where you were?"

I smooth the hair out of her face. "Working late on a client. It's out in the valley where there's no cell service. I must have forgotten to tell you guys."

She stiffens as she draws away. Just barely, I can see her face lit up by a streetlamp through the window. A mix of disappointment and anger. She doesn't believe me.

Only after she's gone upstairs and closed her bedroom door does Waylen speak. "You were with him."

Anyone eavesdropping would think he was a husband accusing his wife of seeing an old lover after she'd promised the affair had ended. Wouldn't it be simpler if that were the truth.

From here, at least, things are familiar. Waylen saying he can't do this anymore, me saying I have to, and him wondering why. It all leads to the same conclusion, which is that he can't bear to lose me, and so he concedes.

He asks why I brought Collette to his sister's, if she was in any danger. I tell him no. And now that I know Bertram was only chasing me down to have that weird little picnic chat, I'm confident that this is the truth. Waylen would accuse me of losing my instincts for being so sure Bertram doesn't mean me harm. I'm always cautious and I never let my guard down. But the more I speak to Bertram, the more I'm convinced that he is just hopelessly out of touch. He's been rich and reclusive for so long, he doesn't remember how to interact with people.

Erin said little about his personality. I didn't press for more details because I could hear in her voice how much she hates him. Even before he stole Budgie from her, he was the golden child of the family, and her resentment is clear. Her feelings toward him are fair, but part of being a good spy is forming a picture based on the evidence presented. And evidently, Bertram is pretty weird.

When my phone buzzes in my pocket, Waylen glances at it as though it's a loaded gun. He's waiting to see what I'm going to do. That phone is at the heart of our marriage, the thing that tethers us and the thing that has the power to destroy everything we've built.

Sometimes I think it's inevitable—that destruction.

"I'm going to check on Collette," I say. It's the only way to end this for now. I can't sit here anymore in the dark, feeling the heat and the weight of his love for me. There are too many strings attached to it, and the more I struggle, the more they tighten around me.

Waylen is afraid he'll say the wrong thing and that I'll leave. I'm afraid he'll say the right things and that I'll stay.

I lie with Collette until she falls asleep, clinging to my shirt the way she did as a toddler.

Only once I'm sure she's really asleep do I check my phone. There are several notes from Elodie asking if I'm okay, to send a signal if I need anything, if I've heard from Mr. X. But her latest, sent just twenty minutes ago, says:

Really hope you're alive, because I've been working on something big.

I text back:

Proof he stole the app idea?

Her reply:

Better!

My reply:

After we drop off the girls.

She gives me a thumbs-up emoji.

I ease out of the bed slowly and make my way to the door. Just before I open it, Collette whispers, "Mom?"

"Yes, honey?"

"You won't leave us? I mean, you won't go away and never come back, will you?"

"Of course not."

"Okay," she says. And she seems to believe me, even if she is starting to doubt many of the other things I say. "Because if you had to leave, I'd want to go with you."

I meet Elodie at a parking garage at a high-end hotel, forty-five minutes from home. There are security cameras in case Bertram decides to follow me again and something were to happen. But it's busy enough that nobody will think it's strange to see two women chatting in a car here.

When Elodie asks, I tell her that Mr. X is doing just fine. He is paranoid about the government monitoring his phone—something about a bitter former client—and he's gone dark on all of his devices until he can neutralize the threat. But not to worry, the plan is still on, and he's still looking out for us.

This is enough of an explanation for her, and I can see that she's about to burst with pride. "I found Mr. Billionaire's girlfriend."

"Annie?"

She shakes her head. Her eyes are practically glittering. "This one is named Skylar. Look." She pulls up the Instagram page on her phone. Skylar Marie. One million followers. Only following one hundred people. Something Collette would call "a flex."

"I told you I've been working on a little side research," Elodie says, preening. "She's some sort of influencer-slash-model-whatever. She's been posting a lot of cryptic stories about having a broken heart and how Mr. Perfect wasn't all he's cracked up to be."

"How did you find her?" I ask. "How do you know it's about Bertram?"

She gives me that pitying *oh, honey* smile. For staying off social media, I'm dubbed the Mennonite of the PTA. "She was on a reality TV show for some streaming platform—one of those who-wants-to-be-a-top-model things. Only lasted a season, but it launched her social media career. I've been following her for years. Here, look."

She pulls up some screenshots of Skylar's now-deleted

Instagram stories. There's nothing identifying about any of these sad professions of love turned resentful. That is until the last screenshot: A photo of her standing in the arms of a man in a tailored suit, a giant eggplant emoji covering his face. But even without his face, I recognize him, and his apartment's fireplace behind them. The caption reads: **The things I know could destroy you, but I know what comes around goes around, and I don't have to say a word.**

"But wait," I say. "He was dating Annie before he even came to America, and she hasn't been missing for very long."

"There's definitely overlap." Elodie is giddy.

"What are you thinking of doing?" I ask.

"Since Mr. X has gone dark on us, it seems we're on our own in terms of research, at least for now." Mercifully, she believes my explanation. She prefers to be in the spotlight where she can collect the glory anyway. She's the perfect match for someone like me who works best in the shadows. "I say we should meet her. She's in NYC, just a quick train ride away."

"You mean just pop up at her apartment and ask her for gossip on Bertram?" I ask. "She's going to turn us away, if she doesn't call the police."

Elodie looks sheepish, and I can't tell whether this is sincere or an act she's putting on for my benefit. "I sort of . . . already handled it."

I rub my temples. "What do you mean, Elodie?"

She launches into a tirade about how Skylar had mentioned in previous posts that her twin nieces are turning seven soon. Elodie direct messaged her and suggested an interior decorator to design a custom theme. She linked her to my minimalist website, which boasts more than a thousand positive ratings. Most of my reviews are fake, but I do aim to please the clients I work with as a front to my secret life.

I don't have much of a web presence, but Elodie used this to her benefit also. I'm very word-of-mouth, very exclusive, and of course I don't advertise. Do the Kardashians use party planners who show up at the top of Google search results? Of course not.

"Imagine if you used your powers for good," I say.

This makes her grin. "You know," she says. "You have such a glowing reputation at the school. Everyone talks about the baked goods you bring, and all the extra hours you put in at the school plays and parties. I'm a little jealous."

Thanks, I think. *Making little things sparkle comes from a deep desire to avoid my larger issues.*

"I like details," I say.

"But what about people?" Elodie asks.

"I like them well enough," I say. But Elodie's mischievous grin pulls a little truth out of me. "In small doses."

If buddy-cop comedies and stakeout episodes of law-and-crime TV shows are to be believed, there's a special bonding that happens in cars. The effect even works on me, because the more time I spend with Elodie, the more I'm starting to think we could get along.

"I can never talk to them about what I really do, so what's the point? 'Wow, Cynthia, sorry to hear you didn't get that promotion. The alleged murderer I'm pursuing under cover of darkness hasn't left enough evidence for a conviction, so I'm also not advancing in my career.'"

Elodie throws her head back, laughing in a way I did not expect. I wonder if I could have had a friend like her if my teen years had been normal. Someone to go to the movies with, or drive around, talking about our silly problems, commiserating over crushes and homework and our parents.

But my teen years were spent locked in a legal battle where I was forced to fight for my freedom. When I met Waylen, he was the only one who had given me a sense of "home" in years; the fact that he wanted to build a life with me endeared him to me more than chocolate or roses or cheesy poetry ever could. *Just try making friends,* he's always saying, in that gentle, coaxing way of his. *You deserve them.*

Curse Waylen and his ceaseless optimism for people. His happy childhood didn't make him much of a cynic.

"Well, I hope we can be friends," Elodie says. "I'm really good at keeping a secret. Or two."

I'm thankful that she breezes forward without giving me time to respond, because I'm suddenly feeling too awkward to reply. "So, what do you say? A train leaves for NYC every twenty minutes or so. We can be there in a couple of hours."

Today I need to go to the hospital to speak with Mr. X's doctors. And then I need to go to his house and secure his computers and documents so that there's no trace of them when he comes home. He will need in-home care, whether he wants to admit it or not. Already the pressure is overwhelming as I realize I'm carrying the weight of all he does for me.

He's protected me all my life. We're all each other has, and now it's my turn to look after him. So I hide how stressed I am. I don't want him to see how hard it is to take over his role and pretend everything is fine. I owe him that much.

How will I keep Elodie safe? How will I keep myself safe?

I don't say any of this, of course. I can't. *I'm really good at keeping a secret,* Elodie just said. But I'm no good at sharing them.

"I'm working on something here," I say. What's one more little lie, if it's for a good cause? And anyway, it's partly true. I do need to figure out a new in with Bertram. "Bertram isn't buying the book angle, so I'm trying something new."

Elodie pulls the ponytail holder from my hair.

"Ow!"

"Your hair is one of your best attributes." She waggles her eyebrows at my breasts. "One of your *three* best attributes. Don't be afraid to use what you've got."

"I'm not going to seduce him," I say. "A little flirting was fun to get us in the door, but if I give him the wrong impression, I could derail the whole thing."

"Nobody said *seduce,*" Elodie counters. "Mislead, maybe. Just to keep him on the hook."

I snatch the ponytail holder from her hand, and she hisses playfully at me, like a cat.

"I'm happily married," I say. Waylen would be beside himself with glee to hear me admit it.

"Yeah, yeah, me too," Elodie says, tapping her wedding ring against mine like two champagne glasses. "But seriously, what's your angle? Maybe I can help."

If I want to communicate with Elodie, I have to mimic

her a bit. Speak her language. Lean into the whole "girl talk" conspiratorial tone she's set up for us. So when I open the car door, I glance back at her with a wry smile. "A magician never reveals her tricks."

Mr. X is looking much better this morning, after a night of fluids and hospital cafeteria Salisbury steak. But he grouses that it's impossible to sleep here, because there's someone waking him up every half hour for his vitals. He wants to come home. I tell him that if he hadn't ignored his illness for so long, maybe it wouldn't be this bad. I tell him that I'm looking into home care options and I don't let him argue. According to his doctors, remission may still be on the table. All he needs to do is rest, and I'll handle everything.

"That isn't the way it's supposed to work, Margaux," he tells me as I'm getting ready to leave. "I'm supposed to look after you."

"We're supposed to look out for each other," I tell him. And then I close the door behind me.

In the elevator, I catch my reflection in the metal doors. For a second, I see the twelve-year-old girl I once was, in another elevator in another hospital, all the way in Oregon. I had just been told my parents were gone, and it felt as though the world was ending.

My brother and I are not those kids anymore, I tell myself. *And nobody knows what we did.*

I stride through the hospital parking garage with new determination. I can handle things while he's infirm—of course I can. First I'll settle things at his house.

Then I'll go to Bertram's apartment. He'll try to turn me away, but it doesn't take much to catch him off guard. He can't say no to me. Elodie is the one who pointed it out, the afternoon that we got lunch after meeting with Bertram. *"You don't come on too strong,"* she'd told me. *"Your sex appeal has softened edges, like a soap opera filter."*

I'm still trying to figure out whether that was a backhanded compliment.

I spent last night planning this part out, given that I couldn't sleep after my argument with Waylen. I'll take a softer approach—as a romantic prospect. He practically handed me this idea on a silver platter.

I'm drafting up a script in my head. How should I play it? Demure and sweet? Confident and cocky? Something to match his energy and reach the real Bertram, not the part he's playing when he has someone to impress. If I get him vulnerable and soft, he'll either open up and tell me the truth about Erin's app and where Annie is, or he'll show me his true colors. Either way, I'll have him.

The screeching of tires echoes throughout the garage. I turn my head just in time to see a black Honda speeding toward me. Even the windows are tinted an impenetrable black.

There's a phenomenon known as the deer-in-the-headlights look. Something is speeding toward you and you know that you'll die if you don't get out of its path. And yet, your feet won't move.

I stand frozen on the gray concrete, smelling the exhaust and listening to the rev of the engine. *Move,* I hear my own mind screaming at me.

And then, suddenly, there's a flash of light, movement,

and I'm on the ground. Something crashed into me, but it wasn't the car. I hear the squeal of its tires as it speeds down to a lower level and out of sight.

My heart is hammering in my chest. Hands grab me under the shoulders and hoist me to my feet, and when I look up, I'm staring into the infuriatingly pretty eyes of Bertram Casimir. His brow is furrowed in concern. "Are you all right?"

"Why is it that cars are always chasing me when you're nearby?"

"Trouble always seems to find me even though I go out of my way to avoid it, and I can see you have the same problem," he says. He has the sense to look chagrined. "Come on," he says. "Get in your car. My driver will follow us out and make sure you're okay."

"What do you mean 'us'?" I ask. "You can't think I'm letting you into *my* car after—well, everything."

The rev of an engine on the lower parking level gives me a rapid change of heart. Whoever is trying to hit me is back, and I have more than a sneaking suspicion that Bertram can offer some insights into this situation. I barely give him time to buckle his seat belt before I throw the car in reverse and peel out of the spot. Mr. or Ms. Black Honda Civic is back and going full throttle.

I am fully aware that Mr. X has limited means of tracking me. He's laid up in a hospital bed with nothing but the Find My app to follow my movements. He can do nothing if I find myself in hot water—which seems inevitable ever since meeting Bertram Casimir.

Bertram must have had me followed, the same way he did when he brought me to that strange picnic.

"Shit," I mutter, as we approach the tollbooth at the exit. There's a striped bar between us and the street.

"Go!" Bertram says.

"But—"

He reaches over and jams my knee down so that I'm forced to slam down when I tap the gas pedal, sending us careening forward. The striped bar snaps like a twig, and I wince at the metal crunch it makes against my paint job. Waylen is going to kill me, if whoever is pursuing us doesn't get the privilege first.

I speed out into traffic, incurring the wrath of a dozen angry car horns. I blow through two red lights, relying on a wish and a prayer to avoid a collision. Somehow, Bertram's driver keeps pace with me, acting as a buffer between us and whoever is chasing us down.

We're five miles from the hospital before I glance in the rearview mirror to see that nobody else is following us. I let out a shaky breath. Beside me, Bertram is just a bit *too* casual about what's happened, as though being chased by a murderous stranger is a routine thing to happen at ten a.m. on a Tuesday. He directs me to get on the highway, southbound, in the lane that will eventually take us to New York.

Mr. X will see my location and wonder what the hell is going on. I'll make up something when he inevitably calls. No need to worry him when he can't help me anyway.

"Okay, what is happening?" I glance at Bertram, who is turned around in his seat and making sure his driver is still following us.

But if I was expecting an explanation, I had another thing coming.

"I warned you to stay out of my life," he snaps. "But you

couldn't stop meddling, and now you've made trouble for us both!"

"Meddling?" I cry. "I haven't done anything. I was in the hospital visiting a friend."

"You know what I mean." His voice is low, not quite seething. "You've been all over the place asking about me. You went to one of the wedding venues I toured. You and that little friend of yours contacted my ex."

"Elodie is *not* my friend. And anyway, no, I didn't—"

"You're lying." He sounds less angry now. There's something else on his face—the darkened eyes, the clenched jaw. If I didn't know better, I'd say he was afraid. *It's all an act,* my logical mind tells me. This man is a murderer at worst, and a thief at best. Knowing my luck, he's both. What could possibly scare someone like that?

I tamp down my argument and switch tactics. I decide to be sweet, a damsel in distress. Exactly his type. "Bertram." I say his name gently. "I'm here with you. I'm doing what you've asked. I'm driving who even knows where, instead of going to work. You have to give me something. What's going on?"

He glances in the mirror, to be sure that his driver is the only one following us.

"I've come all the way across the country to get away from someone, but she finds me wherever I go."

"Who?" I ask.

"An old girlfriend." He sighs. "Her name's Annie."

Oh, Elodie is going to hate me when I tell her that I've come by this revelation without her. Annie Clarke, Bertram's missing ex-girlfriend, is out there somewhere. Maybe she's not dead after all.

Some part of me is relieved, not just because I want this poor woman to be alive for her own sake, but because I need to feel like my radar isn't thrown completely off. I can't bring myself to believe that Bertram is a murderer. Something in my gut tells me there's more to this, and if it turns out that I'm wrong, how will I ever trust my instincts again?

"Your old girlfriend is trying to run me down in a parking garage?" I ask. "Why don't we just confront her?" I need to confirm that she's alive before I bring this to Elodie.

He glances sidelong at me. "You don't know what we're dealing with. She's—unlike anything you've ever seen."

"I can handle myself."

"She's dangerous," he snaps. "Very dangerous."

"So, we'll go to the police." I'm bluffing, of course.

"I can't prove it." He sounds frustrated now. "But she's done things. Terrible things."

I swerve across two lanes to take the exit, summoning a chorus of angry car horns. Bertram grips the seat. I speed down the off-ramp and pull into the lot of an abandoned mechanic. There's nothing here but a termite-ridden sign. His driver didn't have time to get off the exit after us. He'll have to turn around at the next one, which buys me about ten minutes.

"Tell me what's going on, Bertram, or I swear I will take this car straight to the police station."

I see true fear on his face. Finally, we're getting somewhere. Innocent people don't fear the police, but most innocent people aren't reclusive billionaires who fear having a public record of their private lives.

"You won't believe it."

"Try me." I lock the doors for dramatic effect. "Who is Annie?"

Mr. X would kill me for taking such a risk, out here unprotected. But I'll take my chances. Flirting, charming, and playing nice haven't worked. Perhaps Mr. Billionaire will respond to some aggression.

"We were college sweethearts," he says, sighing. "We were going to get married, but it got . . . complicated. We ended things, and I thought she was happy enough to be rid of me, but she started . . . following me. Everywhere. Harassing my family, anyone else I dated, all my friends. She chased everyone away."

From all the articles I've read on Bertram, very few talk about his private life. There's no mention of his parents, his sister, or any friends. I didn't think that was too weird. Once you get successful enough, it's lonely at the top.

Right now, though, I'm astonished by how smoothly he lies, astonished by myself, for not being able to tell his truth from his fabrications. Annie Clarke isn't an old spurned lover. She's an innocent victim who may or may not be anchored to the ocean floor right now. But sure, I can play along.

"So, where is she now?"

"Here—everywhere—I don't know. It's complicated." I never could have imagined Bertram this flustered. "I haven't seen her in a while, but she makes herself known."

He grabs my shoulders. His grip isn't painful, but it's firm. Desperate. "She hurts anyone who gets close to me. She's hell-bent on destroying my life."

For once, I wish Elodie were here. She may love a little gossip, but that's what makes her so good at getting people to talk. I try to channel some of her energy now, batting my eyelashes and leaning toward him. "Bertram, whatever she's done, I can help you. I'm a good storyteller. Finding people and getting them to talk to me is what I do best."

"I don't want you to find her." He's still holding on to me, but he seems aware of it now, and he eases his grip. "No matter where I go, she finds me. That's why I lured you out to the beach, so we could talk somewhere with almost no cell reception and no cameras."

"That's why you were at the hospital, too. You were having me followed because you thought Annie was stalking me, too? Because she knew I was looking for her?"

"Yes," he confesses. "Escaping her in California became impossible, unless I wanted to live out on a farm somewhere. I came all the way across the bloody country, but I know she's here, somehow."

"Since the pandemic, lots of Silicon Valley has gone virtual," I said. "I figured you were here because you like the seasons."

"I don't care about bloody seasons, Margaux!" His outburst startles him and he lets go of me. "I've *tried* the police, don't you think I've tried everything? No one believes I'd be intimidated by an ex-girlfriend, especially one that nobody can seem to find."

"Okay." I take his hands in mine. They're infuriatingly soft. Who knew a tech billionaire would have a moisturizing routine? "Bertram, I'm here. I believe you."

The sound of tires on the gravel makes us turn our heads. His driver is pulling up behind us.

Bertram stares at me, and the fear in his eyes makes him something fierce.

"Tell me," I say, smoothing my hand across his temple. Elodie is right—a little flirting is a powerful truth serum. Waylen wouldn't be able to deny it himself. But still, it makes the hairs on the back of my neck rise. "Tell me what Annie's done. Do you know where she is?"

Waylen lives with the fear that I'll leave him. But it would never be for someone else. It would be for solitude, disappearing into the abyss of my own mind, honoring the wounded little girl inside my heart who doesn't think she deserves to be loved and is afraid to let anyone try. *That's* why Waylen won't let me go.

Bertram, for all his charms, is a symptom of something else. I want to crack him open like a vault to see what's inside. I want to be the one who learns the truth about him, and to be the reason he faces consequences for it.

TWELVE

When I finally convince Bertram to return to his apartment, I'm unsettled by the smoothness of his lies.

I have worked with all types of "clients." From murderers to embezzlers to small-time pyramid-scheme entrepreneurs. Usually, I can smell a lie from a mile away.

So when Elodie and I meet up at the school parking lot an hour before pickup, I decide not to mention my encounter with Bertram yet, nor do I mention that Bertram now knows Elodie and I contacted Skylar. Elodie will want to act on it. She's not one to sit idly by. I'm worried she'll scare Bertram off, and then he'll stop telling me anything at all.

"Margaux, hi!" She jumps out of her SUV, arms extended to give me a big hug. Her message couldn't be clearer: We're being watched. The parents at Westport Elementary aren't exactly peeking at us through the blinds, but a butterfly doesn't fart in this town without someone making a note of it.

Elodie wraps an arm around me and we make our way to the bench just outside the playground. **SHARING IS CARING** is painted onto an oil drum trash can.

"How'd it go with Skylar?" I ask.

Elodie's eyes are bright in that way that tells me she's got a juicy bit of gossip. "Turns out our billionaire was seeing this Skylar person in secret, but Annie found out. He ended things and hasn't spoken with her since."

"But then he ended things with Annie, too. Why?"

Elodie waves her hand dismissively. "Skylar says they were on-again, off-again. But Annie called Skylar directly and put a stop to things over the summer."

I know Annie was confirmed to be alive just a few months ago, but she's been MIA ever since.

"That's all it took for her to back off?"

"Well." Elodie leans in. "Apparently, Bertram tried to reignite things after the breakup with Annie, but he flaked out and ghosted her."

"You got all of this out of her?" I say.

"Of course," Elodie says. "A telemarketer called me, and I broke down crying and yelled at him like he was my toxic ex. Earned her sympathy and made a new bestie for life. She couldn't wait to tell me all about Bertram."

"Sinister," I say. I consider this information against what Bertram told me. I think of how he charmed me with his little picnic but then chased me away. The fear in his eyes and the way he grabbed me when he spoke about it. "So, he's not seeing anybody right now. What's his game?"

"Technically, we're investigating him for stealing that

app," Elodie says. "But his love life is far more interesting, and something tells me that's where the real story is."

"Yes . . ." I trail off.

"What are you thinking?" Elodie asks.

"That I'd like to meet this Skylar."

"Good news, then!" Elodie beams. "I got us a gig planning an event for her in December, two weeks from now."

My stomach fills with dread. "When in December?"

"The first."

Her concerned look fades away, and I'm lost in my thoughts. December first, of all days. Waylen's birthday. The big four-oh. I can already hear the argument now. "Can't we make it for another day?"

"That's the date of her twin nieces' birthday," Elodie says. "That's when the party is, so no. Why? What's up?"

Thankfully, part of being a skilled liar is that I can cover up stress quite well. "Waylen and I had a little something that night, I think, but I'll see about changing it."

"Great!" Elodie clasps her hands together. "I really think this will get the ball rolling on things. Bertram has been infuriating to crack. Have you had any progress on your end?"

"Not yet . . ." I trail off, considering. "I've just had an idea. Annie disappeared while she was dating Bertram. Erin knew about this, despite how badly Bertram tried to hide it. So, if Bertram was seeing Skylar on the side, maybe Erin will also have some insights about that. Maybe she can tell us more about her personality, some ways we can get her to open up to you even more."

"Oooh, good idea!" Elodie is already grabbing her phone and scrolling through her contacts.

"Oh, and I meant to tell you," Elodie goes on. "Finnegan is really looking forward to having Collette tutor her this weekend."

I give Elodie my best smile. "I think our girls can be great friends." It's the biggest lie I've told all week.

The phone rings. Elodie puts it on speaker, and we both huddle together.

"Hello?" Erin's voice is soft, almost dazed, as though we've just woken her up. Mr. X's policy is to call the client at least once during a mission without warning. When you interrupt people being themselves, you can learn something new about them. Even the people who are hiring you to do the work.

Erin, much like Bertram, has been an enigma. Something is odd about each of them, in a tandem way. Something is similar about their mannerisms and their secrecy.

But I don't express this. I continue to observe her, taking a similar approach to Bertram.

"Erin, hi!" Elodie takes the lead. I'm happy to observe how Erin will handle the news. "I'm here with my colleague. Listen, we have a little update for you. I've managed to track down one of Bertram's girlfriends."

"Girlfriends?" Erin sounds more awake now. "You mean Annie? You've found her?"

"Skylar," Elodie says. "Bertram was seeing her at the same time—"

"No," Erin interrupts. "That must be a mistake."

This activates the gossip quadrant of Elodie's brain, and she launches into an excited explanation of how, according to Skylar, it was a loveless relationship with Annie by the end. So Bertram promised Skylar the moon and stars. But then Bertram abruptly ended things with no explanation and left her heartbroken.

I'm tempted to tell Elodie to stop sharing so much. Tact is key in cases like this. But Erin is so hard to read that I decide it's better to see how this plays out.

There's "good cop, bad cop" and then there's "hyperexcitable cop, silently-nodding-along cop." If Elodie overshares and this puts Erin off, I can step in and speak in a softer tone, isolating her and leading her to trust me.

Once Elodie stops speaking, the line is so silent that for a second, I think we've been disconnected.

"Hello?" Elodie says.

"I didn't hire you to snoop into his love life," Erin finally says, in a cool, almost emotionless tone. "I hired you to prove that he stole billions of dollars in investments and funding that should rightfully be going to me."

"This is all connected," Elodie says, clearly flummoxed. "It speaks to his character—"

"Call me back when you have something about that app," Erin says curtly, and then the line goes dead.

Elodie stares at the screen as though it's just committed some grave atrocity against her entire family. "I don't get it. *All* of this information is relevant, isn't it? She asked us to look into Annie's disappearance!"

I put a reassuring hand on her shoulder. "We may not be able to get Bertram on stealing the app. And even if we do, he's got the best lawyers that money can buy. He can tie Erin up in legal fees until she's bankrupt. Finding out what happened to Annie and getting him on her possible disappearance is the best place to start. Once he's in prison for that, he'll be *way* more likely to negotiate with us if we can offer him a lighter sentence."

"Exactly," Elodie says. "It's not like in the movies where the bad guy is just *found* guilty. They play dirty, so we have to play dirtier."

"We should get some vinyl decals made up," I say. "That's a great sales pitch."

Elodie gives me a wan smile, but clearly, she's unsettled by the exchange. She's new to this line of work, and she doesn't understand that charm can only get you so far with these sorts of clients. They have their eye on revenge. It isn't about whether they like us—in fact, most of the time they won't.

But Elodie surprises me by doing something I wouldn't have expected of her. She asks me for advice. "What should we do? This could be a very long process. If she thinks the way we're going about it is all wrong, she's less likely to help us."

Because Erin isn't the subject of our investigation, I haven't had the time to research much about her. And Mr. X, incapacitated as he is, has grudgingly had to put his workload on hold.

But she's a strange one. I've thought that from day one. Estranged from her entire family, unemployed, collecting money from who knows where to pay the rent. She believes her ship will come in if she can prove that Bertram stole Budgie, and that's what I'm here to do for her. But her entire life seems to be on hold until then. It's unusual. I've worked with all sorts of clients who hire me to spy and gain intel on people who have wronged them. Every one of those clients has maintained some semblance of a life. Working, having a family, painting as a hobby—*something.* But not Erin. I've circled by her rental several times, only to find her curtains always drawn and her car always in the parking spot.

I thought it was best to just leave her alone. But Elodie has a point. If she's not on board, it could serve as another roadblock. And Bertram is closed off enough as it is.

"We should go over there tomorrow morning and talk to her in person. Explain the process and give her the notes we've compiled so far about Annie. I wish we could give her more information, but right now, the more time we spend investigating, the more questions we have. We'll see what she can answer for us."

"A house call!" Elodie is excited again. "I'll bring croissants!"

The doors to the school open, and we rise to our feet. Finnegan is one of the first students out of the door, bouncing happily toward Elodie, as Elodie assumes her position directing the pickup line.

Collette is somewhere in the middle of the sea of students. She walks gracefully and deliberately. When I was a kid, I had a cat that moved in a similar way. It used to nap on the shelf where we kept the wineglasses, its long, slender body curled deliberately between the glasses without moving them so much as a centimeter out of place.

But I don't tell Collette about my cat, or anything else about my childhood. I don't tell her about what I do after she's gone to bed.

She gives me a small smile as we get into the car.

"Why are you parked in the lot?" she asks me as I buckle my seat belt. "You usually pick me up in the line."

"I was early, darling," I tell her. "So I had a chat with Mrs. Blevins."

In the rearview mirror, I see Collette wrinkle her nose. "Do I have to tutor Finnegan?"

"If you're open-minded about it, you may just make a friend," I tell her. "Look at me and Mrs. Blevins. I didn't think we'd get along, but we have a lot in common."

"Like what?" Collette asks.

"Well . . . we both like croissants."

Collette rolls her eyes and stares out the window. That's new. Who is *this* child? I switch gears and ask her, "How was school?"

"Fine."

"Can you elaborate?"

"I got a ninety-seven on my book report for *Mrs. Frisby and the Rats of NIMH*. I said it was timeless, because teaching the rats to read and write isn't all that different than using AI to create art."

It is a clinical and yet impressive response that leaves me stunned. "That was only worth a ninety-seven?"

"I misspelled 'genocide.'"

This time last year, Collette was decorating the back of the seats with unicorn stickers, the glitter from which has never fully vacuumed out of the upholstery. She was bubbly and all too excited to tell me about her day. Now she tiptoes around my questions, giving me just enough to have technically answered me.

We ride in silence for the rest of the way, and as I pull

into the driveway, it occurs to me that Collette has spent eight hours away from me, and I have no idea what she's done in that time, and she isn't going to tell me.

She tells me that she's going up to her bedroom to do her homework, and I tell her that she can come and ask for her iPad once she's finished and I've checked it.

I hear the familiar clack of Waylen's keyboard as I head up the stairs, and I find myself craving the sameness of it. Waylen never changes, never does a single unpredictable thing. Most days, this puts us at odds because it is our biggest difference. But today, I find it oddly comforting. Before I open the door, I know I'll see his familiar silver hair, his tense, hunched shoulders. He'll close the laptop screen, swivel in his chair, and say, "What's up?"

That's exactly what happens. But the smile on his face is guarded. We haven't been on the best terms since our disagreement. Well, string of disagreements, really.

I sit on the small couch by his desk. "Can we talk?"

There's concern on his face. "Is everything all right?"

God, I hope this doesn't blow up our marriage. We're already on a tightrope. I decide to cut right to the chase. Waylen may hate my line of work, but he at least appreciates straightforwardness. "In two weeks, I have to go into the city. For work."

"For design work?" he asks. "Or . . . work?"

I tug nervously at my hair. "A bit of both. There's someone out there who needs a host for her event, and she'll definitely have valuable information. The only thing is that it has to be on that exact date, and there's no wiggle room."

His eyes change. "What date?"

"December first." The words are glue in my mouth. I

dread the argument that's coming. The days of awkward family dinners, Collette picking up on the tension and neither of us knowing what to tell her.

He's still sitting in his computer chair. His eyes gaze downward, and there's a long pause. Then he nods.

"I was doing a little snooping into this case. I hope you don't mind. This billionaire you're tracking down—he's gotten himself into some sketchy shit, yeah?"

I'm so shocked that at first, I can't think of a response. I was expecting a fight. A passive-aggressive huff as he turned back to his desk. A preplanned monologue about why I should give up on this and all future vigilante endeavors.

I was not prepared for Waylen to ask me questions. I didn't anticipate the interest he shows me now.

"Tell me what you're planning," he says. "Tell me how you're going to make him pay."

It's been years since he's asked me about a case, and I find that I'm still eager to talk to him about it. I tell him about Bertram's dodgy love life, how I'm the only one who can make him fry for the murder of his missing fiancée. How he'll be exposed as a fraud and lose everything. And the whole media machine will wonder who brought down one of the tech world's most powerful men, but only Waylen will know it was me.

For just one moment, our diverging worlds meet. I want him to still love what we used to do together. He wants me to come home to him. It isn't often that we get both.

"Promise me," he says.

"What?" I ask.

"Promise that this is the last one. After this, you'll quit."

If I can't solve this case, there are no stakes that the world will see. There will be no news outlets reporting my failure. Nobody in the world is expecting to hear about it, which is the case for most of the projects I take on. Even when I've succeeded, I'm never the one who takes credit.

I don't answer him.

Waylen and I know the real stakes. All these years, Waylen has been waiting for me to let one slip through the cracks. He's been waiting for me to finally meet the client I can't help, and give up on the case I can't solve. Because then, I'll be all his.

THIRTEEN

To: ProfJArtler@Yale
From: Jennifer Smith

Dear Professor Artler,
I'm a journalist writing a piece on Bertram Casimir. It's my understanding that he's a former student of yours. He's cited you as a big inspiration. I would love to set up a time to chat, if you're available.

Sincerely,
Jennifer Smith

I send the email at three a.m., when I'm sure I'm the only one awake. I've sent the same email to half a dozen professors at Yale. It's desperate, but one of them must have worked with Bertram while he was a student there.

Never overlook a lead, no matter how small. While Elodie

chases Bertram's love life, I'll dig into his academic one. He may be a reclusive billionaire now, but he was a run-of-the-mill upper-class college boy just a few years ago.

CEOs, millionaires, and tycoons pay big bucks to scrub their past lives from the internet, but if you look, there's always a crumb left behind.

So, was Waylen mad?" Elodie asks.

"What?" I realize only now that I've been staring off into space, my mind numb. I'm exhausted. I slept horribly last night, disturbed by weird dreams of Bertram Casimir throwing Annie's body from a jagged seaside cliff. In one bizarre dream, as Annie's body fell in slow motion, he offered his hand to me to tango along the edge.

"When you told him that you had to work on December first." We're in Elodie's car, about to turn onto the block of Erin's condo complex.

"Oh, that," I say. "No, he understands."

"Really?" Elodie says. "That's great. Todd is being a miserable son of a beach because the twins are such a handful. I said: You think playing Roblox is a handful? Try pushing them out your vag like you're a human water slide, and then come back and tell me about hard."

I laugh, but she glances at me as she pulls into a parking space. She can smell gossip from a million miles away in a snowstorm. "What's the matter?"

"Nothing," I say. "Just—thinking about how we should handle this. You did all the talking last time. Maybe I should try. She doesn't seem to like how friendly and open you are."

"You mean she's got a stick up her butt."

"Exactly," I say. "I can see how she's related to Bertram. They're both so serious about things."

"I meant to ask how that's going," Elodie says. "You've spent more time with him. Anything stand out?"

"It's a dead end," I tell her, though I'm not entirely sure that's true. "I think Skylar is a better lead."

Elodie smirks. "You can tell me, you know."

"Tell you what?"

"If you sleep with him." She says it without her usual flair for the dramatic, which somehow makes it worse because I know she's being sincere.

"I'm not going to sleep with him," I say, not giving her any emotion to play off of.

"But have you ever? You know, for the good of the cause."

"Nope. Look, we're here." I unbuckle my seat belt and reach for the door.

"Wait," she says, her harried tone so uncharacteristic that I freeze with my hand on the lever. "I'm sorry. That wasn't appropriate. Todd is always on me about that, you know?"

"It's fine," I say. I can sense another buddy-cop bonding moment, and I'm desperate to end it before it begins. *Let it go, Elodie. Let me be surly and quiet and unapproachable in peace.*

"No." She locks the doors just as I pull the lever. "Please listen. I know what you meant earlier about not having enough to say to all of those other parents at the girls' school. None of them knows about my . . . brief stint with law enforcement. Mr. X promised to purge it from any public records when I agreed to work with him. And it isn't much—clearly, you've been doing this a lot longer than I have—but I wanted to say I admire your ability to stay so calm."

The words surprise me. After years of hearing Waylen beg me to quit, I realize this is the first time someone is telling me I'm good at what I do.

"Thank you," I say.

"But also," she goes on, "I wanted to say that doing this work is lonely. You're allowed to have a friend."

I can tell by the bright, eager look in her eyes that she's inviting me to partake in a brand-new mission, one much messier and more difficult than trying to catch a billionaire murderer. Navigating a friendship is something I haven't done since I was a child. Being easy to like, showing up with a good casserole, and heading a riveting discussion on that month's book club pick? Those things I can do. But a real friendship is too terrifying a thought to entertain.

So, I do what I'm best at: I give Elodie a friendly smile, and I nod. Later, I'll bake her some cookies and recruit Collette to have a playdate with Finnegan. And I'll hope that's enough to satisfy whatever it is Elodie wants from me.

"I'd like that," I say.

"Really?" Elodie is beaming.

"Of course. But we're here, so let's get to work."

She scrambles to keep up with me as I stride to Erin's front door, determined not to miss out on even one precious second. It helps, having something to do today. A clear task: Explain our next steps to Erin. Get her on board. Try to wring out a few more details that can help us.

And do not—absolutely do not—think about Waylen and what happened yesterday.

I knock assertively on Erin's door, and I swear I'm only a little bit satisfied that Elodie is breathless when she finally catches up to me. She busies herself with straightening her hair, smoothing out the faux fur that trims her winter coat.

A few seconds pass and no one comes to the door.

"That's odd," Elodie murmurs to me. "Her car's here."

I knock again and ring the bell. It's nine thirty. Still early, if you're unemployed and don't have any young children. Maybe she's sleeping.

Elodie pulls out her phone, but I touch her wrist to stop her from dialing Erin's number. "Wait," I say. "This feels wrong."

For a second, I allow myself to entertain the thought that's always at the back of my mind, which is that my radar is off, my instincts are wrong, and Bertram could be the greatest liar I've ever met. Despite his anxious front and his soft, smooth way of speaking, he's actually hiding a violent side. He killed Annie. He's figured out that Erin has sent me to investigate him, and he's killed her, too.

My stomach drops. Shit. What if that's what happened? I peer at the window, but the interior is well concealed by the curtain inside.

This is why I need Mr. X. He knows everything that happens in this town, and he would be the one to warn me when I'm about to step into danger. Whether or not I listen is on me.

Elodie takes a step back. Despite her nettling curiosity, self-preservation wins out. "Do you think—"

The door creaks open, making both of us jolt. It opens just enough for Erin to peer out at us. Despite the sunny winter sky, the inside of her condo is dark.

"What are you doing here?" she asks, clearing her throat.

I open my mouth to speak but stop short when I get a better look at her. She's set back, as far as she can stand from the door so that she won't be spotted by her neighbors.

"Erin." My voice is hushed. "Is someone in there with you? Are you in danger?"

"No, thank you," she says, suddenly loud. "I'm not interested in donating to the ASPCA today, but I appreciate you stopping by."

She tries to slam the door, but I jam it with my foot. She scowls but quickly hides it. Is that bruising on her skin?

"If you're in danger, blink twice."

She only shakes her head. "Everything is fine. Please don't stop by unannounced again. You may call me when you have updates about my brother." She pushes on the door so hard that I feel my shoe starting to bend, and I withdraw before she crushes my toes.

The door closes and then there's the click of the lock.

Stunned, Elodie and I make our way back to the car. I direct her to park around the block, at the top of a parking garage that will allow us to see Erin's complex but keep us out of her view. I suspect that Erin is watching for us.

"What the hell was that?" Elodie rasps. "Do you think Bertram was in there? Do you think he's going to kill her?"

"He wouldn't be that stupid," I say. From up here, Erin's condo looks like a dilapidated little dollhouse. But it's identical to all the others in its row, nothing amiss. "He would be seen. And besides, if he attacked her and we intercepted, she would be thrilled to have him arrested. And if he was there to intimidate her, then she would have told us to stop the investigation. None of this adds up."

"Speaking of things not adding up," Elodie says, "what did you mean when you said 'this feels wrong'?"

"You didn't find all of that suspicious?" I ask.

"Yes, I did. But you said it before Erin opened the door." Her bubbly demeanor is gone now, replaced by an unsettling soberness. "You know something."

"I know as much as you."

"Bullshit." She kills the engine on the car. "You've been spending a lot of time investigating Bertram while I've been pursuing other avenues. I've told you all my leads. What aren't you telling me? Why is Mr. X suddenly only communicating through you?"

I knew Elodie was smart. She presents herself as a shallow, self-obsessed PTA mom, but she's proven her intelligence more than once. It's my fault for not having good answers to her questions, for not being able to pull up a little white lie that satisfies her.

I'm just so tired. Mr. X's doctors have been forthright with me, and they're not optimistic. Collette is starting to pick up on the fact that I'm not all I seem. Waylen— *No, don't think about that, Margaux, there aren't enough hours in the day and you have enough to do.*

My shoulders drop, and it's as though my whole body is a deflating balloon. "Please, just trust me."

Elodie wraps an arm around me. She's taking the sympathetic confidant route. A thinly veiled and yet effective tactic.

"You don't have friends," she says.

"Thanks a lot."

"I mean, you're likable. *I* like you, but you don't seem to want friends."

I look at her. *What's your game, Elodie? What is this?*

"Are you trying to cheer me up?" I ask dryly.

"I'm saying that I'm the same way. I get it." She sighs but doesn't release me from her arm. "I don't know how to have close friends, either. In fact, Todd and I have talked about moving back to California in a year or two. But this thing we're doing needs to be a partnership. Fifty-fifty. That means spilling the beans, sister."

We can never tell anyone, do you hear me? Mr. X—my brother—said those words to me after the fire that killed our parents. We were standing in the cemetery, and I turned my head to look at the CPS car that was parked at the edge of the grass. I knew that I was only being given a few minutes to attend the funeral before they would take me away again.

I want to go with you, I told him. *I don't want us to be separated again.*

He stooped to my height. The summer sun made his blond hair so bright that it was reflective and painful to look at. *It's going to be okay, but only if we never, never trust anyone but each other.*

That was it, and then our time was up. A social worker led me back to the car. A parole officer came for my brother, and I could hear the clink of the shackles at his ankles and wrists as he was taken back to jail.

My mind jolts back to the present, where the car smells

like Elodie's sugarplum hand lotion. In a different world, where I wasn't so warped by the things that had happened to me, maybe she and I could be friends. Then again, in a different world, I wouldn't be here doing this. We'd have to bond over cookie recipes.

Still, I need to give her something. I weigh it carefully before I speak.

"Bertram gives me friendly-next-door-neighbor vibes. You know on the news when some guy kills his whole family, and all the neighbors talk about what a nice guy he was and how he always waved? That's him. Usually, I can tell when someone is suspicious, but he's throwing me way off."

Elodie nods. "He's a creep for sure."

"But what *kind* of creep? It worries me that I can't tell."

"Did he say anything to give you a clue?" Elodie asks. "Think."

"He told me that someone is following him. Actually, he said that Annie is stalking him. But when I called his bluff and suggested going to the police, he kept insisting that she knows how to stay hidden. And apparently she does, because we still haven't found her ourselves."

Elodie balks, and at my startled expression, she eases up. "I'm sorry," she says. "It's just, killing your girlfriend and then blaming her for her own murder is like, chapter one in the Creepy McCreeperson handbook."

"Maybe you're right," I say. "But . . . it just isn't adding up."

"Yes, it is," Elodie insists. "Don't feel bad. I could almost buy his bullshit, too. But that's how he's been so successful at getting away with murder and stealing his sister's app.

Annie Clarke isn't stalking him. She's probably buried at a construction site somewhere, and our job is to figure out how he did it." She nods to Erin's condo, far below our parking spot.

Everything Elodie says makes perfect sense. I've already thought the same. What are we missing?

I pull up my phone and type Bertram's name into Google, looking for any new articles, as though they will contain some kind of hidden clue. Despite Elodie's logic, I can't explain my apprehension. I can't justify why my instincts are telling me Bertram may be telling the truth. I can't find any evidence that he's the monster I thought he'd be.

The top result is a YouTube link for *Business Insider*'s channel. I tap and it takes me to a live stream. The host is on one side, talking against a living room backdrop. And to the right is Bertram, his back against the fireplace in his sterile penthouse apartment.

Elodie huddles against me to look at the screen, and I wonder if Californians are more comfortable with physical contact than us New Englanders. "Is that live?" she asks.

"Seems to be."

"No way it's prerecorded?"

I turn the volume up. "Looks like they're answering live questions from the comments right now."

We watch as Bertram chats in real time. Elodie even throws a comment into the quickly churning comment section, and while it doesn't get addressed by the host, many of the other comments do.

"A frustratingly solid alibi," she mutters, and then

glances at Erin's condo. "But if he's not there, why wouldn't she feel safe telling us what happened?"

"Unless it wasn't him," I say. "Maybe she has a more complicated life than we realized. Maybe she's not such a recluse."

Continuing to watch Erin's home for the next hour yields no results. The live stream ends with Bertram cheerfully thanking the host for his time.

"Well, this was a bust," Elodie says.

"I'll see what I can squeeze out of Bertram," I say. "What's your plan?"

Elodie seems to remember something that makes her grin. "I slipped an AirTag on Erin's car, so I'll keep an eye on where she goes today."

"You sly fox," I say. "I didn't even see you do it."

She beams. "That's the idea. Never get caught, right? Here, share your phone's location with me, so I'll know where to come looking if things go sideways with Mr. Millionaire."

I do, but only select the "until end of day" function. Her name appears on a little map, next to Mr. X. The blue dot representing him is still fixed at the cancer center, ten miles away.

"When all of this is said and done," Elodie says, "I'm treating us to lattes. Full-fat, with whip, extra syrup. We'll have earned an overpriced drink."

There it is, that glimpse of what my life could have been if only I'd taken a different path so many years ago. I've always dismissed the idea of truly enjoying these little things, but deep down I think I envy the people who can.

Elodie and I part ways, and I drive home first. I leave my

phone in the garage, texting Elodie to say I have to take care of some things at home and won't be able to get to work for a couple of hours. Then I head to the hospital, sans phone.

As I drive, I think about Elodie's offer of friendship, and then I chide myself. *You don't know how to have friends, Margaux, remember?* When Waylen pushes me to lead a normal life with him, when he tells me I need to make friends, and especially when he tells me I need to shield Collette from my work, it's easier to disregard the thought.

But Elodie's words reached me in an unexpected way. I never tried to open myself up to other people, and yet here I am forcing Collette to be social.

As I drive to the hospital, I imagine it. Elodie and me, conspiring over lattes as we read the latest headlines on our phones. Browsing obscure message boards to find cold cases, talking in whispers about how we'd get the criminals who walk free. Like scratching the ultimate itch. And then sitting on a bench, watching our daughters' dance rehearsals.

Is it possible to form a true friendship? Not in the way my husband proposes—which would require me to ditch my little side hobby entirely. But with someone who gets it, and who's willing to entertain the thought with me from time to time. You know, for fun.

When I make it to my brother's hospital room, he's asleep. But he jolts awake as though I've just burst through the door with a marching band procession. "Margaux," he blurts. But he doesn't mean me, the grown woman standing before him. He means the twelve-year-old who was separated from him when we were young.

He's been dreaming about the night of the fire. I can tell. I have the same look on my face when I dream about it, too.

One look at his expression, and all thoughts of a friendship with Elodie dissipate from my mind. A real friendship is founded on honesty. It's the same as a marriage in that way, isn't it? And I can never be honest with Elodie about what really happened that night.

But I don't say any of this to my brother. We've agreed never to speak of it, and we don't. Whatever alternate life I might like to lead, this is the one I have. There are no friendships. No true, soul-deep connections over Starbucks lattes. Only the memories that haunt me, and the regrets I don't think about.

"Hey." I draw up a chair and sit by his bed. "You look good. I thought you were supposed to be sick." What I'm really thinking is that he doesn't look as bad as I thought he would, based on how he sounded over the phone. I won't let myself think about him getting worse. One thing at a time.

He smiles, despite himself. "What day is it?"

"Wednesday. You up for a little recap?"

He nods, and I summarize everything I know about Bertram and about Erin, who was always a bit strange but may be worth a closer watch.

"A lot of my clients go deeper than we expected," he agrees. "She may have a complicated life, but she only hired us to resolve one aspect of it."

"Yes, but if she gets murdered by an ex-boyfriend or a violent neighbor, we can't exactly give her the answers she's looking for."

He stares flatly at me. "You know better than anyone that people keep their secrets for a reason, M."

"Her secrets weren't of any use to me at first," I say. "But now I wonder if there's some connection. Something happened to her. She looked terrified when Elodie and I showed up unannounced. I could have sworn someone was in there with her."

"You're sure Bertram had an alibi?" he asks.

"Airtight."

He nods. He pushes the button to recline his bed and slowly brings himself to a seated position. God, he looks so pale. I should have ignored his demands for privacy and checked in on him. Maybe if he'd gotten to a doctor sooner . . .

Don't think about it, Margaux. Don't go there. He'll be fine.

"Okay," he says. "I think Elodie is right that you should let her share the lead with you. See if this Skylar woman pans out. I'll think on some questions you should ask her and get them to you today."

"I don't trust Elodie to—"

"I didn't say anything about 'trust,'" he interrupts. "I said 'let.' You always try to do everything yourself, and it's worked out, but this one is big. There's something that even I am missing. We started this to figure out how Bertram stole his sister's app idea, but we may not find the evidence for that outright, so chasing down any other leads that might land him in prison is another thing to focus on."

I tilt my head. "Do you realize we've been talking for the better part of an hour, and you haven't worried at all about whether I'm staying safe? That's usually your entire MO."

He smiles wanly. "I trust you. You've done dozens of cases with my help, but you never really needed me."

"Bullshit," I say. "Why aren't you pestering me about leaving my location on, and wearing AirTags as earrings, and committing the license plate of every car behind me to memory?"

He doesn't answer right away, and I'm sorry I asked, because I have a pretty good guess at what he's about to say.

"Margaux, the reason I picked this one is because it's big. You could retire off of it."

"I thought we don't take pay—"

"I'm not talking about money, and you know it," he says firmly. "I mean this is the one that will finally even the score and give you peace. If you can nail this guy, avenge the woman he's likely killed, *and* get his sister the payout she deserves, you can let go of what we did. You can see that you are a good person. You can stop trying to prove it to yourself, and go enjoy your life."

The words are too much, and I can't process them. I feel that steel wall coming up around my heart, preventing me from feeling what it's so desperate for me to feel. But the questions still filter through: What if it's not enough? What if I can't be redeemed?

But all I say is, "Where is this coming from?"

"I know you still feel guilty about that night with the fire," he says, breaking our cardinal rule. "I replay all of the accusations too. And the trial. The way they separated us."

It's amazing how words cause us to time travel. One moment I'm in the hospital with my brother, and the next I'm a small child in a courtroom, as a lawyer in a three-piece suit explains in detail that my brother and I deserve to be in jail for the rest of our lives for what we've done.

The night of the fire, our childhoods died along with our parents. Our innocence. Our dreams.

The truth is that I wouldn't have turned to petty crimes. I wouldn't have been so angry at the world. I wouldn't have been so willing to throw my shot at happiness away. I really would be like the other parents at Collette's school, snipping at my husband about leaving his towel on the floor or flirting with a waitress. Maybe I would be an interior decorator full-time and enjoy it. Maybe I would have more children, not bound by the paralyzing fear that they'll end up broken like me.

I've never allowed myself to want those things. I've looked on from the outside, into the pretty, well-lit windows of the neighbors' houses, past their manicured lawns and flower beds. I've told myself they're all unhappy. Their lives are shallow. Their marriages are falling apart. Their kids are driving them crazy.

I have to pity and resent them. I have to stereotype their wealth, beauty, and personas. It's the only way I can bear being on the outside. It's the only way I can live without regret.

"This is it for me, kiddo," he says, using the nickname he's had for me all my life. "I'm not going to be here for much longer, and this is the only way I can think to make sure that you'll be okay."

Don't you do it, don't you cry. I scoff. "You'll live to be a hundred just out of spite," I say. "And besides, I'm not quitting."

"It was always inevitable we'd have to stop somewhere,"

he says. "You may not want to stop now, but what about when Collette is old enough to ask real questions? Do you really expect to sneak out of the nursing home to chase a lead when you're eighty years old?"

He says that like it's a bad thing.

"You sound like Waylen," I say, crossing my arms.

"I've never liked him," my brother says.

"You hired him, you twit."

"Yeah, because he's a criminal."

"*Was* a criminal," I correct. "And barely even that."

Waylen was always pristine. Even now, he's impeccably groomed. He folds his laundry before putting it into the hamper. He's quiet as a mouse when I'm sleeping. He's gentle and soft-spoken, a great cook.

He's the sort of person I would have fallen in love with anyway. I know that much. If I met him at a party, or on a bus.

"You owe yourself a good life, Margaux," he says, not taking the bait and arguing with me.

"Bit late to sound all brotherly, isn't it?" I bite. I don't know why I'm so angry. It's this place, this illness that's eroded him so much and so quickly. It's the guilt I carry for not knowing sooner, and the anger that he hid it from me so well.

"You want me to retire so that I can go be a housewife, all of a sudden," I accuse.

He only smiles, which makes everything worse. "I want you to go be Margaux," he says.

"Who the hell is Margaux?" I ask.

"Don't you think it's time to figure that out?" he asks.

I thought it *was* figured out. I thought we were in this

together. And now he's telling me that he's leaving—checking out, dying, forcing me out into the world by myself. Catching this alleged murderer billionaire is his final gift to me. He thinks it will redeem me, but what if he's wrong? What if nothing does?

"Go get 'em, Margaux," he says. "For both of us."

FOURTEEN

I don't want to see Bertram today. When I leave the hospital, I'm especially annoyed about having to go anywhere else.

When I ask for him at the front desk, a part of me hopes I'll be turned away. Let Elodie charm him and I'll go play social media influencer with Skylar. Even as I think it, I know it would never work. She's too aggressive for him, which works well as my research partner, but not as the one manning this particular helm. Bertram needs to be finessed. Billionaires and murderers have that much in common. It doesn't matter whether he's just one of those things or both.

I can feel the absence of my wedding ring on my finger, and it makes me think about my brother's words. I imagine myself talking to the alternate version of me—the Margaux whose parents are still alive, and who went to college, and who met and married her husband in the typical way.

The Margaux who has a normal career, friends, and lunch dates. I imagine telling that Margaux about what I'm doing with my life.

Why? she would ask me. *It's an awful lot of work. Surely you know you can't save the world.*

I don't know, I would reply. *It's just what I have to do.*

The man at the desk ushers me to the elevator, and I'm on my way to the penthouse.

Bertram stands in the foyer when the elevator doors open. He nods to the security guard who rode up with me, and we're alone as soon as the doors close behind me.

His expression is guarded as always, but there's something different about it today. Something I can't put my finger on. Elodie warned me not to come here—she wanted me to meet Bertram someplace public. But Bertram doesn't do public, and it's far too cold for another impromptu seaside picnic. My argument was that this is the safest place to meet him, in a building where every exit is marked by security and cameras are watching us at all times. *"Not if he flings you from the balcony,"* Elodie said. I couldn't work out whether she was being hyperbolic.

I'm loaded up with pepper spray and a switchblade just in case.

Inside, the apartment smells like freshly ground espresso and cinnamon. It's a light, pleasant scent that definitely wouldn't cover up the stench of a dead body if Annie Clarke was buried under the polished floorboards.

"You don't listen to instructions, do you?" Bertram asks in an eerily neutral tone. He leads us to the couch. "I've told you that it isn't safe for us to keep meeting."

I shrug. "Yet you let me in."

"What do you want?" He sits and leans one elbow into the couch behind him. He crosses his ankle over his knee, like he's posing for the cover of *Fortune*.

We have more in common than he realizes. We both dress and groom ourselves immaculately and then hope nobody sees whatever it is we're hiding.

"I'm a storyteller, as you know," I say. "And I've been thinking about what you said. Nobody believes you about Annie, and you won't go to the police, but you say that she's ruining your life."

He looks like he's bracing for the other shoe to drop, for me to accuse him of making the whole thing up. Maybe he realizes how ludicrous the story sounds now that I'm relaying it back to him. But all he says is, "Right. Yes."

"Well, I believe you. And my experience has been that people will believe the written word when there's no name attached to it. When they don't know who the author is, there's no one to scrutinize. Nothing to judge but the story itself."

He raises a thick, neatly trimmed eyebrow. "I don't understand."

It would be easier to do this Elodie's way. I could undo the top buttons of my blouse, bat my eyelashes, and be exactly what he's into. I've seen the women he dates. I know how to mimic.

I could seduce him. He's the type who would be chatty in bed, trying to impress women with his vulnerability. It's something I did once or twice before I got married. Back when it didn't matter, when I didn't even like myself enough to have a code of ethics. Waylen is the one who changed that, as perplexing as it is for me to grapple with.

Our marriage is one of the few things about my public persona that isn't an act.

But seducing a man like Bertram isn't the *only* way to get him to talk. I can make his ego an offer that it can't refuse: the opportunity to speak about himself for hours at a time to a captive audience.

"I can write it as though it's fiction. A novel, with the names all changed. I have connections at major publishing houses, and I can practically guarantee it will sell."

"I see." Bertram gives me no reaction to work with. "How does this help me?"

"Didn't you see that Netflix show that turned out to be a true story after the fact? Something about a stalker, not that different from your story. Anyway, point is, millions of people watched the show for the entertainment factor, and then people did a little digging and realized a lot of the story was true, and the victim got vindication."

"And this person who stalked the victim . . ." Bertram says. "Did that person go to jail?"

"I don't think so," I admit. "But there was retribution in the form of social stigma. Everyone sided with the victim."

Come on, Bertie. Take the bait. A covert narcissist should be chomping at the bit to have a book written about their supposed life experience. He can indulge me in every lie he's been desperate to tell, make himself the innocent victim, and that's when he'll make a mistake. He'll accidentally tell the truth. Yes, I'll have to wade through thousands of pages of bullshit and lies, but I'll find the pearl in that polluted sea.

He shakes his head, exasperated—but, I note, not entirely resistant to the idea. His body language suggests he's been listening. "Why do you want to help me? Why are you so bloody persistent?"

"It isn't about helping you," I say coolly. "It's about getting to the truth. That's my line of business." *Truer than you realize.* "And sure, there's something in it for me. It could make my career."

He stands and then strides across the living room with such gravity that I think he'll shove me back out into the foyer. But instead, he sits beside me, leans in so closely that I can smell his aftershave, like breathing in cedarwood smoke on a cold winter night.

He opens his mouth, and my eyes go to his beard, the smoothness of his lips, the square jaw. It's a shame that he chose sketchy business dealings as his bread and butter, I think, because he could have made a small fortune as a model. But a small fortune wasn't enough, I suppose. He wanted it all.

When he touches my chin, I look up into his eyes, startled by their softness. Oh, he's good. He's done this countless times before. This is a manipulation tactic. These are the eyes Annie looked into as he killed her.

How did you do it, Bertram? Give me something I can work with.

"All right," he says, almost as though he's reading my thoughts. "I'll tell you about Annie. But you can't write it down."

"What would be the point of that?" I ask. I have to clear my throat before the words come out.

"You're a writer, Margaux," he says. "Surely you know the importance of context."

"If I don't write it, there's no story," I say.

"I assure you there is."

Christ, his voice is so smooth. All I do is nod. I sense that something important is about to be shared, and I don't want to compromise it by saying the wrong thing.

"I was never very adventurous growing up," he begins. "Polite, quiet. I'd never even been out of the country until I'd attended college and then started pitching my app to software developers. Not the successful one, but another idea I'd had that never went anywhere."

Interesting. So, he tried to make it on his own before stealing from his sister. But he doesn't mention his sister—I suppose he wouldn't.

"Annie was studying at Oxford. Her parents wanted her to be a doctor. But she was far too restless to commit to any one area of study."

He sits back, crossing one arm behind his head as he eases into the couch. His lean, muscular physique is captured by the morning sunlight through the floor-to-ceiling windows.

"What she saw in me, I may never know. I hadn't ever had time for romance before. I was barely twenty at the time, and I'd spent my whole life studying. I'd never even been kissed."

This has to be a lie, I think. Bertram, for all his faults, is a natural beauty. There are no photos of him online before his thirties, and I try to picture him as an awkward, shy college freshman, to no avail.

Then again, apart from Annie and Skylar, nobody has come out claiming to have dated him, or to have any sort of past with him at all. No childhood friends, neighbors, ex-lovers. It could be that he existed in a loner's vacuum all his life—that certainly fits the profile of many notorious criminals. Or it could be that he's gathered up a portion of his fortune to pay them all off. A few thousand dollars would barely be a drop in the bucket for him.

"With Annie and me, the attraction was instant," he goes on. "I don't mean romantic strolls through a garden or lovely picnics in a park." He closes his eyes, remembering. "I mean wild, frantic, ridiculous passion. Something out of a tawdry romance novel."

He stops speaking, and I try to read the expression on his face. Pained, yet fond. Longing with desperation and despair. He's either a world-class actor or telling me the truth. As ever, I still can't work out which one it is. I could swear he's a bit embarrassed, too. Like recounting the details to me is baring his soul.

"I tried to resist her at first," he says. "My parents wouldn't have approved of me settling down so young. They wanted me to focus on work."

"But you were an adult," I say.

"That hardly mattered to them." He opens his eyes and looks at me now, some of that long-ago memory still living there. A part of him will always be a young man in love—or so he wants me to think. I can't reconcile my confusion. I want to believe him, which is rare in my line of work.

I lean in. "What made her so irresistible?" I ask.

He opens his mouth to speak. Then, from the kitchen, something begins to beep in a shrill, repetitive pattern. He sighs. "Excuse me," he says, standing. "I've just backed this startup company, and they've sent me a prototype for their coffee machine. But it's been firing off random alerts. I'll unplug it."

"That's all right," I say. "Mind if I use the restroom?"

"Of course. You remember where it is."

As I walk down the hallway, I wonder how many others have been in his apartment enough times to know where the bathroom is. I pulled up all of his live streams online and never saw any indication of another person, no noises coming from another room. It doesn't appear that he ever talks to his family or has any friends. His social media presence is clinical, business only. Although thousands of people post questions and replies, he never tags anyone socially. He only follows companies and public figures.

How has he managed to so neatly erase his personal life?

In the bathroom, I lock the door behind me, and I text Elodie to let her know that I'm working on the lead we discussed. **What should I ask him?**

After a moment, she replies: **Record everything on voice memos on your phone.**

Can't, I respond. **It's a two-party-consent state.**

Oh Margaux, seriously, is all she texts back.

But we aren't talking petty theft or small crime. We are trying to get him on a murder, and if I obtain the evidence illegally—like by recording him without his consent—there won't be enough to blackmail him with, because the confession would be thrown out if we brought it to the police anyway. Connecticut is a two-party-consent state, meaning all recordings in a private place require the knowledge and approval of everyone present.

If I get him on *murder*, the recording won't be enough, but the evidence he provides may do it.

Still. I open the voice memo app and consider it. I tap the

record button, but all I'm going to pick up in here is silence. Silence is innocent. But it's not just any silence—it's the silence in a billionaire's apartment. It's the silence that exists between his minimalist furniture. The silence into which he confides his secrets when he's alone, and the thoughts he will never say while I'm around him.

What has this apartment seen? Was Annie murdered here? Did he sit at his desk and plot it out like he was playing a mental game of chess?

What does he think about me while I'm sitting across from him?

How do I get those secrets out? How do I find out what he's done?

There's a soft knock at the door. "Margaux?" he says.

"Yes—I'm almost done." I run the sink as though I've just washed my hands.

"Actually, this is going to sound a bit strange, but could you stay in there? For just a minute?" he asks.

"What?"

"I'd like to tell you something, but—and this will sound absolutely crazy—I don't think I can look at you while I say it."

What is he playing at? "Oh—of course," I say.

I hear the soft thunk of his body leaning against his side of the door. I move closer, my hand hovering over the smooth, polished finish, not quite touching it, as though it's a looking glass and I could step through it and be with him in his memories.

"Annie and I were on and off for many years. You could say we grew up together in a way. By the time we were in our mid-twenties it seemed like it was time for us to do what people do—get married, maybe talk about having a family. By then, she had her degree in medical science, but she hadn't committed to pursuing it further. She told her parents that it had never been her dream and that she wanted to be an anthropologist.

"Of course, I supported her. I'd sold some programs to developers and we were making decent money, so we traveled for a while. It was so . . . liberating. Neither of us having to do anything. We hiked in Machu Picchu, went swimming in Greece, went diving off Kahekili's Leap in Hawaii. It was magical, wild, passionate.

"Before we were to officially tie the knot, we went to Havasu Falls in Arizona. Her family lived nearby, and she was going to break it to them. They were going to be unhappy, of course. In their minds, I was the one who had corrupted their perfect daughter and derailed her from being a doctor. Even though I was making enough money to support the both of us, it wasn't nearly as much as she'd be making if she had seen medical school through."

I close my eyes and I can picture it. Traveling the world with the person you love, just the two of you on a floating island above everyone else, unreachable by logic or persuasion or responsibility. No mortgage, no careers, no crushing guilt.

I breathe in, and I can feel the mist of a waterfall on my face.

"There's this little pocket along one of the cliffs where you can stand under the water," he says. "The night before, as Annie slept in the hotel room, I'd gotten the call that my app was sold. I knew it was going to be big. The preliminary offer was nearly seven figures, and with investments it would quadruple that in the first year.

"I hadn't told her yet. I wanted it to be special. I wanted to tell her that I would take care of her, that I wanted to make all of her dreams—all of *our* dreams—come true. But standing there with the water moving over and around us, I looked at her and thought she was so beautiful that I couldn't speak."

I try to picture Annie, but the only public photo of her is taken from a distance, her face and hair blurred by the motion as she turns her head. But Bertram's tone when he speaks of her is filled with desire, and as he recalls her, I can see how beautiful she is. Her rosy cheeks and light eyes, her wet hair sticking to the curves of her shoulders as she looks at him.

"We'd been together a hundred times before, but never like that," he says. "I'd never been so in love."

Bertram tells me more than I would dare to ask. That they gave everything to each other, that they cupped their hands over each other's mouths and laughed into each other's palms as some tourists swam in the pool below where they were making love.

The details are so vivid that I can't tell what he's told me and what I'm imagining. Annie straddling his waist, her eyes burning bright with love for him. His corded arms around her. Her finger in his mouth. The way he leaned forward and bit her lip.

He's been dying to tell someone about this love affair. Not just me, but anyone who would listen. I can hear it in his voice. I can see the loneliness leave his face when he gets lost in the memory. He wants to speak the words out loud just to prove that it happened. Now someone else knows about it, too.

"I didn't tell her yet, even though I'd planned to," he says. "I just wanted the moment to be what it was. I didn't want to talk about our future yet."

I lean against the door, my legs suddenly unsteady. God, what is it like to be with a man who isn't so obsessed with the future? One who doesn't plan everything and try to push me into the labyrinth of calendars. Christmases with his parents. Summers at the beach. Saving up for a very structured tour of Venice, with Collette in tow.

What is it like to be wild? To not care if strangers see your bare ass bouncing up and down through the curtain of a waterfall?

When Bertram opens the door, I nearly stagger into him. He catches me, his hands tight around my forearms. I can feel his pulse thudding through his fingertips.

"Sorry," he says, breathless. "The lock doesn't work. I should have asked."

Wake up, Margaux. I've had some version of this dream before, where I'm running but my legs won't work. I'm screaming, but marbles fall out of my mouth and I can't make a sound.

He's a liar. A killer. A con man. A strange lone wolf with a *Vogue* model face. I had thought his eyes were the same as Erin's, that light, champagne-bubble green. But now I think there's more darkness in his, like the deep heart of a wilderness somewhere. I'm in an episode of *I Shouldn't Be Alive*. I'm a hiker who went too far off the trail, missed the markers, and has spent days wandering through evergreen needles and vines, all tangled and lost in him.

I stare, even though I'm telling myself to look away. To break the spell. To wake up. But he's staring, too.

He touches my face, and his fingertips are soft. He rustles through my ponytail like a breeze.

"What happened?" I ask him. I'm desperate to know. "How did you tell Annie that you were going to be rich?"

This awakens him from some sort of trance. I see the sobriety fill his features, and then they turn sad for a flash before he locks them away.

"That's enough for now," he says softly, and he lets me go. "All of this was off the record, of course."

FIFTEEN

"Well?" Elodie asks, by way of greeting when I call her. I'm in the parking lot, leaving Bertram's apartment.

"I thought we were getting somewhere, but as usual he cut me off. More than that, really. He practically shoved me out the door." I shiver at a gust of cold November wind. A lone raindrop falls on my nose, a sign of a pending storm.

"What did you find out?" she asks. "Anything good?"

"No," I lie, as I climb into my car. Poor Elodie. She wants to be my friend because she's realizing how lonely it is to live a double life. She hasn't learned yet that we're so good at what we do—and were selected by Mr. X—because of our ability to keep secrets. She'll learn soon enough.

"What about you?" I ask her.

"I've just gotten off the subway," she says. "I'm headed to see Skylar now. I thought—screw it, why not go in person and turn the day into a shopping trip?"

"Naturally," I say. It would be nice to spend the day looking at designer bags and playing Harriet the Spy; maybe I should have gone with her instead of wasting my time here. I'm irritated that Bertram kicked me out just when I thought I was getting somewhere. The sudden emotion on his face, the intensity when he looked at me, was an open door. But he slammed it shut before I could walk through it.

I need to speak to my brother. He'll know where to steer me, if I'm honest with him about what's just happened.

Elodie and I say goodbye, and I make my way to the hospital. When I glance in the rearview mirror, I see a purple gel pen that must have fallen out of Collette's backpack, and I catch myself thinking of her.

She doesn't know anything about my family, apart from the fact that her grandparents died before she was born. She doesn't know that she ever had an uncle, or that he's dying.

Maybe they should meet. I can trust her to keep a secret. Hell, she barely tells me what's going on in her own life anymore. But Collette is observant, and she'll ask questions. She might even try to research him in secret, without telling anyone, and go fishing for details she doesn't think I'll tell her. The apple doesn't fall far from the tree.

One thing I have learned in my line of work is that the truth always comes up. Not right away. Not next week. Maybe not even next year. But someday. When she's twenty-five, or thirty, or cradling a baby of her own, she'll come across the information somehow and she'll want to know why I kept it from her. Because if my brother dies, his existence doesn't die with him. Yes, I've lied to Collette about her family, but if I never tell her the truth even after he's gone, every year will be a lie, too. When I'm bringing her flowers at her college graduation, or helping her pick out a wedding gown, or coming with her to her seaside vacation to celebrate her new promotion—I'll know something that she has a right to know.

I keep secrets from everyone, and I have my reasons. But Collette changes the game. My secrets belong to her by extension. Your child is different from your husband or your neighbor, or even yourself.

And my brother is dying. That's the truth, even if I don't want to admit it. In a few weeks, or months, maybe a year, he won't be conscious enough to speak. He won't know who's coming to visit. He won't be able to answer her questions, or tell her how much she looks like our mother.

"Damn it," I mutter to the purple gel pen. Life was so much easier when the only person I had to hurt was myself. Having a daughter is like giving birth to a mirror that you can't help glancing into.

As though in response to my frustration, the rain picks up, smashing down on the windshield so hard that I can barely get visibility even with the wipers on high.

The rain is so loud that I don't hear the metal grinding sound or the low sputtering sound until I try to turn the steering wheel and the car doesn't move. Then all the lights in the car go dark as the engine shuts off.

"No, no, no," I say, pushing the start button and pumping the brake over and over. "Why are you doing this? You're a new car!"

Thunder roars outside as the rain turns angry. I grab my

phone and start googling for everything I can think of. *Car suddenly stopped working, Car lost power.*

I'm just about to call roadside assistance when there's a knock at my window.

Of all people, Bertram Casimir is standing outside in the rain, holding a sleek black umbrella that hardly shields him as the rain falls sideways. He gestures for me to get out, but I shake my head. He tries the handle and the doors are locked.

Did he do something to my car? I was with him all morning, but he could have hired someone to mess with the engine. Why, though? If he wanted me alone, he already had me there in his apartment. He's the one who kicked me out.

He knocks on the window again, this time frantically. I shake my head. I'm not getting out. Not without knowing what his game is.

Seconds later, my phone rings. It's him, holding his own phone pressed against his ear as he stands in the middle of the street.

"Margaux, goddamn it, you're in danger," he snarls at me. With his other hand he's pounding on the glass so hard I think he'll shatter it.

My heart is hammering, and I clutch at the hilt of the box cutter I keep in my pocket. If he tries anything, he may be stronger, but I know where the jugular is. "What are you talking about?" I demand into the phone.

"This is her doing, I know it."

"Annie?"

"Yes—please. I'll explain everything if you just come to my car where it's safe."

A pair of high beams floods my car as he says the words. There's a car coming toward us, bright lights on and penetrating through the gloomy, cloudy day. It's nobody important, I tell myself. Just someone trying to get a little visibility on their way home from the store. But it speeds through a stop sign, makes it to the end of the street, and then swings back around in a U-turn.

Muttering curses, I unlock my door and allow Bertram to rush me to the back seat of his car, and his driver speeds us away.

My wet hair is plastered to my face, and a bit of it slaps him in the face when I turn my head to look at him. "How did you know something would be wrong with my car?" I demand. "Did you have something to do with it?"

"N-no," he says, more flustered than I've ever seen him. "I just had a terrible feeling, and with the weather, I—"

"Bad weather doesn't make a car shut itself off!" I cry. "Bertram, what's going on?"

The car is tailing us, and when I glance at the speedometer, we're exceeding eighty miles per hour in a city grid, blowing through stop signs and swerving around the few cars that are out on the road in this weather.

"Don't tell me this is your ex-girlfriend," I say, turning in my seat to look at the black car with the tinted windows. It's the same one that was in the hospital parking garage.

"I warned you to stay away from me!" he cries.

"Oh, not this again." I grab his arm, my fingers digging tightly into his muscle. "Annie is dead, isn't she? And this is all some sort of scare tactic to stop me from finding out about it." Being charming hasn't worked. Being sweet, being romantic, and even being blunt. This has gone far enough, and it's time to switch gears. "Admit it!"

The shock in his eyes is immediate. "What?" he rasps. "Of course not. Why would you think that?"

"Because Annie Clarke doesn't exist, Bertram. I've looked. It's the twenty-twenties; *everyone* has some sort of social media profile. But there isn't a trace, not even an embarrassing college Facebook photo from decades ago."

Apart from the thunder and the splash of the car hitting the puddles as it speeds through the city, there's silence. I crash into Bertram as we take a hard turn, and he steadies me.

"I never told you her last name," he says softly.

"What? You must have."

"No," he says, with deliberation. "I know I didn't." He stares at me. "Oh God, she's sent you, hasn't she? That's why she's following me again, just when I thought she had finally eased up. Just when I thought I'd made my life so boring, stripped myself completely of *any* personal relationships, made my life *nothing* just to get away from her, you've gone and brought her back."

I'm so confused that I don't know how to respond. He sounds so certain that I begin to wonder if he's suffering from some kind of delusion. I'd almost think Annie Clarke didn't exist at all, except that his own sister confirmed it when she asked me to look for her.

He pulls at his hair and then strikes out and hits his fist against the door. The sound of it makes me jump. "Why is this happening? I'm not the one who ended things. I loved her!" I don't know if he's talking to me or to some painful old memory that keeps following him like an apparition. "After that day under the waterfall, I woke up the next morning and she had gone. Abandoned our whole vacation and flown home to her parents. They convinced her to go back to medical school, and she didn't have the nerve to tell me, so she just left."

I blink. "She's the one who left you?"

"It would be years before I saw her again," he confesses. "We tried to rekindle—we even got engaged, but I wasn't the same person as when we first met. Neither was she. The fire had gone out."

"But then why was she so angry?" I ask. "Why is she doing all of this to you?"

"Like I said, she just isn't the same." He steels his voice. Whatever emotion he's feeling, he doesn't want me to see it. "All those years of trying to please her parents, and realizing it was all for nothing. She thought our engagement would undo all the time she wasted, but it didn't. I couldn't fix it for her. I wasn't the man she fell in love with back in college. She hates me for that."

"Sir, I think we've lost the other car," Bertram's driver interrupts us. We've veered into a parking garage affixed to an office building. Nobody else is here, and I let myself breathe a sigh of relief, but Bertram doesn't seem at all soothed.

He's staring at me, and I see some lingering trace of that desire he showed me earlier. But it's crowded now by something else, something resembling anger and fear. "Margaux, if Annie sent you, you must tell me."

He pulls me once again under his spell, and even as I

feel it happening, I struggle to resist. If he was right, if Annie were somehow still alive and she had been the one to put me up to this, in this moment I would tell him.

"She didn't," I say softly. "I thought she was dead."

"Why would you think—"

The car lurches forward with a roar of the engine. The car is behind us again. It makes no attempt to be subtle, honking and flashing its lights as it chases us. But there's nowhere for us to go.

Something occurs to me.

I go through my purse as Bertram's driver exhausts the last of the possible turns, narrowly missing the parked cars as he rounds the corners. Bertram seems well and truly terrified, but a resigned calm washes over me, mixed though it is with a new sort of dread.

"Don't you have bodyguards?" I ask him as I paw through my zippered compartments.

"I'm not Elon Musk," he snaps back. "People might try to hack into my bank accounts, but why would they assassinate me?"

"You seem to think your ex-girlfriend wants to kill you."

"Not me," he says. "She wants me alive so she can hurt me."

"Sir, we're at a dead end." The driver sounds only marginally less panicked.

Frustrated, I dump the entire purse onto the seat, flustering Bertram. I shake the empty bag vigorously, sure I hear something clattering inside.

"What are you doing?" Bertram asks.

I pull at the lining until I find it—a tear so minuscule that even I hadn't noticed it. The fact that it's cleanly slit with no loose threads tells me that it must be new. I root my finger around inside until I feel the smooth, curved edge of something roughly the size of a quarter. I already know what it is before I've extracted it.

An AirTag.

It can't be. It truly fucking can't be.

I open the door, and Bertram lunges to close it, but I'm too fast for him. I ignore his shouts for me to get back inside the car. When he realizes I can't be stopped, he gets out after me, demanding I stop as I pound on the tinted window of the car behind us.

Suddenly in a less murderous mood, the driver of the vehicle throws it into reverse, and I lunge for the hood, clinging to the windshield wipers. I know who's in that car, and it's not Annie Clarke. I won't let him get away. If he wants to speed away, he's taking me with him.

But Bertram has other ideas. He pries me from the hood. "Damn it, woman, have you lost your mind?" he says. His muscles lock. He's too strong for me, and in one fluid motion he's propelled me behind him. He guards me with arms held out at either side.

Finally, the car door opens. I recognize the suede Aldwin lace shoes, the wedding ring on the hand that grips the frame of the car door as he gets out. Waylen, the sneaky son of a bitch.

Days earlier, when he and I argued—not for the first time—about me quitting my vigilantism, he got out of bed in the middle of the night. I heard him rummaging through the kitchen to make himself some coffee, and I went back to bed.

In the morning, my purse had fallen from its hook by the door. I'd assumed Collette had gone through it looking for gum.

It's been more than a decade since Waylen and I worked together, but our whole marriage has been a mission unto itself. And tracking people down was a specialty of his. He's been so soft for so long that I forgot he had it in him.

But Bertram has never met Waylen, except on paper when he was stalking my personal data. He has no idea that the man standing before us now is the very same one who catches spiders under a glass and uses a bit of cardboard to release them into the yard, who sat patiently as our daughter snapped barrettes into his hair and used my old makeup brushes to pretend that she was his agent and he was America's Next Top Model.

There's a loud click. Bertram's driver has a cocked gun trained on Waylen, who holds his palms up and utters a soft, "Whoa, whoa." The same tone he uses on the rare occasion that one of our arguments leads to me yelling.

"Don't shoot him!" I say, and rub the bridge of my nose. "He's not dangerous. He's just an idiot."

Bertram has shoved me behind him again, as though pulling me out of a valley of flames. There's a concerned crease on his brow, much like the one he had when he coaxed me out of my broken-down car.

Was my engine dying also Waylen's doing? I stare at him, not fighting Bertram's protective force field. I see a glimpse of the man he was before we were married. Soft-spoken and mild, until suddenly he wasn't. It was that unexpected edge that lured me in, made me give myself to him. It's the reason we ended up conceiving Collette one winter night beside a roaring fireplace in his apartment.

But he'd put that side of him away when we said our vows and he gave up this life. I had forgotten it existed—almost.

"You know this man?" Bertram asks. "He works for—"

"He doesn't work for Annie," I assure him.

"Who?" Waylen asks, when the driver finally lowers his gun. But he at least has the sense not to take another step, and to keep his palms visible.

"He's my husband." I sigh, and turn on Waylen. "What are you doing here?"

He hesitates, but the anger in my eyes—despite my cool tone—scares him more than any gun ever could.

His shoulders drop, and then his hands. He sits on the concrete. The sight of him in his pressed khakis and white blazer—which he so lovingly ironed with the Sunday laundry—is distressing and yet somehow so romantic in a way that only I would see. He's broken.

"Please, Margaux," he says, staring down at the ground. It's stained with puddles of old oil. "Please, I just want you to come home."

Bertram doesn't stop me when I approach Waylen, perhaps because he's too perplexed by the sight before him.

I crouch in front of Waylen, my thighs burning because I refuse to sit on the dirty concrete in my clean dress.

He won't raise his head to look at me, but I see the bleariness of his eyes. Are those—tears?

I want to hug him. To pity him. To revert back to the young twentysomething I was when we met and his eyes could melt me like a puddle. But I have been married to this man for more than a decade now, and I know what will happen if I turn soft. We'll go home, make reckless, passionate love in the middle of the day, and he'll hope that my hazy post-sex brain will forget all about it. That's what he wants. That's who he thought he was marrying, and if I give up my vigilantism, my edge will go along with it.

At least, that's what he thinks.

"Waylen, really," I say. "What are you trying to do?"

"I just want you to come home," he says.

I grab his chin, forcing him to look at me. He swallows hard. "Collette is a mess, can't you see that?" he says. "You're forcing her to socialize with Elodie's horrible daughter, and don't get me started on Elodie. The choices you're making, the things you're getting up to. I don't even recognize you anymore."

"That doesn't answer my question," I say, staying firm. "That was you at the hospital, too, wasn't it?"

I feel a sick dread at the thought of him following me with that AirTag, knowing everywhere I've been. Has he figured out that Mr. X is in the hospital? If so, he'll wonder why I'm going to visit him when I've never met with him in person for our missions together. He'll want to know why I'm speaking to his doctors, why I care so much about his health. Worse, if he finds out how sick Mr. X is, he'll be glad. He'll hope this means that my spy work will die with him.

I can't let him find out about my past. I can't let him know that Mr. X is my brother. He'll piece too many things together and ruin everything.

Isn't it enough that I've given you my stupid, traitorous heart, Waylen?

I would prefer he accused me of an affair than know the truth about my past. In his mind, Mr. X was never more than a boss to me. I thought about telling him the truth, but I can only stand to share so much.

But if Waylen is wondering what I was doing at the hospital, he doesn't ask. He only nods. "Yes. Yes, it was me."

"Every time?" Bertram asks.

Waylen doesn't look at him, seeming almost to have forgotten he was standing behind me. "Yes," he says. "All of it."

"Why are you following us?" Bertram asks the question before I can get the words out.

I stand, and when Waylen doesn't follow suit, I grab his arms and force him to come up and face me. There's a flash of something angry in his eyes—something jealous and dark—and then it's gone, traded once again for contrition. Nobody saw it but me. I'm the only one who ever looks closely enough. Blink and you'd miss it.

He looks at me like a man defeated, as though I hold the strings to his heart and the fate of our marriage. "I did it for us," he tells me, ignoring the fact that it was Bertram's question. "I hoped you would finally see how dangerous this all is, and it would scare you into quitting."

"Dangerous?" Bertram asks. "What's dangerous about writing a book?"

My hands, still gripping Waylen's arms, dig into his skin. *Don't blow my cover,* I'm telling him.

"It's not the writing; it's the research that's dangerous," I tell Bertram, glancing back at him. "My husband knows that I'll go to any lengths for a story. Last summer, I was considering a scuba-diving class so I could write a murder mystery where the plot twist is that the victim was actually eaten by a shark."

Bertram runs a hand through his hair, grasping it in frustration. "So, it isn't just me, then," he says. "You're a natural-born risk-taker."

"Something like that." I nod to the car with the tinted windows—the very same one that has been chasing me down for days. "Rental?" I ask. Waylen nods.

There's been no unusual activity on any of our shared bank and credit card statements, so this means he has a secret stash of money somewhere.

"Darling," I say softly. Waylen's brow furrows. The term of endearment and my dulcet tone are out of character. "I'm only writing a book about Mr. Casimir's life because he has a fascinating story to tell. And if I sell this one to a publisher, it'll help us pay a lot of bills. We've talked about this. I'm not doing anything risky." I turn to Bertram. "I'm sorry about this."

It's so strange to see him standing across from Waylen. Two different aspects of my world colliding. And although Waylen stands calm, even penitent, I can feel something simmering just below the surface—a quiet, jealous rage that only I can see, because only I know who he was before he gave up this life for that of a respectable book editor.

He knows what Bertram has been accused of. If I know Waylen, he's dug into message board conspiracy theories, read the fan fiction—and, yes, there is some of that—and formed his own conclusions.

He knows that he can't persuade me to quit. And now

he knows that he can't stalk me while I'm working this case. I wouldn't put it past him to do something drastic.

I have to get him out of here before things get ugly.

What the hell was that?" I say, once Bertram and his driver are out of sight. I'm staring through the darkly tinted windows at the stormy city as it speeds by. It's still raining.

"Should we go home, or should I take you to your car?" Waylen asks. He at least has the awareness to act guilty.

"As if you don't know the engine's dead," I snap. "It broke down *right* before you decided to come chasing after us."

"The engine's dead?" he asks, his voice soft in that way he gets when he's being thoughtful.

"What did you do?" I ask him. "I know this was part of your master plan to scare me into being the perfect wife and mother. What's phase two? Creating an Instagram account and getting brand sponsors? Tampering with my birth control so I have another baby?"

"Margaux." He sounds just angry enough, and I know he's standing on some sort of edge, daring me not to push him over. "I didn't touch your car, or your birth control."

Suddenly I'm not so sure. Calm, even-tempered Waylen has always been easy to read. But he does have a side that comes out when he feels threatened. And nothing threatens him more than the thought of me leaving him.

"I was just— I'm worried about you," he says. "You seem to be spending a lot of time on this one."

He's pulled up behind my car, broken down on the shoulder, in a puddle of fresh rainwater.

He moves to open his door, but I grab his arm, making him look at me. "Do you think I was sleeping with him? With *Bertram*?"

He flushes, averts his eyes. "I—"

"Waylen, he's a monster!" I say. I'm trying to convince myself because I know it to be true, despite some nettling voice telling me to believe his lies. "I'm trying to find evidence that he killed his fiancée, since that's the only way to get him locked up. There won't be enough proof that he stole his sister's silly little app."

"I know that," he says. I'm still gripping his arm, and he puts his other hand over mine and looks at me. "But I'm not entirely sure *you* know it. And he's so—well, he's just a hero from a romance novel, isn't he? Rich, manicured, edgy, British."

"He's *not* edgy," I say, breaking the tension with a small laugh. "Far from it. He's scared of his own shadow, or at least that's the act he puts on." I soften. "I'm taking all the right precautions. I'm so close to a breakthrough, and then I'll never utter the name 'Bertram Casimir' again. I promise."

There's something that happens whenever things have been tense between Waylen and me for a long time. It's a magnetic, irrational, kinetic attraction that forces both of us to throw logic out the window. It happens again in this moment, with the heavy pattering of rain on the metal walls of the car.

He is fueled by the jealousy that the thought of me being alone with Bertram evokes. My mind is racing too fast for me to catch my thoughts—the words he said to me last night about quitting this work, the passion it must have taken for him to go to such great lengths to scare me out of it. The demons of my past and present always lurking in the dark somewhere, and Waylen being the only thing that can silence them.

But he kisses me and I melt, and neither of us gives a thought to what will happen tomorrow, or today, or where we've been. Who we are and who we pretend to be.

He plays with my hair, which somehow got tugged out of its ponytail.

"Waylen?" I murmur, touching his face, tracing my finger over his lips.

"Yes," he says. It's not a question, but a profession. *Yes. I'm yours, whatever it is you need. Yes.*

"What did you do to my car to make it break down?" I ask, still talking softly to him. "I'm not mad, but I need to know the truth."

"I didn't."

"Waylen."

"You're the smooth liar, not me." His fingers tighten around my hair, giving it a firm tug that gets my attention. "Why would I have to mess with the car, my love?" he says. "Wherever you go, I always want you to have a way back home to me."

SIXTEEN

Collette, smart girl that she is, can sense that something has changed in the air. She doesn't comment on the fact that Waylen and I pick her up together, in his car. She doesn't even comment that we're late, because I made Waylen stash away the Honda in a parking lot until it can be returned.

I'm the first one to speak when I glance at her in the mirror and ask where she got the glittery purple lip gloss she's wearing.

"Finnegan," she says matter-of-factly. "We wanted to do makeovers at lunch, but her ColourPop palette got taken by the cafeteria monitor. It was so dumb. But she had lip gloss in her other purse."

Of course Elodie Blevins's kid would take two purses to school.

"Be careful, kiddo," Waylen says from behind the wheel. "You shouldn't be sharing that stuff. Germs."

She only nods.

"I'm glad that you're making friends with her," I say. "I know it hasn't been easy."

"She's okay, I guess," Collette says. "Actually, she's kind of nice when she's not with her other friends."

I could say the same thing about Elodie, come to think of it. I think again of her odd offer of friendship. I've seen other groups of friends and wondered how they started—if they met in college, or at a bar, or if they made small talk while standing in line at a store somewhere. It never occurred to me that it would be as simple as just asking, "Would you like to be my friend?"

By the time we get to the house, I've gotten a text from the mechanic that they've received my towed car and they'll give me a call tomorrow morning.

"What did they say it was?" Waylen asks.

"They'll look at it and get back to me."

He smiles, as cheerful as the sun that's starting to peek through as the rain clouds disperse. "Since you don't have your car, we should take a family trip." He turns to look at Collette, who is shouldering her backpack and about to step out into the driveway. "What do you say, 'Lette? We could go to the grocery store and get the stuff to make one of those famous TikTok recipes you've been talking about."

"I have math homework," she says, clearly confused by the break in our routine. Waylen isn't exactly known for his spontaneity.

"We'll get to it!" Waylen assures her. "Mom and I will help—not that you need us anymore." He turns to me. "She's smarter than either of us, isn't she?"

"Yes," I say, cautiously guarding my responses. What is this? What game are we playing?

I decide to let him take the lead. He drives us to the grocery store that we dubbed the "ritzy market" because it only sells select brands, all of which are organic. Collette acclimates to the change in routine and asks us if she can add some LaCroix to the cart.

When we get home, the kitchen is soon filled with the aroma of simmering broth for our homemade spicy pho, to be accompanied by strawberry cheesecake muffins that have to go back into the oven three times because the center doesn't pass the toothpick test.

We watch *When Harry Met Sally* on Collette's iPad as we eat dinner at the kitchen table. Through the bay window, warm kitchen light spills out into the autumn darkness, where the rain has given way to light flurries. Like something Norman Rockwell would paint. And after, as promised, Waylen and I help Collette with her homework. Waylen catches two small misspellings in her book report. I struggle my way through sixth-grade geometry.

But I begin to feel that I'm in a geometry puzzle of my own, driving a car that isn't mine through the strict confines of a grid drawn by my husband. None of the lines leads to Bertram, or my brother, or the past I've been running from. It all just leads back to this.

At eight o'clock, Waylen goes to his office to catch up on a deadline he says he can't put off any longer. At ten o'clock, I check on Collette, whose bedroom is softly lit by the spinning rainbow of stars cast by her night-light. She's in bed, breathing softly, her back turned to me.

"Mom?" she whispers as I'm starting to close her door.

"Yes, darling?"

She sits up. In the dim light, her eyes are two black pools. Her face looks too old and too serious for her age. "Do you have any family you don't talk about?"

My heart simultaneously aches and beats faster. "Grandma and Grandpa died when I was a little girl. You know that."

Collette nods. "But didn't you have any other family? A brother or sister? Cousins? Aunts and uncles?"

My family sat in the courtroom, listening to the list of charges being read aloud. I tried to make eye contact with them—someone, anyone—but they all turned away, except for two. They still haven't forgiven me. They still say it was all my fault. Not that I've contacted them recently to see if they've changed their minds.

"My grandparents died before you were born, honey. They were very old. But I know they would have loved to meet you."

"Maybe we can visit their graves," Collette says. "What if no one ever visits them? What if no one mows the lawn or takes care of it?"

"Their graves are very far away, Collette." I don't mean to snap at her, but I see her wince. It's so rare for me to lose patience that she's forgotten I even can.

I close her door and sit on the edge of her bed. She crawls up beside me.

"What is this about?" I ask her. "We've already had this conversation."

"Not really," she says. "You only told me that everyone

is dead. But—Dad's side has Grandma, Grandpa, Aunt Linda and Ellen, and all the cousins. I just thought there might be someone you aren't telling me about."

There are a lot of things I'm not telling you about, my love. I study her. Where is this coming from? I know it wasn't Waylen—he readily accepted my story about being adrift with no family to tether me elsewhere in the world. It's even why he loved me so much and so fast when we first met. He had never been someone's whole world before, and that was what he wanted. It still is.

My brother said it was for the best that it stays between us. He's got his hands into too many messes. The cases he's helped me work were all researched on his hard drives, following coordinates he sent and using vehicles he procured. He's so careful, but if there's ever a lapse and he's caught, he doesn't want any of it traced back to me.

"No," I lie, and of all the lies I've told, this is simultaneously the easiest and the most painful. "There's no one else."

She seems disappointed. "Could we road-trip to Oregon sometime? Where you grew up?" she asks. "Could you show me?"

"It wasn't in a big city like Portland, or anything you'd see on TV," I assure her. "It was basically just wilderness."

"Camping trip," she says. "We could go, just us."

I stand, pulling her blankets up. "Come on," I say, mustering my best cheerful tone. "That's a conversation for another time. Get some sleep."

She climbs under the covers and asks for her iPad, insisting she just found a new meditation app that helps her fall asleep.

I concede, just this once, and leave her with the sounds of a Tibetan singing bowl and babbling brook, while a soothing voice murmurs affirmations about how strong she is.

When I get into bed, I'm just about to check my voicemail when Waylen enters the room. He sighs tiredly and starts to undress.

I watch him, considering the man I married. He is like a tall building with infinite windows, and when I peek through, I can't be sure what it is I'll find playing out inside him. Most days, he's sensitive and kind, the long-suffering girl dad and attentive husband. Evidenced by the now faded unicorn sticker on the glove box of his otherwise pristine car from when Collette was little and used to pretend to drive while he washed the car in the driveway.

When it's my night to host the book club, he brings trays of wine and veggie spreads into the living room, making polite small talk before jogging back upstairs to work. The ladies swoon and tell me how lucky I am, before regaling me with some story about how their own husbands are useless when they host parties.

But there are windows I haven't peered into, or won't. I assess the situation I'm in now: no vehicle, no privacy to check in with Bertram, or my brother, because the engine mysteriously died. Bertram thinks that Annie has been stalking him since they broke off their engagement in the summer, and found him again—at least that's his claim—but it was Waylen.

But I could see the panic in Bertram's eyes, in the driver's eyes, as we raced around that parking lot. Does that mean Bertram was telling the truth, and he really did think someone was out to get him? But who? If he *did* kill Annie, he would have known it wasn't her. Could there be someone else?

I pull up my messages with Elodie so that I can ask her to pick me up tomorrow morning. I'll say I had car trouble and that it will be fun for our girls to carpool together. But when I open up our conversation, I see a message that was sent hours earlier: **Call me, ASAP. Big development.**

I glance at Waylen through the doorway of our bathroom, brushing his teeth now. If I get out of bed now to call Elodie, what will happen? Will he try to stop me, or say nothing but then find a way to listen in?

Whatever it is can wait until morning. I have no way to leave anyway.

When he comes to bed, he leans in to kiss me, and we make love quietly, our jagged breathing doing the talking for both of us. After, he goes to the kitchen and brings up two glasses of wine and turns on the TV. We snuggle up in bed to an old black-and-white film on TCM. Something about a beautiful young woman who meets a reporter who offers her a deal if she'll let him write a story about her life.

That's Bertram, I think: a beautiful subject with a dark story that I want to write. Only it's not for the reasons he thinks.

Waylen kisses the top of my head. "We should go on vacation for Christmas," he says. "We'll both be done with work by then."

He says it with such confidence that I wonder if I told him I'd be done working on Bertram's case before December. I try to scour my mind, but I'm too tired to think clearly.

"Sure," I say.

"Can you think of anywhere you want to go?" he asks.

I don't tell him about Collette's strange request to visit my family's graves in Oregon. That's one state line I never plan to cross again.

"Maybe a beach in California." I yawn. "Nothing too expensive."

"Don't worry about the cost," he murmurs, drawing me closer. "I'll take care of it. I'll always take care of you."

It isn't my alarm that wakes me in the morning. Rather, it's the opposite of my alarm. The house is so quiet that I hear the neighbor's car backing out of the driveway, the splash of a puddle from yesterday's torrential rain.

I can't remember the last time I felt so well rested. For a moment I bask in it. I stretch my arms and legs in the crisp, newly laundered sheets.

Then I look at the clock.

Ten a.m.

I bolt upright. Collette is late for school. I never answered Elodie's texts. I have so much work to do with Bertram—

"Morning," Waylen sings, walking through the open doorway with a mug of coffee for me. "Collette and I finished off the frittatas, but there's some fruit salad in the fridge if you'd like breakfast."

I'm already climbing out of bed. "Why didn't you wake me? I was supposed to take care of a million things today."

"Whoa. Hey." Waylen sets the coffee on the night table and then gently takes my shoulders and guides me back to bed. "I thought you might want a break, so I took care of getting Collette to school. Don't worry, I made sure she had her homework. Besides, how were you going to do anything without the car?"

I put a hand to my head, as though I can grasp at a memory that I can feel is missing. How did I sleep so late? It feels incredible. No lingering tension headache, no urgent need to go somewhere or do something. No crushing sense that the entire house will fall apart without me to spin all the plates on all the sticks.

Waylen smiles at me pityingly. "You can take a day off, you know," he says. "Until you get the call back about your car, at least."

The car. I glance at my phone, resting face down beside the coffee that Waylen has brought me. It all comes back to me: The car breaking down. The heat of Waylen's body as he kissed me on the side of the road. The picture-perfect evening we had.

Waylen was always full of surprises in the beginning. That all changed once we were married and he became predictably predictable. But now, for the first time in more than a decade, I can't fit the pieces all together. He tracked me down like a bloodhound when I was with Bertram. If he was able to do that without my noticing, how many times has he done it before? Has he gotten into my phone?

He doesn't know about your past, Margaux, I assure myself. It's not as though there's any physical evidence or spoken memories from that time. Mr. X and I have never spoken about it, much less put it into texts. And it happened so long ago, before the age of archiving small-town news articles online. Googling my name will yield hundreds of unrelated results.

But he knows more about me than I wanted him to. Falling in love made me stupid and chatty. I consider my options carefully. It could be pure coincidence that my car broke down at the same time Waylen started his desperate ploy to stop me from working. Or it could be that he's lying to me—only telling the truth about one part of it to throw me off the trail.

It could be that following me around to scare me was his whole plan. A sweet one, really, and easy to see through. This would mean he's lost his touch. He's admitting that he isn't as clever as me—he's always hated the sneaking around—but hoping that he can reel me in.

It could also be that he expected me to catch him yesterday and that he's hoping I'll let my guard down because he's planning something much bigger in the near future. What, I don't know. This would mean that I'm the one who's lost my touch. It would mean that I am no longer the one in this marriage who's always a step ahead. Or that I never really was.

I glance down at the steaming dark liquid, swirling with just a bit of almond milk. It looks normal, smells normal. So did the wine I had last night.

Did he do something to my drink to make me fall asleep, or was I simply so tired that I slept in because he'd muted my alarm? When I first met him, part of why I fell in love was because of how calm he made me. I slept better by his side. I forgot about my past when we were laughing together or taking long walks to look at the autumn leaves.

Last night, I was similarly calm. It was like our little

house was the only one in the world, and we were immune to the frigid wind that blew against our windows.

There's a flash in his warm eyes. A challenge. A dare. A spark of the man I first lusted after. I call it lust because it was only meant to last for the short weeks that we were paired together on our vigilante mission. And we had fun. Ill-advised, wild, reckless fun.

But the Waylen I've been married to all these years is the man I love. Love is a more practical emotion. Love means taking turns washing the dishes after Saturday morning pancakes. Love is when he takes my car to get an oil change, and I remind him about a conference call he's got on the calendar when I overhear him making plans on the phone. Love is striking that balance of remaining young and fit, and simultaneously eighty years old and comfortable.

Love is a nice house on a quiet street, and the promise that we can trust each other.

Is this the man I love? Or has this all been an act? Did the structured family man marry a skilled liar, or are we tit for tat?

I've never questioned it before. I can't decide if this makes me a good wife or a bad spy.

I smile sweetly at him, because I don't know which of those two realities I'm living in. I nod. "A day off sounds nice. It's been so long, I don't even know what to do with it."

"Funny you should say that," he replies, handing me the coffee. "The Christmas sales are starting to hit. I was thinking it's the perfect time to shop for Collette."

It is with great caution that I agree. He tells me he'll go wrap up some emails and wait for me to get dressed.

Once he's gone, I retreat to the bathroom and call Elodie.

"Where have you been?" she demands by way of greeting. "I haven't been able to get ahold of you all morning. Since Mr. X is all off the grid doing God knows what, I thought we'd be relying on each other."

I was not expecting her to sound so livid. It's the way I sounded when Collette let her phone die last month and wasn't waiting at the front door when I picked her up from dance class. That mix of moderate annoyance and nagging fear of worse things we don't want to entertain.

"I'm all right," I assure her. *I think.*

"It wouldn't kill you to return a message," she says, starting to come down from her anger.

I think about that word she used the other day. *Friends.* Would that look like the things we saw on nineties sitcoms as kids, meeting up on a couture couch in a coffee shop? Should we be having these conversations by a picturesque fountain, sprinkling in mentions of our meddlesome mothers-in-law?

"You will not believe the strange week I'm having," I tell her. For just a second, I think about telling her my concerns about Waylen, if only so she'll assure me that it's all in my head.

"Well, maybe not," Elodie says. "But I'm pretty sure your week hasn't been stranger than the one Skylar Marie is having."

That's right. Elodie went into the city yesterday to finalize our event-planning cover for Bertram's ex. "Did you find anything else out?" I ask. "Did Skylar give you any new information?"

"No, I'm pretty sure Skylar won't be giving us anything new," Elodie says.

I run a washcloth under the tap and scrub my face. "Don't tell me she's backed out."

"Oh, she's backed out, all right," Elodie says. "She's dead."

SEVENTEEN

New England is known for its autumn beauty, but that transition into the Christmas season is what makes us the stuff of cheesy television romances.

There's a bite to the chilly air, and I've taken out my winter coat and Waylen's. They're the same shade of beige, mine with a faux-fur trim, his with a lambswool collar. When we park at the store, he sprints around the car to open my door for me.

He's a living Norman fucking Rockwell painting, I think.

While we browse the arts and crafts section for things our daughter will like, amid the glitter unicorn slime kits and the glow-in-the-dark bracelet kits, I am thinking of Bertram Casimir. He called this morning while I was sleeping, no voicemail.

The thought occurs to me that Waylen could have deleted it. But then, why leave the missed call in my log? He holds my hand, asks my opinion on a makeup palette. I tell him Collette is too young.

Here is what I know: Waylen wants me to quit my vigilantism so badly that he rented a car just to chase me around town and scare me out of it. Someone is hurting Erin—who, by the way, has not answered her phone since that incident at her apartment. Elodie did a drive past her place to confirm she was still alive, spotted through the curtains while they were briefly opened. Annie may be dead, murdered by her billionaire boyfriend, or she may be alive, operating under some mysterious cloak of darkness to torment Bertram. Skylar *is* dead, although it's been ruled an accidental drowning. Slipped and fell over into the Hudson River. It's believed she was crouched down, looking for her phone, which she may have dropped. It's a way that people die in movies, but not so much in real life.

Elodie went into a panic when I didn't answer my phone, thinking that Bertram must have gone on a killing spree and that I'd be on his list of women to take out.

"He's not done using me," I'd said. "He wouldn't kill me now."

"Not exactly reassuring," Elodie had replied.

She was upset when I told her I couldn't meet up today, but reassured when I said it's because I'd be with Waylen. "Oh good, you'll be safe," she'd told me before we hung up.

Am I?

Waylen is humming "It's Beginning to Look a Lot Like Christmas," slightly out of time with the store's radio.

He loves me. The question is, how much? Enough to kill for me?

My phone vibrates, and I break my hand out of his grasp. "I think this is the mechanic," I say, and sprint toward the restroom.

The mechanic tells me it's a fuel-pump issue. They can order a new one, but it will take until Monday at the earliest, since we're heading into the weekend. I ask what could cause something like this, and I can practically hear his shrug through the phone. "These things just happen."

"Hang on," I say before we hang up. "I heard this story on a podcast about a woman whose car was being tracked so that a would-be thief could follow her home and steal the car later when the family was sleeping. He put something under the car, I think? Can you check for anything like that, or is that completely crazy?"

"We can check," he says. "Can't always guarantee we'd find something like that. For what it's worth, I've never seen anything like that in my years doing this."

"It would make me feel so much better if you could look," I say with a sheepish laugh. "I know, my husband is trying to get me to stop listening to all this true crime."

I thank him profusely, and he assures me that you can't be too careful these days and he'll do his best.

When I return to Waylen, he asks about the car and I tell him I'm stuck until Monday. He can barely hide how thrilled he is about this.

"I was thinking," he says. "Do we really need two vehicles? I work from home anyway. There's no reason we can't share one. And your car has the most cash value. We could sell it, catch up on a few bills."

Waylen was the one who insisted I get that car. I was

more than happy with my dinky old Honda that I brought with me into our marriage. He was the one who wanted our lives to be perfect, right down to the smallest detail.

"Oh!" Waylen says, before I can respond. "We can use the extra cash to spend next Christmas in Hawaii."

"Wow," I say, trying desperately to stall for time before I commit to an answer. There's no way I'm selling that car, and he must know that. Is he feeling me out for something? "Let's wait and get the repairs done first. Then we can talk about it."

"We won't talk about it," Waylen insists, standing beside a row of garland lawn reindeer. "We'll argue once, maybe twice, and then it will hang in the air between us like all of our unresolved fights."

It isn't like him to be so insistent. Then again, it isn't like him to rent a car just to stalk me. If he's this desperate to get me to quit my work, what else has he done? What else would he be willing to do?

I have been neglecting him. I can admit that much. But then, that's who he married. "I was never Carol Brady," I say, keeping my voice measured, not just because we're in public, but because I haven't figured out what he's angling toward.

He braces himself to speak the same diatribe he's given a thousand times before, but I put a finger to his lips. He stays silent, his eyes wide with surprise.

You catch more flies with honey.

"I realize that I've been working too much," I say. "I need to be better at the work/life balance, but that doesn't mean I'm quitting my job, or that I'm quitting us." Somewhere in the distance, a customer pushes the "try me" button on a dancing Santa, and a synthesized version of "Jingle Bell Rock" begins to play.

"How about this," I go on. "Who says we have to wait until next Christmas? Our anniversary is in three months."

His eyes light up with hope and warmth. "Really?"

"I don't know about selling the car, but we have some money tucked away. We can make it work."

He wraps his arms around me, hugging me right there in the aisle.

He smells like aftershave, coffee, and the synthetic fibers of his coat. He's always so clean, somehow. His hair falling perfectly back into place even when he tugs nervously at it; I've never felt the barest prickle of a five-o'clock shadow; his nails are neatly trimmed and manicured, his hands broad and thick, but soft. Everything about him screams to my senses that he's what I'm attracted to, the perfect man.

It's always men who look like him, though, isn't it? The ones who surprise you.

I imagine him creeping into Erin's condo, lurking behind the door until she comes home from a trip to the grocery store. I imagine him threatening her, pinning her down when she tries to scream. Punching her in the eye with hard knuckles that hide behind his moisturized skin. When Elodie and I come to speak to Erin, we don't see him hidden in the shadows, glaring at Erin so that she won't betray his presence.

And then I imagine him taking the train into the city. Trying to intimidate Skylar the same way. But something went wrong, the struggle got out of hand, and she ended up dead. I can see him accosting her as she takes a brisk morning walk along the Hudson, shoving her so hard that she bashes her head on the railing before her body topples over.

Does he have it in him? The images play out like scenes in a noir film. Underlying them are the images of his tear-slicked face when he held our daughter for the first time. Or the gentle way he touches the small of my back as he passes me on his way up the stairs.

He loves me. He tells me every day. But does he love me so much he would kill to keep me safe?

Without my car, I begin to realize that I'm trapped. It isn't as simple as getting a ride from one of the other carpool moms, or stealing away to make a private phone call. Waylen is watching me. He's keeping track of me. And either I am making up elaborate scenarios that have no basis in reality, or I have underestimated him.

"Are you all right?" he asks.

I'm slipping. Usually I'm able to hide my pensiveness. This Bertram case has me all mixed up, and I'm getting distracted. It's dangerous.

I nod, smiling. The scenes I've just imagined disappear. Of course it couldn't be Waylen. Not *my* Waylen.

At home in the bathroom, I count my birth control pills carefully—just to be sure. Twelve little pills remaining neatly in their oval case. When Waylen returns to his home office, after we've stopped for a nice lunch on the way home, I rummage through the kitchen and bathroom cabinets. I don't know what I'm looking for exactly. A big cartoon bottle that says "sleeping pills" or "ACME memory erasers."

In any case, I find nothing out of the ordinary. I try to add up the pieces Bertram Casimir's case has given me: a missing girlfriend, a dead girlfriend, a sister with a dark past.

Waylen would never hurt me. He wants me all to himself, yes, but not in a *Kiss the Girls* way.

That means that I'm the one who's slipping, then. He didn't give me sleeping pills—I'm just exhausted from trying to catch Bertram in a lie when the man seems too clean to even be human. Waylen didn't tamper with my car. Bertram—or someone he hired—gained access to it while my brother is incapable of monitoring the security cameras I park under. The little partnership I have with my brother is slipping. *I'm* slipping.

"It was always inevitable we'd have to stop somewhere," my brother told me from his hospital bed. We've been running from ourselves for most of our lives. It's this desperation that has made us so good at what we do. I understand how well people are able to hide what they're capable of, even from themselves. I force them to confront it. I offer them a saving grace, or a just punishment. I don't think that I'm any better than they are, because I've been forced to do the same.

I hear the creak of Waylen's chair against the hardwood floor upstairs. He'll be preoccupied for a while. And since I don't have my car, he knows I'll be home. That alone seems to satisfy him—at least for now.

I take my laptop and my phone, and I slip into the basement.

It's cold and damp. The walls are unfinished, fluffy pink insulation contained between wooden frames instead of plaster, and exposed pipes and beams where a ceiling should be. Plastic bins of old books from Waylen's college years, and old toys of Collette's that we never got around to donating are stacked like giant bricks.

I can see the spines of Waylen's old paperbacks through one of the bins. Murder mysteries, psychological thrillers, and textbooks about MLA and APA stylings. Before he became an editor, he considered being the next James Patterson.

If you want to know the truth about a family, go to their basement. It's the one part of the house they don't decorate to impress you.

The cell service isn't great down here, but I know it's the only place where my voice won't carry throughout the surrounding rooms.

My brother answers on the first ring. "Is everything okay?" is how he greets me. He sounds so tired.

"I need advice," I say. "I'm stuck on this case."

"The billionaire? You're a clever fox. You'll get there."

"My instincts are way off," I tell him. "Everything points to him being clean."

"Margaux, come on," he says. I hear the distant beep of some machine, reminding me that he's in a hospital. Reminding me that my foundation is falling apart. "Think. He's got a sister whose entire life has been ruined by him. Erin hired us because we're the only ones who would work for free, but also, Bertram has bought out every legal avenue she could have pursued. There isn't a lawyer in the world who would touch him."

"Skylar is dead," I say. "Bertram's other ex."

"What?" Mr. X's voice is raspy. "When did that happen?"

"An 'accidental drowning' yesterday. No coverage in the news at all, just like when Annie went missing. Skylar had a family, people who loved her, but there's nothing online, nothing in any news articles. Her Instagram was deleted, and the most I could find are some vloggers asking what happened to it."

"It's just like his parents," Mr. X reminds me. That's right—there's nothing available online about them either. I've been so preoccupied by Bertram's love life that I haven't given much thought to his past. In most cases, I don't need to go back any further than the date of the crime. "You never did like to spend time analyzing the criminal's history."

"Because it's a waste of time," I say. "It doesn't matter if he wasn't hugged enough as a child, or he tortured birds. My interest begins the day he stole that software from his sister. Or maybe even later than that, on the day Annie went missing."

"Your interest begins there, but does the case begin there?" He pulls the phone away from his face, and I hear him coughing, muffled, as though into a pillow. I pretend I didn't hear it, for my own well-being as much as for his.

"Where would I begin to look?" I ask.

He catches the desperation in my voice. "Margaux." His tone changes. "What aren't you telling me?"

Oh, nothing, brother dear. Just that I need to prove Bertram is the one who did the evil deeds. Bertram was the one who killed Annie and then made up some ludicrous story about her stalking him. Bertram is the one who found a way to kill Skylar—maybe not directly, but through his power and influence, using someone he could hire. I have to prove that Bertram was the one who messed with the engine of my car.

Because if Bertram's guilty . . . the man I married is innocent.

I *have* to prove that Bertram is guilty. The idea of Waylen being behind this case spinning out of my control is too crazy to say out loud, despite his renting a car to stalk me throughout the city to scare me off of it.

"Tell me," Mr. X says. It's a demand, but it's given gently. He was always good at that. I found it so calming after our parents died. Someone was looking out for me. Someone kept me on the right track, made sure I did the right thing, even if everyone in the world thought the worst of us.

What I hate is how well it works. This is one of the reasons I rarely speak to him on the phone. He's the only one who can coax my secrets out of me.

"Why did you hire Waylen? All those years ago?" I ask him, attempting to deflect. "I know you wanted a small-time criminal, but there were dozens to choose from. What was it about him?"

He plays along, knowing it's the only way to get me to talk. I was never good at getting right to the point. "I liked that he was cool as a cucumber. I always thought that he could survive a proper CIA interrogation. He never betrayed anything he was thinking. Normally that's a good thing in our line of work. But a bad thing when we're talking about the person who marries my sister."

"But you thought he was honest, right?" I say. "I mean, there was something you could trust."

"I don't trust anyone, Margaux. You know that. Neither do you."

"But we're broken," I say. "That's why we can't trust." *That's why I'm suspecting my own husband of something he could never do.*

"Everyone is broken." He's losing patience, or maybe he's just afraid he's running out of time. "Tell me what this is about."

"It's—" I pause. Upstairs, I hear Waylen's footsteps moving through the kitchen. I hear the beeps as he pushes the buttons on the oven timer. I move farther from the bottom of the staircase, lowering my voice to be sure he won't hear me. I'd told him that I was going to take a nap, so he thinks I'm in the bedroom. "You don't think that he would hurt anyone, do you?"

"Tell me what happened." My brother's voice is deathly serious. "Did he do something to you? Are you hurt?"

I say the words quickly, because I want to be rid of them. I say them like I'm throwing a hated object down a dark, endless well where I'll never see them again. I recount the strange events surrounding Bertram, and how many of them line up with times that I can't confirm Waylen's whereabouts. I tell him that Waylen was tracking me with an AirTag—which could have been a misguided attempt at him trying to save our ailing marriage, or a hint at something insidious. I confide that I don't know if I can trust him, and that I don't trust my own instincts. That things since meeting Bertram Casimir have not added up.

"Margaux, listen to me," he says. "I want you to take Collette and get out of that house. I've got your location on your phone, so keep it with you. I'll get to you as soon as I can."

"You're in the hospital and you're staying there," I insist. "I don't want to overreact. He's never done anything to make me doubt him before. Maybe it is me—"

"Get out of that house," he insists, and his tone makes the hairs on the back of my neck rise. "I have ways of finding out where he's been and whether it checks out. I'll contact you when I know. Until then, take Collette to my house. He'll never find you there. Don't take your purse or anything he could have placed a tracker in. Just your ID, a credit card, and your phone, do you understand me? I'll make sure he can't trace your location."

"I—"

"Do you understand?" he repeats.

I stare at a spiderweb in the concrete corner, lit up by a scrap of sunlight coming in through the small window. A fly is trapped there, struggling fruitlessly. I feel similarly trapped.

A shrill alarm pierces the silence. One long, loud whining that breaks out into a vibrato.

I know that sound too well. The fire alarm in the kitchen. The memories come back to me immediately, too visceral for me to stave off. I'm only vaguely aware of Mr. X's voice on the phone, still asking me to confirm that I've heard him, that I'll do as he asks. I don't remember hanging up, but I must have, because in the next moment my phone is in my pocket, and I'm sprinting up the stairs.

The house is burning down. Everything is turning to ashes.

The smell is so thick that I'm already choking on it. I expect the doorknob to be hot as a coal when I touch it, but it's still cool against my palm.

I see flames, thick gray smoke, and the charred skeletal beams of the house for a moment, before my eyes register what's actually in front of me.

It's golden sunlight—not smoke—that fills the kitchen, the first sunny day we've had after weeks of gloomy autumn skies. Things are tidy, the way I left them. Waylen is standing by the stove, waving an oven mitt in front of the smoke detector. "Sorry," he says, when he hears me walking up behind him. "I left the water boiling too long and scorched the pan."

Whatever else he was going to say dissolves when he turns and sees the expression on my face. He must see that I'm not the woman he knows, but a scared little girl, screaming for my family as the flames come up around me.

I try to put on the mask I've been wearing since I was twelve, but for the first time, it won't go up. My emotion is laid bare on my face, and I'm exposed.

"Margaux?" Waylen approaches me like I'm a frightened animal in headlights. "Sweetheart, what is it?"

I shake my head, take a step away before he can touch me. *It's nothing. Tell him it's nothing.* But the words won't come out.

He takes my shoulders. My back is pinned to the wall. "You're shaking," he tells me.

"I—I thought the house was on fire," I manage to croak out. "That's all. I guess I haven't been getting enough sleep."

He wraps an arm around my shoulders, and just like with Bertram, I feel completely thrown off my game. My instincts are firing in a hundred different directions. Is Bertram a master liar? My mind tells me he's not. But then again, I'm not even sure if I can trust the man I married.

He guides me gently into the living room, sits me on the couch, and places himself before me on the edge of the coffee table. His eyes are big and soft, so much like Collette's in this moment.

"It's okay," he tells me. "You're safe. You can trust me."

These are the exact words the social worker told me. What a crock of shit that turned out to be. I was young and trusting and I didn't realize that everything I said would become evidence in the trial.

Waylen doesn't know about that. He knows my parents died in a fire, but not that my brother and I went on trial for starting it. And not about anything that came next.

"Where are your keys?" I say, unable to control the hysterical edge to my voice. "I need to get Collette from school—I—"

"It's barely even noon," Waylen says. When I try to stand, his gentle grasp turns firm, and I realize I can't stand. He won't let me.

The bruise on Erin's face. Skylar's body on the surface of the river. I was so busy tracking Bertram's whereabouts that I never thought about the fact that I didn't know where Waylen was when any of it happened.

Take Collette and get out of that house. Mr. X's words fill my mind. He's the only one who's ever been able to tell me what to do, the only one who really knows me.

When I try to stand again, Waylen forces me down, and I kick him in the shin so hard that he staggers back into the coffee table with a loud thud. I run for the foyer and he leaps over the couch, grasping the collar of my sweater for only a second before I wrest it away. I hear his footsteps chasing me as I scramble into the kitchen. His keys are where he always leaves them, in a bowl on the counter beside an old tube of ChapStick and some paper clips.

I struggle with the lock on the kitchen door, which leads out to the backyard. We haven't opened it since the summer, when the weather was still warm enough to use the patio furniture. Now it all sits there, covered up in tarps like the old ghosts of the life I thought I was living.

"Margaux, please!" he calls after me, desperate. I trip on a rock in the yard but manage to save myself from toppling face-first into the mud.

I'm begging Waylen to stay away from me, not to touch me, and he's saying that I've lost my mind and I'm scaring him. But somehow, I make it to his car and lock the doors before he can get to the handles. Now it's his turn to try to cling to the car while I speed off, but he can't do it. He gets to the end of the driveway and staggers, and I leave him standing there as I gun it down the street.

EIGHTEEN

Elodie answers on the first ring. She's on edge because the Skylar situation is freaking her out.

"Margaux!" she cries, by way of greeting. "I thought something happened to you."

"Actually, I—"

"Listen," she carries on, talking in that hyper way she does when she's got an idea. "We need to talk to Mr. X. I know you know more than you're telling me about how to get ahold of him. We're in over our heads on this, and the deal was that he'd be watching out for us. This is getting unsafe."

"You're right," I tell her. "I know where he is, but I can't tell you yet. I promise I will—" *Once he's dead and his secrets don't matter to him— No, Margaux, don't go there.* There's another way out of this. There has to be.

"Listen, Elodie." I keep my voice calm. "We're both in danger."

"Like—right now?" she asks, bewildered.

"Right now," I say. "Go to the school, get our girls. You might get a call from Waylen, but don't answer it."

"The girls?" Elodie rasps. "What's going on?"

"I'm not sure, but I'm going to find out if it was really Bertram who killed Skylar." Am I remembering the anger in Waylen's grip as he tried to keep me in the house? Was he screaming, or was he just concerned? Are my instincts about anything right, or am I losing my grasp on reality?

"As opposed to who?" Elodie is asking. Of course she won't just concede all the control to me. "Is there someone else?"

"No! I— Maybe there's another explanation."

I can still smell the smoke from the nonexistent kitchen fire. I wake up from dreams sometimes with it in my nostrils. It never truly goes away. No matter how fast I drive, I can't evade my past.

"Take the girls somewhere safe," I tell her. "Somewhere nobody knows about." My heart breaks for Collette, who will be so scared and wondering where I am. She asked me if we could go to Oregon together, just to see the graves of grandparents she's never met. Why didn't I see it sooner? *Just us,* she said. Not Waylen. She wants to be away from him. She's been too scared to tell me.

"Where will you be?" she demands. But I hear her keys jingling and I know she's doing as I ask.

"I'm going to see Erin," I say. "Whoever killed Skylar is the one who hurt her. Who else could it be? I need to figure out what's going on, and she's the only one still alive to talk. Get the girls somewhere safe. Do *not* tell me where you are. Don't tell anyone, do you hear me?"

"I know a place," she says.

"Stay with them and wait for me to call you," I say.

"I'm on it. And, Margaux . . ."

I'm just about to hang up. "What?"

"I'm going to be really pissed if you get yourself killed." It's the closest she'll ever come to admitting that she likes me.

"Ditto," I say, and then hang up.

If I want to be safe from Waylen's tracking, the best way to do it is in his own car. He wouldn't think to have placed an AirTag here. It's been so long since I've driven it that I've lost the muscle memory for it and I keep confusing the turn signal for the high beams. He'll check the school first. Only a parent is authorized to take Collette out of class, but Elodie has her connections.

Mr. X calls just as I'm pulling into the parking lot in front of Erin's condo. "I'm safe," I say, by way of answer.

"Really? Because my phone says you're at Bertram's sister's," he snaps. "I didn't think I needed to specify that it's time to abandon the mission, Margaux. Get somewhere safe."

Forget the mission? He's not thinking clearly. He's heavily medicated, in more pain than he'll let on. Nothing is more important than learning the truth—he knows that. "Erin is the only one who will have answers," I tell him. "If Waylen hurt her, or—or if it was someone Bertram hired, she'll talk. I'll make sure she knows she's safe with me."

"Take Collette and get to my house." He isn't even listening to me. "All of my work will be for nothing if you get yourself killed now."

I shut the engine. "What do you mean?"

"Come on," he says. "You're not dumb. Do you really not see what this has all been about? It's about absolving you of your guilt."

"You're not making any sense," I say.

"You aren't seeing reason," he argues.

"I'll call you back." I hang up.

I stride toward Erin's door with the confidence of a woman possessed. Something happened to her, and this time I'm not leaving until I find out what it is.

I knock. No answer. I knock again. "Erin," I call through the door. "It's me. I'm alone, but I need to speak to you." Nothing.

I try calling, and her number goes right to voicemail.

No, no, no. Damn it, she's dead. Someone got to her. Last night, Waylen was asleep beside me, wasn't he? I think about how restful I felt when I woke up, how calm, for once not plagued by nightmares or fitfulness. More than eight hours, during which I can't account for my husband's whereabouts. Has Erin Casimir been lying here dead while I've been out Christmas shopping and accusing her brother of murder?

"Erin!" I pound desperately on her door. In a moment of panic, I try the knob, and to my surprise it turns. I bolt inside as though I've arrived in time to stop whatever has already happened here.

I make it two steps inside and then I stop in my tracks. The air is stale and cold. The heat has been turned off. I try the light switch. Nothing.

Heart pounding, I venture into the kitchenette, where Erin prepared tea for Elodie and me during our interview.

I recall now how stilted she was, how closed off. Was she in danger even then?

"Erin?" My voice is softer now, and far away, as though someone else is speaking. There's a heady, metallic smell to the air. The kitchenette is tidy, but something feels off about it. There's a mug in the sink, and the leaky faucet is drip-drip-dripping against the brim, making a faint, echoing beat.

I move down the narrow hallway. Her bedroom is tidy, even though the bed is unmade. There's nothing but a dresser and a laundry hamper. There were no trinkets in the living room, no excess. Erin leaves a small carbon footprint. Even the way she sits, moves, and speaks has the mark of someone who wants to leave as little trace in the world as possible.

I stop just before the tile threshold into the bathroom. There's a drop of blood right where the carpet ends. A cut from a glass she broke, or menstrual blood, or a nick from the razor when she was shaving her legs.

But when I look up, I see what deep down I already knew. This was no small accident.

Blood is smeared all across the tiles on the floor, the wall. Red handprints grapple at the edge of the porcelain sink.

The shower curtain is ripped open. A pink ring stains the sides from bloody water that has since been drained.

My breath hitches. I stumble back.

There's no body. I force myself to keep looking, but all I see is blood and a clump of Erin's dark hair.

It isn't the carnage that frightens me. I learned long ago

about the terrible things that happen in this world. I've even learned that anyone can surprise you. The sweet old lady who keeps offering you lemonade and complimenting your garden shot her husband and keeps his body in the freezer as she collects his retirement checks. The handsome young man all dressed up and nervous for his first date is stealing millions from crypto investors.

We are all the tip of our own iceberg, with secrets that range from little white lies to crimes that can get us put away for life. And you can never truly be sure.

No, this blood doesn't tell me anything I didn't already know about humanity. But it may have told me something I was afraid to admit about my own life, about the father of my child, and the game we've been playing since the day we met.

He couldn't have done this.

It was Bertram. It has to be.

My husband was sleeping beside me all night. Yes, he tried to scare me off the trail with the rental car. His possessiveness has a bit of an edge. But he's so sensible, his moral compass so strong that there has to be a limit.

"Everyone is capable of anything," my brother's voice says.

I expected Bertram Casimir to be a simple case, but his whole story is like a puzzle with half the pieces missing.

As though reading my thoughts, my phone rings, making me jump. Bertram.

"Hello?" I'm standing in the living room now, and realizing that it's *too* pristine. The carpet—old and faded after years of tenants—has been freshly vacuumed. Neat horizontal lines in the nap show that every inch was covered.

There's the faint smell of disinfectant. The couch cushions are damp, as though they've been recently steam-cleaned.

"Are you all right?" Bertram asks. "I've been trying to get ahold of you all morning. Listen, I know your marriage isn't my business, but I'm worried that Annie may have gotten to your husband."

"No, my marriage isn't any of your business," I say. I'm noticing how bare the apartment is. Was it always like this? As I backpedal to the front door, I drag the edge of my shoe against the carpet to erase my footprints. I wipe the prints off the doorknob with my shirt.

He sighs. "I'm sorry, Margaux. Everyone in my life gets caught up in this. It's why I'm so selective about who I speak to."

"Then why are you speaking to me?" I try to keep my voice neutral. I don't want him to know what I've just witnessed. *Did you do this, Bertram?*

My heart is pounding, though I appear calm as I walk back toward Waylen's car.

"I'm worried about you," Bertram says. "I—"

I shush him, and he stops speaking. There's a police car turning into the complex. *Okay,* I tell myself. That's not too unusual. But then the driver locks eyes with me as I grip the handle of Waylen's car, and the lights and sirens come on.

"Margaux?" Bertram says.

Waylen called the cops on me. He broke the cardinal rule of our line of work—even though he gave up this life, he still knows what something like this can mean for me. For our family. And it isn't just about the fact that I stole his car—technically. He must have told the police that I was a danger to myself. That's why all the fanfare. The officer gets out of his car, hand on his holster. "Are you Margaux Blue?" he asks.

"Margaux." Bertram's voice is urgent now. "Is that a police siren? What's going on? Where are you?"

"I'll call you back," I say.

And then I run.

NINETEEN

To: Jennifer Smith
From: ProfArtler@Yale

Dear Ms. Smith,
Apologies for the delayed response. I would be happy to speak with you. I'm available until noon or after 5 p.m. on weekdays.

Sincerely,
Professor Jim Artler
Yale University

I'm hiding in the alleyway between a laundromat and a Chinese takeout when I see the email. It comes amid a flurry of texts that I don't bother to check, missed calls that I send straight to voicemail.

I sprinted a mile before pausing here to catch my breath, in a haze that smells like detergent and fried shrimp.

But being crouched in the damp and cold for the past several minutes has given me time to think about how to approach Bertram.

I've organized my thoughts into neat little categories, like building the frame of a puzzle before sorting out the middle. All of the pieces must be here; I just haven't found them yet. And here's a chance to add some more.

I dial the jolly professor's number, and he answers, all tweed-business-casual, having no idea that he is the key to my salvation from across the pond. I introduce myself, cheerfully apologizing for the poor cell reception as what I'm pretty sure is a rat skitters across the shadows behind me.

"I wanted to ask you about a student named Erin Casimir. Bertram's sister," I say. "The piece also dives into his relationship with his family. It's part of a profile series we're doing on the human side of tech influencers."

"His sister?" The professor is thoughtful. "I'm sure I've seen her on campus, but I can't recall if she was ever in one of my classes."

Police sirens wail in the distance, making my blood run cold.

It can't be for me, I reassure myself. Nobody is going to go through all this trouble just to recover a vehicle that Waylen reported stolen. Besides, I left it in the parking lot and tossed the keys on the driver's seat before I bolted. Problem solved.

"Bertram mentioned in our interview that his sister was

a software developer too. Maybe he mentioned her influence in some of his programs."

"I'm sorry, he didn't." I can barely hear the professor's voice now. The sirens are piercingly loud as they get closer. He's saying something else, something that I can't hear.

I plug my other ear and duck into the shadows. It reeks of garbage. That smell must be to blame for the sick feeling that's taking me over, I rationalize.

I ignore the call that keeps trying—over and over—to interrupt my conversation with Bertram's professor. I ask him what Bertram was like as a student, and he tells me all the typical platitudes. He was always enthusiastic, polite, helpful—the things you could say about Ted Bundy before you knew.

Something is pressing at me, some dark sense that I've tied myself to Bertram in some inextricable way. *Those sirens aren't for you,* I tell myself. But why are they getting louder?

"Did anything ever seem unusual about Bertram?" I blurt. "Did he ever . . . do anything that concerned you?"

"I'm sorry," he says, "what did you say the name of your publication was again?"

"You've been incredibly helpful, thank you," I say, and hang up.

Elodie is calling me, and not for the first time, if the little red bubble by my phone icon is to be believed.

"I can't talk," I say in a hushed tone when I answer.

"You had better talk!" She sounds livid. "I've just gotten a call from your husband. He's beside himself. You stole his car? You've just involved me in taking your daughter away from him? You may not want to talk, but you'd better start, sister."

I pinch the bridge of my nose. "You didn't tell him where Collette is, did you?"

"I pretended my cell reception was bad and hung up," she says, still sounding like a swarm of kicked hornets. "But he sounded like he was about to come over and break my door down if I didn't answer him. Todd is at home with the twins, Margaux. I can't have your husband going down there, exposing what I've been doing."

"He won't," I assure her. Waylen is a lot of things, but he isn't rash. He's a quiet planner. This past week has reminded me of that much.

"I'm going to get the girls," she says. "I don't want this kind of trouble, and you refuse to tell me what's going on. Mr. X hasn't answered my texts for days—what kind of Podunk operation is this, exactly? I thought we were professionals."

"Don't get Collette!" I cry. "Tell me where she is, and I'll get her."

"You're in no position to be making demands of me," she says. I've seen Elodie blow her top about a minivan double-parked in the school lot. I've been present for her lectures to the vice principal about expanding the budget for the upcoming Christmas pageant because *no way* is her little girl going to show up in hand-me-down velvet for the *Nutcracker* chorus.

But this is a different kind of mad. Like when your mother pulls you out of the street so you don't get hit by a car, or your spouse catches you in bed with your boss. This is the life-changing anger that ruins trust and damages everything you've built.

I'd love to heal it now, but I can't, because the sirens are back and they're loud enough to drown out Elodie, who is demanding that I come clean on all my lies. She's telling me that I've lost my mind, that I'm scaring her, and has any word to come from my mouth ever been the truth?

I'm so sorry, Elodie. You've learned the hard way that I'm not friend material. If I had the time now, I'd say that I wish it could have been the way she wanted. How nice to have a true partner in crime. It isn't that I wanted to be a lone wolf. It's just the only thing I do well.

"Damn it, now the police are at my house. I see them on the doorbell cam," she says.

"What?" I rasp.

"What have you done, Margaux?"

She hangs up before I can reply.

TWENTY

"Goddamn it," I mutter, because the most horrific thing about this day is what I've just come to realize: With my brother out of commission, Bertram Casimir is the only one with the resources to help me now.

I run until I no longer hear the sirens, and I ask Bertram to meet me there.

He arrives in record time—without his driver, and in a beat-up old Honda Civic. "Borrowed from a friend," he tells me as I climb into the passenger's side and tug the hood of my coat up over my face.

"I thought you didn't have friends," I say.

He quirks a brow. "Careful," he says. "It sounds like you're not in a position to be picky. What sort of trouble have you gotten yourself into?"

"Where were you last night?" I ask, catching him off

guard. We're still parked on the side of the road, the occasional car zipping around us.

"What?" he says.

"I can't explain now, but if you can prove where you were last night, I can help you."

"Help me?"

"With Annie," I say. "With her disappearance, and with what happened to Skylar." I don't tell him about Erin, who is very likely dead herself. But by whose hand? If it was Bertram, I'll know soon enough. And if it wasn't . . . I have to contend with reality about the man I married. If my instincts about Bertram's innocence are correct, then I've been sleeping next to a stranger for the past eleven years. And if I'm wrong, and Waylen is innocent, that means Bertram was able to fool me so effectively that I've been questioning my own reality for weeks.

I don't know which is worse. But I'll know soon enough.

My phone buzzes, distracting me from the fact that he hasn't answered my question. A text from Elodie:

> **You're a murder suspect. They think you killed Erin. Don't try to explain here. I'm deleting all our messages. Don't reply.**

I reply anyway: **Keep Collette away from Waylen. Please.**

Now Elodie is regretting trying to be my friend. I'm sure of that. This case has gone over both our heads.

My blood runs cold and rushes through my ears so loudly that I don't hear Bertram asking me where we're heading. I was seen leaving Erin's apartment. Who but the guilty party would leave a scene like that without calling for help?

Numbly, I tell him which street to turn down.

I need to get in touch with my brother, but I already know any calls placed to him at the hospital will be easily traceable. For once, he can't help me.

"Park here," I tell Bertram, when we reach an abandoned building at the end of my brother's block. It's a small, unassuming neighborhood. Lower income. If he wanted, my brother could have afforded a suburban McMansion like the one Waylen and I occupy. Our parents' deaths left us with a decent inheritance.

But he takes what he needs to fund his elaborate surveillance setup and leaves the rest of the money to me. It's in a joint account that only he and I know about, under his name so that it can't be used as leverage if Waylen and I ever have a bitter divorce.

Or if Waylen ever goes to prison for homicide.

"Here?" Bertram asks, looking at the boarded-up building on a plot overrun with weeds. "It looks—um."

"I need you to wait here," I say. I get out of the car and sprint down the street, hoping Bertram won't follow me to see where I'm really going.

No such luck. I hear the click of his Marzeri Buranos against the uneven pavement. To look at, Bertram passes for normal. If you don't follow the world of big tech—and most don't—he looks like a manicured CEO, or the overachieving assistant manager at Staples. But there are little details, like his thousand-dollar shoes, the color of a lacquered wooden floor at a gastropub, and the severe part in his short, dark hair, or the fact that his cuticles are perfectly tended to. Even Elodie would envy how well groomed he is.

He grabs my arm and whirls me around. “Margaux,” he says firmly. His voice is a rugged whisper—he knows better than to let it carry through the empty street. Someone in these shuttered houses around us may be listening. “I’m not stupid. There were police sirens when you called me. Someone is looking for you. What’s happened?”

I stare back at him, startled by how badly I want to believe in his innocence. *Don’t be foolish,* I remind myself. There’s a tactful way to handle everything. When I know without a shadow of a doubt that my target is guilty, I don’t go storming into their home with guns blazing and a police force behind me. I handle it quietly, giving them ample security, letting them check their mail after pulling into the driveway, pouring themselves a cup of morning coffee as they enjoy the sunrise on their porch on a Saturday morning.

Slow and effective, and always lurking in the shadows so that they don’t know what hit them. They never know who was spying on them, or where I came from.

I suppose this is also true if my target is innocent. I don’t know, because it’s never happened before. By now, I’ve always proven their guilt. I’ve always had my brother to help me.

“You said you can help me with Annie and Skylar,” he says. “But—how do you know about Skylar? How can you possibly know about Annie, when even I haven’t seen her in months?”

"I know more than you think," I tell him. "But before I answer your questions, I need you to answer mine. Where were you last night?"

"I was home! I'm always home, because there's nowhere else for me to go!" he cries. "You don't realize how much Annie controls my life. I can't have friends, I can't speak with my family; everyone I come into contact with is in danger. No matter how I try to explain this to you, there's no way you can realize what she's put me through! You wouldn't believe me—nobody would ever believe me." He loses it for just a second, his impatience bobbing to the surface, like the bodies of his former lovers from their watery graves.

He's still gripping my arm, but then he realizes it and eases up a bit.

I stare at him, matching the intensity of his gaze. His glittering eyes, clenched jaw, and a worry vein that strikes his temple like a bolt of lightning.

Is this elusive Annie as powerful as he says, or is she another dead girl in his string of ill-fated lovers? How can one woman have a billionaire with all the resources, security, and power in the world running so scared? Or is he just that good a liar?

What's the truth?

I look over my shoulder. I can see my brother's house from here. The grass has been mowed recently. The only expense he doesn't spare is what he needs to keep the place looking boring, tidy, and unremarkable. Nobody would know that there are shelves blocking the windows and doors. Or any of the things that the cheerful, tacky yellow curtains hide.

There was a time when bringing an outsider here was

unthinkable. But he's dying, and all the rules are broken. This is the last big case of my vigilante career, he said. Crack the code, and I'll be absolved of all my guilt. I'll be able to live a normal life.

A "normal life" scares me more than anything, but in this moment, I hope he's right.

I look to Bertram again. He's patiently waiting for my reply, even though nervous energy is brimming off him.

"There really isn't a violent bone in your body, is there?" I say.

"What? Of course not."

I hesitate. "What if I say that I believe you—about Annie, and about everything?" I ask him. "But the proof I need to not feel like an idiot for trusting you is in one of these houses, and I have to go and get it."

"You—believe me?" His face lights up with a desperate hope that makes me so sad, because I can see immediately that I'm the only one who's spoken these words to him in a long time.

"Those police sirens were for me," I say. "I'm being framed for murder. Or maybe I was just at the wrong place at the wrong time. Either way, I know I'm innocent, and I need to prove that *you're* innocent, so I can trust you."

"Murder?" he rasps. And then he releases my arm and takes a step back, rakes his fingers through his hair. "Oh God," he says. "She's killed someone."

"Her, or my husband." Saying the words out loud feels surreal.

Bertram doesn't press for details. Maybe he realizes he's in no position to scrutinize my situation, given the nuances of his own.

I make a decision—one I think Mr. X would approve of, but only because he's not long for this world. I take Bertram's hand and lead him to my brother's house.

Bertram is tall, muscular, but lanky at the same time. It's comical to see him climb in through the back entrance of my brother's house and navigate the labyrinth of boxes and wires as we make our way upstairs.

"What was that?" he whispers, in response to a faint skittering sound.

"Probably a mouse," I say.

He shudders.

I've come to admire how stalwart Bertram Casimir is, how stunningly adaptable. He doesn't complain or grouse, and he doesn't ask the glaring questions, like, "What the hell is this place?" and "What are we doing here?"

I realize now that this is why my instinct feels so correct. Someone like Bertram is well groomed and media trained. He can handle himself with aplomb in any interview, from *Good Morning America* to the most niche of tech podcasts. But the real test is how he carries himself when there are no interviewers, no public to dazzle. Just a woman who says she believes him, and a whole lot of wires.

He sits on the only chair at the kitchen table that isn't covered with boxes of hard drives and old phones—everything from Nokias to iPhones to Androids. He doesn't ask any more questions.

"Don't touch anything," I say, and he nods.

In the living room, I find what I'm looking for. The last time I visited my brother in the hospital, he told me that he'd hacked into the security cameras at Bertram's building. The videos upload to a custom cloud he created, in thirty-second segments. "It was just Ring cameras, if you can believe that," he told me. "You'd think these big, swanky places would have some top-of-the-line, closed-circuit surveillance, but this is usually what we're dealing with."

I sit on the edge of a chair that's covered with my brother's things. I don't let myself look around, because it will make me too sad, like I'm sitting in the center of his heart. He's brilliant, and he should be out there somewhere, giving his own interviews like Bertram does, inventing world-changing technology, coding and programming for NASA.

But the fire killed us both. It took away whoever we might have been. And rather than try to heal, my brother has spent all this time carrying and living in the pain, so that I could at least pretend to have a happy life. Being an actress in a role that fools everyone else is something, isn't it? Being a good liar is better than facing the truth.

There's the live feed of Bertram's building. I click through the folder of auto-saved clips from the feed, but there are hundreds of them, between the lobby and the elevators and the parking garage and the penthouse. It would be so much easier if there were a camera inside Bertram's apartment, because then I'd doubtless have hours of him toiling away doing whatever it is he does in there. But I have to locate the last time he entered the building and prove that he never left. It's a task that could take hours—time I don't have.

There is Bertram entering the parking garage with his

driver after we parted ways. Progress! I save the file and continue, following him into the elevator and to his penthouse apartment. Now to prove that he hasn't gone anywhere since this morning, when he came to get me.

My phone rings. An unknown number. Normally it's the sort of thing I'd ignore, but today is different, and I know that whatever is on the other end of the line is important.

"Hello?" My calm voice doesn't betray the anxiety I feel. I'm still clicking through the clips. No sign of Bertram for hours after his return home. He's right—he really doesn't go anywhere. A delivery person leaves food at the front desk, and the doorman brings it upstairs at ten p.m. Once the elevator dings and the doorman has gone, Bertram answers in his bathrobe, takes the food inside, and closes the door. The only sign of life.

"Mommy?" Collette's voice sounds small, the way it did when she was a little girl, nothing at all like the maturing eleven-year-old who forever tries to carry herself like she's twenty.

"Collette?" I rasp.

I hear the faintest murmur of a voice somewhere in the background, and then she says, sounding scared, "Mommy, can you come pick me up?"

These aren't her words. Collette is too much of a stoic to confess when she's afraid. She bottles it up for days, sometimes months, until it manifests in a violent panic attack. But as she gets older, she's gotten better at hiding them. I know, because she gets it from me.

Someone is listening to us and coaching her, using her as bait. Waylen? The police? Elodie?

I have to be very careful about how I respond. I recall our conversation several weeks ago, when I was driving her to her aunt's house. I thought Bertram was following us and that our lives were in danger, but really it was Waylen trying to scare me into retirement. Collette—smart girl that she is—was the one who suggested a code word. *Nail polish.*

The next set of videos shows no sign of Bertram leaving his apartment. I'm almost done with last night's footage, making my way through to this morning. If I can prove he didn't leave his building until I called him for help, I'll know he wasn't the one who killed Erin.

And my celebration will be incredibly short-lived, because that means Waylen is still in the running to be a suspect. He has been more and more desperate for me to quit spy work, and he has a motive.

I can't communicate any of this to Collette. All I can say is, "I'm looking for that nail polish we lost. It's important that I find it."

Where are you? I want to say. *Are you frightened? Are you hurt? Has Waylen locked you in a closet and forced you to call me?*

He wouldn't hurt Collette, surely. The past forty-eight hours have made me rethink everything about him. Insidious intention can be applied to so much of what I thought made him safe to be around.

"Um . . ." Collette's voice trails off. She's looking to whoever is with her for direction. Smart girl. She knows better than to give a poorly coded clue and put us both in jeopardy. After a beat, she says, "I think you gave it to Elodie. The red and blue nail polish."

The line goes dead just as a male voice in the background was starting to murmur something to her. I couldn't make out the word being spoken, but I already knew that the low timbre didn't belong to Waylen.

Red and blue. She's with the police.

I'm still furiously scanning the surveillance footage as I work it out. Finally, I reach this morning, wherein Bertram emerges from his apartment for the first time.

He was telling the truth. If the circumstances weren't so dire, I'd be leaping for joy. This means I can trust him. When someone was making a bloody mess in Erin Casimir's apartment, he was miles away in his apartment. I know Erin was alive at least twenty-four hours before the bloodbath because she'd texted me for a progress update. I didn't answer because I didn't have an answer for her yet.

But someone did kill her, and now I'm being framed for it. And until I prove my innocence, the police won't stop looking for me.

When I finally muster up the bravado to approach Bertram, it's so that I can break the news that his sister is dead. Not only is she dead, but she hired me to prove that she was the true inventor of his lucrative app, and *someone* didn't want me to find out the truth, so they silenced Erin—for good.

"Bertram," I say, coming into the kitchen, "I—"

His phone rings. Both of us go silent, staring at the screen. An unknown number. He's about to decline, when I say, "Wait! Answer it." He looks at me quizzically, but he does as I ask.

"Hello?" He sounds cool and professional as ever, his accent rhythmic even in those two syllables.

"Bertram Casimir," the voice says, matching his confidence. "Thank you for taking my call."

"Waylen," I whisper.

Bertram furrows his brow. "How did you get this number?"

"I have my ways," Waylen says. "Especially when it comes to her."

My blood runs cold, and even though I can't predict what Waylen is about to say, something deep within me already knows and is dreading it.

"There are things you don't know about my wife," Waylen goes on. "I'm not sure what she's told you, but I do know that it's all lies. She's not just a pretty face and a delicious hourglass figure. She's dangerous."

How have I never noticed how soft Bertram's facial features are? Standing over him now, in the dim light of my brother's curtained kitchen, I see the gentle slope of his nose, the smooth corners of his eyes. I bet the world only sees the chiseled jaw and the muscled forearms. He presents himself as strong, confident. But in this moment, I see what I haven't allowed myself to notice in our time together: a sensitive, empathetic layer just below the surface.

He looks at me now, as though Waylen's words are breaking his heart. All this time I was thinking that he was a liar with an edge, like me, Bertram was thinking that we were the same for a completely different reason. He thought that I could be sweet, that I really wanted to help him.

How do I convince him that I was lying before, but I'm telling him the truth now?

"Hang up." I mouth the words to him. But he doesn't listen.

"I know it's hard to believe. I fell for it, too," Waylen is saying. "But I've slept beside that woman for more than a decade. I know her in a way that nobody else ever will. I know her more than she knows herself."

I kneel before Bertram, my hands clasped in supplication. I am begging him to end the call, to trust me. But why should he?

"I know she's with you," Waylen goes on. Bertram hasn't said a word. He doesn't need to. "Did you know that she's wanted for murder? The police can place her on the scene. She walked right out the front door with blood on her shoes. Look, she needs to turn herself in."

My head perks up at that. If Collette was being coerced earlier, then Waylen is being coerced now. Turn myself in to the police? He would never suggest something so—straightforward. He knows I'm listening in, surely. He knows there's nothing he could say that would make me approach the police to turn myself in. Whatever he *really* wants me to do is going to be communicated in code.

Bertram still hasn't said a word. He's looking at me with that devastatingly scrutinizing gaze, and I can't tell whether he believes a word that's being said. He's been lied to by everyone he's met in his adult life. Success has brought him money and fame, but it hasn't brought him a single soul he can trust.

Or maybe he's thinking what I'm thinking, that anyone

who's married to me and knows me as well as Waylen already knows I won't go to the police.

"She isn't with me," Bertram says, cool as a cucumber. "But maybe I can get a message to her, I'm not sure. What should I say?"

Waylen laughs—a dry cackle he reserves for when he puts on his phony charm during one of my book clubs with the ladies from the PTA.

"You tell her that she knows where to go," Waylen says.

In a flash like a bolt of lightning, I remember the night Waylen and I first made love, when he told me that the safest place to weather a storm is in a building full of wires and pipes. He wants me to meet him at the parking garage of the mall. We first scoped out the area years ago, but at least once a year we go by and note that the archaic surveillance cameras have never been updated. The lights still flicker; the security guards are still too understaffed to bother with it.

Mr. X has confirmed as much. He's told me it's a stupid place to ever go alone. But then, he's never trusted Waylen.

Bertram doesn't have to ask me if I know what place Waylen is referring to. He can see the color draining from my face as I try to work out what to do. Did Waylen go to the police? Will I be swarmed the second I enter the parking garage?

"Margaux, I love you. I just want you to be safe," Waylen says. Then he hangs up.

It's that word—*safe*—that lances through me. I play that one word over and over. Was he saying it with menace? In earnest? I hear it in a hundred different tones each time I try to remember, although it was only a few seconds ago.

Bertram takes me by my arms and gently pulls me to my feet. "What's going on?" he asks me, with the precautionary tone one might use on a rabid dog.

"I'm not dangerous," I tell him. "But I am a liar. Or—I can be. Sometimes. Not always."

He puts a finger to my lips, halting me. "You said that you believe me," he says. "I'd like to give you the same chance to tell me the truth."

TWENTY-ONE

I understand now why it meant so much to Bertram that I'd believe him about Annie. He's used to being surrounded by yes-men who will nod along to whatever he's saying, whether they care or not. Unlike them, I don't want anything from him, except for the one thing I'm bad at giving myself: the truth.

I've taken for granted how easily everyone has always believed me in recent years. The teachers, the fellow yoga students in my Sunday class, my daughter. Speak with enough confidence and they'll have no reason to doubt you. They'll question themselves before they entertain the idea that you did anything untoward.

But that was before I was wanted for murder.

Here in the curtained house that belongs to my dying brother, I am the most vulnerable I've been since the fire—which I do not tell Bertram about. I keep that memory buried deep down as always, hoping it will stay put.

Instead, I tell Bertram about the operation that Mr. X has been running for the past fifteen years, and some of the cases I've secretly uncovered without claiming credit. I tell him that I was hired to prove he stole his winning app software from someone else. But since it's so hard to prove plagiarism, I would be better off uncovering his role in the disappearance of his ex-girlfriend, Annie. Annie, who *is* still very much missing, and whose digital footprint is nonexistent. She is brilliant, I'm learning, in the worst kind of way.

I tell him about Waylen's involvement in my dealings with Mr. X—how he left the life years ago to live in the suburbs, but how he never truly lost his edge.

Bertram doesn't bat an eye. He listens to everything with the quiet patience of a man who has learned not to react emotionally.

When I'm done speaking, he weighs everything I've said carefully. "So, you're not a writer."

"No." I'm breathless, as though I've just run a marathon. It occurs to me that I've never told anyone what I do. "Technically, I'm an interior decorator."

"And you don't take any money for this?" he asks, an eyebrow raised.

"Not one thin dime."

"Then why do you do it? You and this—Mr. X, was it?"

I didn't tell him that Mr. X is my brother, or that he's dying, although both of these things play a huge role in why I've just confessed so much to him. I think back on what Mr. X told me, about this mission being his gift to me, a way for me to be redeemed and then retire quietly.

This is the part I hang on to. I've never admitted why I do this, not even to myself.

I avert my eyes. Only for a second, but it's long enough for Bertram to see that he's hit a nerve.

He reaches out and takes my hands, somehow pulling my gaze back to his. "We're trying to trust each other, remember?" he says.

"I—I've never told anyone what happened. I don't think I can say the words, but I can show you."

I lead him upstairs, and he follows without complaining about the darkness, or commenting on how, despite the boxes and old monitors and wires everywhere, there isn't a speck of dust to be found. My brother is a fastidious housekeeper, even if his methods wouldn't make sense to anyone else.

There's a closet just at the top of the stairs. I turn the combination of the fireproof safe on the bottom shelf, sitting on the ground as I tug it open. Bertram sits beside me, crossing his long legs elegantly, like an exotic, deadly cat that would only be found in some untapped jungle.

My brother never told me what he kept in this safe, but I've always known. It is the tangible beating heart of this house, the reason he lives in shadows as he does.

I extract a stack of newspaper articles bound together by a single elastic band.

They're in chronological order—of course they are. Yellowing and tearing at the edges. More than twenty years old.

Silently, I hand them over to Bertram. I am giving him something that I've never shared with my own husband, or with my daughter. I realize that I've wanted to share it with someone for years, but every time I came close, I ended up pushing it farther to the back of my mind.

"I've been trying to convince myself that this doesn't define me," I say. "But the more I insist that it doesn't, the more it does."

The headline of the top article reads: WALLOWA MOTHER AND FATHER KILLED IN FIRE.

I don't read over his shoulder. Why should I, when I already know the story? The investigation turns to suspected arson. The couple's two children—a boy, fourteen, and a girl, twelve—are being looked after by relatives. Rumors abound as people speculate that the children conspired to collect their inheritance. Turns out, the parents had a sizable fortune in the bank from a string of wise investments in a little company called Apple. They chose to live simply, to secure the money for their kids' future. How could the kids do it? Did greed mean more than the lives of their parents? Something was always off about them, the neighbors say when interviewed.

Neighbors who once waved at us, sent their kids to play in our yard, and talked to my dad about lawn care. We went from victims to monsters in a blink. Soon enough, it was like we had never been human.

Then the trials began.

Bertram stares at the headline and then at me. "Is it true?" he asks. "Did you kill your parents for the inheritance?"

It's an accusation that has haunted me for most of my life. But the way Bertram asks it, as though he'll accept whatever answer I give him, offers me a chance to explain that hasn't been given to me before.

You killed them. You're both monsters. You should be in jail. You should be in hell. The voices all meld into one, until I can't remember whose words belonged to whom, not that it matters. And then my brother, taller than me, crouching down before me with his reassuring, gentle eyes. *"Don't say anything,"* he told me. *"Not to anyone."*

So, I didn't. Neither of us did. And with nowhere to go, the words have been trapped inside me.

"No," I say, my voice hoarse. It's as though I'm breathing in the smoke again. "Not exactly."

Bertram sets the articles down, neatly returning them to their original pile and wrapping the elastic around them. He doesn't read the remaining headlines. He's telling me that he'd rather hear it from me.

"We're trusting each other, remember?"

I nod, trying to work out how I got into this situation. My instincts have never steered me wrong, but now I don't know whom I can trust. All evidence leads to Waylen killing Erin Casimir. I can't account for his whereabouts. He's been acting out of character lately, tracking my location and trying to scare me out of my spy work. He's told me that he'll do anything for our family. Would he kill for us?

Not just that, but I believe Bertram is telling the truth about his ex-lover, Annie, being the one to wreak havoc in his life. Maybe Annie killed Skylar. Or was that Waylen, too? I can't work it out. Too many pieces are missing.

And here before me is Bertram, the man I've been trying to put in jail, offering me redemption. Telling me he'll believe whatever I say.

"I was twelve," is what comes out. *The truth, Margaux. Of all the things you blurted out, you had to tell him the truth.*

But why not? If I'm expecting him to confess his sins, then confessing mine is the least I can do, besides which, I'm desperate. For the first time, I'm not sure if I can trust my own husband. Elodie is being watched by the police. I don't know if Collette is safe. I can't afford to hold on to my secrets anymore. They've caught up with me. "My parents both died of smoke inhalation before they could get out. They never even made it to the door. The firefighters found me out on the lawn sitting under the sprinklers."

Maybe in its own way, telling the truth is still being deceptive. Nobody in my life knows this story—not my daughter, not my husband, not any of the Westport Elementary parents who are forever trying to out-perfect each other's lives. I've hidden the little girl I once was from everyone. I've tried to kill her, exorcise her, erase her with tapping and past-life-regression therapies. But the best I've been able to do is lock her away in a tornado shelter underground, where I'm the only one who ever hears her muffled screaming to be let out.

"I refused to talk for weeks," I say. "Or maybe it was months. It was a sticky summer night when the fire happened. We kept the sprinklers on a timer because the grass kept dying in the heat. And I remember it was snowing when I went to the therapist's office for the first time."

I had been paraded through the offices of many child psychologists by that point, each one some brightly painted version of the one before it. Finally, I was sent to someone who didn't specialize in children at all, but in PTSD, trauma, and something to do with inmates—my grandmother found that last one especially important to repeat.

"She deals with prisoners, for God's sake. Surely she can handle a little girl."

"She was the first one who didn't try to get me to speak," I say. The therapist's office was on the third floor of a larger office building. I had to pass a bunch of smiling faces when I went in. Were their lives really as safe and pretty as they seemed, or were they liars like me? "She gave me a journal. Told me to write anything I wanted, she said, but it had to be the truth. So, I wrote about the things I missed. The way the beach towels all smelled like chlorine in the summer no matter how much we washed them. The ugly pink ruffled curtain on the window above the kitchen sink, and how I went through the wreckage later and saw that it had somehow survived the fire."

Bertram is so quiet that I might think he'd up and walked away if I couldn't still feel him reaching out and touching my hand.

I can't even hear him breathe.

"Therapists love when their patients open up like that. She called it a breakthrough, told me I was excellent at communicating. I just sat there and stared at her like I was in a coma, and since I wouldn't speak, she flipped through the pages and read my words back to me. She did this for weeks, and it made me so—mad. Hearing her speak my words in her voice, speak my memories like she owned them."

Because I wouldn't speak, all the previous child psychologists treated me like I couldn't understand them. They talked to my grandparents like I wasn't in the room. All of them said some version of the same thing: That I was disassociating; that I willed myself not to remember what happened; that any memories I did have were playing on a screen in my mind, and that screen was slowly dimming down.

I remember listening to their assessment and wishing such a thing were true. But there was no screen then, and there is no screen now. I remember it like it happened this morning. All of it. It's been more than two decades. I've stuffed my life full of beautiful memories in that time. I had a romance novel love affair and met my husband. I have the house and the life and the family I've always wanted. This is who I am now. Margaux the adult, not the troubled little girl.

But I can't disassociate. It's always there. It's always the truth of who I am.

"Then what happened?" His voice is the soft coo of a lover. I can't make myself look away.

"One day, I couldn't take it anymore," I tell him. "I took the journal out of her hands and I ripped the pages apart, everything I'd written in the weeks since she'd given it to me. I started screaming as I did it. That was the first sound I'd made since the fire, and it was awful. It felt like it would never stop."

For a second, I can see the flakes of paper and remember the feeling of being caught up in a snow globe, a claustrophobic prison. I feel the rawness again in my throat as I think of all the screaming. I had always been calm as a child. Quiet. Eager to please. I'd stayed quiet even through my grief because I thought it was what was expected of me. I thought it was the only way to make others happy.

But in that moment, I realized there was no one left to make happy, and that it had never truly mattered. Everything I knew was gone. My family wasn't coming back.

"I screamed because I realized I couldn't just put it behind me," I say. "They wouldn't stop asking me about the fire until I told them everything I knew."

He doesn't look at me with pity, and I'm thankful for that much. "So, what happened?" he asks, his voice low. "What caused the fire?"

Even if I can still remember being a little girl, I'm not one anymore. And I'm prepared for his question.

"I don't know," I tell him. "I was asleep when it started."

The lie slips out like a flat note in an otherwise perfect aria. I've lost my ability to lie, and Bertram knows it. Worse, he knows he's the cause.

I avert my gaze, starting to tremble, like when Collette was five and we asked her who'd spilled flour all over the kitchen.

I expect Bertram to scold me for going back on our little agreement to be honest with each other. He'd be justified in storming out and leaving me to sort this mess myself. After all, *I'm* the one who's wanted for murder. For the second time in my life.

But I can't speak the truth of that night. Having conjured it up, I suddenly can't speak at all. The air is stale and stifling, and I think I hear the piercing wail of the smoke alarm. Bertram is trying to talk to me, but I can't hear his voice over the sound, though I suspect it's an imaginary sound.

He puts his arms around me, and I'm only vaguely

aware of him hauling me to my feet, saying words I still can't understand. It's almost as though he's leading me out of a fire.

For a second, I feel safe. And then, in the next instant, we hear the police sirens right in front of the house.

TWENTY-TWO

I believe that Bertram is innocent. My instincts have never failed me in the past, and I've spent this entire case ignoring them. No more of that. His innocence is the only thing that makes sense. He didn't kill Erin—he doesn't even know she's dead. He didn't steal her app. So, why did she frame him? Is she just a jealous kid sister who wants her piece of the pie?

And because he's innocent, he has no reason to hide from the police. It's aiding and abetting to protect me. As the sirens wail, accompanied by the red and blue flashing lights around the edges of the curtains, I know that it's over.

I'm already mapping it out in my head. He'll go to the door, shove the bookshelf out of the way, and let them in. But moving the bookshelf will buy me some time to get downstairs and hide.

"Margaux." He's grasping my shoulders. How did we

both get to the bottom of the stairs? I don't remember moving. "Did you do it? Did you kill someone?"

The smoke alarm going off in the kitchen. Waylen chasing after me as I frantically started the car. *"There are things you don't know about my wife."* The creak of Erin's door. Elodie's voice through the phone saying, *"What have you done, Margaux?"* And the pages of my journal falling around me like confetti—all my secrets and rage and sorrows like snow.

Did I do it?

Of course not.

Right?

But Bertram doesn't wait for my answer. He's shoving me toward the basement door, telling me to move. We scramble into the darkness as the police continue to pound on the door and announce themselves.

"Can we go out through the same window?" Bertram asks.

I shake my head. "We're surrounded by now," I say. "They think my brother is hiding me."

"This is his house?" Bertram says, but now isn't the time to answer questions. It doesn't matter. If we're lucky, the police will figure out eventually that he's got the world's best alibi—being in the hospital, surrounded by security cameras and nurses, too weak to Spider-Man his way down the side of the building to come help me.

There's no escape for me, either. All I can do is hide.

Bertram follows me behind a pile of boxes—just one pile among dozens. A billionaire and a liar, hiding in a musty basement from the police. I want to tell him that he can go. It'll be better for him if he just comes out and tells them the truth: that I lied to get him here, that I called him for help and he thought he was doing the right thing.

But I don't say anything, for the same reason I told Waylen I'd marry him: I don't want to be alone. Despite years of convincing myself that I didn't need anyone, I have never wanted to be alone.

The door breaks open upstairs. They must have used the pry bar, which means they really think I'm here, and they want to take me away. Is Waylen still tracking me somehow? Is he trying to set me up? Is Elodie?

I hear the footsteps thundering upstairs, then the abrupt stop. The police must be looking around in surprise, because from the outside this was a normal house, but inside it's the most organized technological hoard you've ever seen in your life.

This was it, my brother told me. The last mission he ever wants me to do. Neither of us could have known it would end like this, but deep down we knew it had to end somehow.

The officer is calling for his colleagues to come in and take a look at what he's stumbled upon. Dozens of computers, hundreds of hard drives. All of them are password protected, but it's doubtful they're interested in looking at what's on them. The sheer volume alone is what's so fascinating. My brother is an obsessive, fastidious record keeper. He has footage from every security camera in every building I've ever occupied. Except, of course, in the past twenty-four hours when I'd need them the most.

Did you do it?

I push the question from my mind. Of course not—right? I also push away the image of my state defense attorney and my therapist testifying in my trial to determine whether I conspired to kill my parents. And I fear that my brother was wrong. There is no redemption. No amount of good deeds to cancel out the bad.

Bertram notices my ragged breathing before I do. He puts an arm around me. I'm not sure why he comforts me instead of turning me in. He should be running up the stairs, shouting, "She's here!" But instead, we both listen as the footsteps move through my brother's things. He tugs me farther into the shadows when the glow of the officer's flashlight sweeps through the basement.

It feels like an eternity before they leave. It's not illegal to have an ungodly amount of technology, and they have a murderer to catch.

"They'll see your car," I whisper.

"It's parked down the street," he reminds me. "And it's not a real license plate."

I look at the silhouette of his face in the darkness. "Annie," he says. "She always seems to find me, and I never know when she'll pop up. So, I arrange for rentals under fake names."

"Maybe we can prove that she's stalking you," I say. "We're sitting on years of surveillance footage. I bet there's something."

"She's too smart for it," he says. "And anyway, it's not like what you see in the movies where someone slinks around in the darkness wearing a trench coat. She has other ways of keeping tabs. Just when I think I've adapted, she gets at me again."

Upstairs, the voices and footsteps trail out the door. I hear someone give the all clear. I'm officially not here.

Maybe Annie and I would be friends, we're both so good at staying invisible.

Even so, we wait until we're sure the area is clear before we slink out and make our way back to Bertram's car.

He starts the ignition, but before I can ask him where we're going, he turns to me. "Tell me this," he says. He takes a deep breath. After all that's just happened, this is the first time he's seemed nervous. "You said you were hired to investigate me. Who hired you?"

I've never betrayed a source. Not even as years have gone on and some of those sources are long since dead.

But Bertram is right, I do owe him that much, after everything he's just done for me. More than that, because he's the only one offering to believe me. It's obvious that Waylen has gone to the police and is trying to lure me into our spot at the abandoned mall under the guise of helping me.

And it's obvious Bertram isn't going to drive anywhere until I answer him. I'm once again reminded that he isn't the one facing a murder charge. I am.

"Your sister," I tell him. I think it's time for a full recap. Maybe he can make sense of it. "She contacted us—me—because she's accusing you of stealing her app. She hired me to expose you, so I've been pretending to write a story about your success to try to gain information. I was able to track down the names of your exes, Annie and Skylar. But Annie has been impossible to find. I thought she might have gone missing, but it's as though she doesn't even exist online. And Skylar is dead. Erin insists that you're to blame for all of it. I thought that if I could prove you did it, I could put you in jail. But you didn't do any of it, did you?"

Even as I tell the story to Bertram, the pieces fall apart. Pieces that I was so sure about days ago.

But Bertram seems to have retained only one key detail. "My . . . sister?"

"Yes. Erin," I say gently. "But, Bertram—"

"She's been living out in Seattle for years," he says. "We haven't spoken in months. Why would she want to take credit for my app? She's never been remotely interested in software development."

That may be true, at this point. It could have been pure greed that motivated her. But it doesn't matter now. "It gets worse. Erin is the one they think I've killed."

With frenzied speed, I tell him everything that happened since she hired me. The strange behavior that night she answered the door, while Bertram was confirmed to be doing a live stream. And the blood all over her apartment now. The police chasing me away from the scene, clearly thinking I had something to do with it, because who would stumble upon a blood-filled apartment and *not* call for help? So now Waylen either thinks I killed Erin, or he's done it himself. I'm not sure which is worse.

Bertram's eyes are glassy and far away as he considers this. He shakes his head. I watch as he pulls out his phone and dials his sister, listed in his contacts only as ERIN. I watch the color drain from his face as it rings and rings, and then goes to a generic robot-voiced mailbox.

"Where was she staying?" he demands of me now. "We have to go there."

"It's swarming with police," I say.

He shakes his head. "This isn't like her—we weren't in touch often, but we got along. She wouldn't do something like this." Even before he's gotten the words out, I know what he's going to say. "Annie must have blackmailed her."

My stomach feels queasy. I wish Mr. X were here. He would tell me if my instincts are off. My theories are going in so many different directions that I don't even know if any of them are plausible.

Annie. Why do all roads always point to Annie, the one person in Bertram's past who is impossible to find, save for one blurry paparazzi photo?

Bertram doesn't wait for me to tell him where his sister has been living. After a brief search for something on his phone, he starts to drive at breakneck speed, his tires squealing.

"Where are you going?" I cry.

"You said her place is swarming with police and you're wanted for her murder." His jaw is clenched. "It wasn't hard to do a basic internet search."

"You can't go there!" The desperation in my own voice terrifies me. I grab the wheel, but it's locked in his iron grip.

"Then what's your suggestion?" he fires back. "You tell me that my sister is dead"—he blows through a stop sign, pressing hard on the gas—"and that you're the last one to see her alive. You tell me that you've been working for her to *spy* on me, and you blame all of it on your husband, while he blames all of it on you! Which is it?"

I have a flashback of my aunt and uncle—the only time I saw them after the fire—shouting, demanding to know what happened, demanding that I speak. I can see the raised palm of my aunt's hand as she rears back to slap me.

Never again, I'd told myself after the trial. I'd grow up

and go somewhere far away, where nobody knew what happened. I'd never be accused of doing something horrible again.

But here I am.

When Bertram finally comes to a stop—at a line of cars idling at a red light, I open the door and undo my seat belt.

"Where are you going?" he asks me. "The police are looking for you. If you stay with me, I can protect you."

"No, you can't," I tell him. "They'll find me."

"Get back in the car," he insists. I want to—how to tell him that? I trust him. So far, he's only tried to keep me safe. It's everyone else I don't trust. It's me. "I don't want Annie to hurt you, too. Whatever is going on, I can get to the bottom of it. We're trusting each other, remember?"

"I can't go back there," I tell him. Already the flashbacks are taking over and I can smell the smoke. It isn't just Erin's apartment, but the memories. I can never go back to that place again.

Bertram's phone rings, and we both glance at the screen as it lights up. Bertram's shoulders ease, and he ignores the angry honking of the cars that now have to navigate around us with the light turning green. He holds up the screen to show me the blond woman with a shy smile, holding up a handful of paintbrushes.

"Who's that?" I ask.

"Erin," he says, relief flooding his voice with that one word. "She's calling me back."

My blood runs cold. I've never seen that woman before in my life.

Numbly, I climb back into the car as Bertram answers the call.

Am I losing my mind? I remember Erin as a slight brunette with green eyes and fair skin. Nothing at all like the woman on the screen.

But then I hear the voice coming through the Bluetooth speaker in Bertram's car, and that is the voice of the Erin Casimir I know.

She says, "Hello, Bertram."

Once again, the blood drains from his face. His lips struggle with the word, but when he finally spits it out, some of the millions of pieces come snapping into place. "Annie."

TWENTY-THREE

Hello, Margaux," Annie says, ignoring Bertram's bewildered greeting. "I've just seen the news this morning. It looks like you're being charged with my murder. Congratulations, that's quite an accomplishment. Bertram has been trying to catch me for years. He even staged a fake engagement to try to trap me."

The blood all over her apartment. The real Erin's face on Bertram's phone—she is calling from the real Erin's number. But how?

"What have you done with my sister?" Bertram demands, suddenly snapping out of his daze. "She has nothing to do with this."

"Doesn't she?" Erin—Annie—responds. "We're all just sisters and brothers here, aren't we?"

"Cut the bullshit," he rasps. "You framed Margaux for your murder just to get at me? Why?"

"I didn't frame anyone," she says coolly. "How was I to know she was going to show up at my little hideaway this morning? Actually, she ruined my plans by intruding before I had a chance to clean the place up." Everything was lies.

Mr. X won't believe it when I tell him.

I open my mouth to speak, but Bertram stops me with a hand on my wrist and a shake of his head. It's futile, he's telling me. Whatever she says is going to be a trap. I nod because I know that he's right, and I don't try to stop him when he hangs up.

Annie is too good. She had me doubting my own marriage. She's unlike any suspect I've ever faced because—well, I haven't exactly faced her. She's been pulling all of her strings from the shadows.

"We have to find a way to get in touch with my brother," I say. "I can encrypt my phone to evade the police, and then he'll know how to prove that Annie's alive, no matter where she's hiding."

But Bertram's mind is elsewhere. "Could she have spoofed my sister's number, or does she have her? If she has her, we have to get to them before—"

"We will," I say.

Before Bertram can reply, the phone rings again. "Don't hang up," Annie says, with playful glee. "There's someone here who wants to speak with you."

"Mom?" Collette's voice is tight, the way it gets when she's holding back tears.

"Collette." I grab the phone. I want to scream. To run to her. To beg her to tell me where she is so that I can fix this. But I know that's what Annie wants, and that it will only make things worse. So I keep my voice calm, even as every nerve in my body is on fire. "I'm here. I'm right here."

"Mom, you have to come and meet us. Everything will be okay if you just come." Again, her voice, but not her words.

I look at Bertram, his wide eyes mirroring my own terror. Annie has his sister and she has my daughter. Bertram kept his parents and sister at a distance—I realize now—to protect them from danger. I stupidly slept under the same roof as my daughter. Even more stupidly, I love her, a fact that I've never been able to conceal from anyone, much less my enemies. If I really loved her, I should have forfeited her. Never told Waylen I was pregnant, sealed her birth records in a closed adoption and never looked back.

But it wouldn't have mattered. The past always comes back to find out. And the dangers of this world always know how to hunt us down.

"Where are you?" I ask Collette, still maintaining my calm voice, even as I feel my whole body go hot with fear, my pulse thudding in my temples. If a single hair on her head is harmed, Annie won't need to frame me for her murder. I'll gladly go to prison for the rest of my life for what I'll do.

In response, a song comes blaring through the phone's speaker, tinny and echoing, like someone is holding a device up against their phone. I recognize it immediately. A song that tormented me throughout my childhood. A song the other kids sang as I sprinted away from them, and wrote in Wite-Out on my locker, and scrawled on my notebooks. That is, until I moved away to where no one knew what had happened to me.

. . . The roof, the roof, the roof is on fire
We don't need no water, let the motherfucker burn
Burn, motherfucker, burn . . .

I know exactly where they are.

Bertram doesn't protest when I commandeer the driver's seat, and he doesn't say a word when I stomp the gas pedal to the floor. He is a man who doesn't fear speeding tickets. He has all the money in the world. But he only has one family. That much, we have in common.

I veer into the parking lot of the abandoned mall. The one that Waylen and I set up as our safe space. I'm positive that this is where Annie is.

Is she working with Waylen? Was all of this a conspiracy orchestrated by both of them? But why? Because he wants me to quit my vigilantism so much that he has to scare me out of it, and chasing me around in some blacked-out cars wasn't enough?

But if Erin—Annie—isn't dead, then whose blood was in the apartment? And if she isn't dead, that means Waylen didn't kill her. But—as the sick feeling in my gut suggests—he did bring her here. He knows that most things don't rattle me. I've dealt with killers, fraudsters, con men, and loan sharks alike. I've ventured into dark shadows and damp basements without so much as a hair standing up on the back of my neck.

But for the first time in years, I'm terrified of all the unanswered questions. And because I know better than anyone that things aren't always what they seem.

SISTER, BROTHER DUO IMPLICATED IN FIRE THAT KILLS PARENTS

The parking garage is blocked off, so I abandon the car at the entrance and run inside, Bertram at my heels.

"Erin!" he's shouting. I can hear by the way he says her name that he loves her. It was ingenious of Annie to assume Erin's identity when there's virtually nothing about her online. Bertram's entire family keeps a low profile. I suppose it's the same principle that compels all major tech figures to keep their families offline. They know better than anyone how their apps are used to spy on us. Someone, somewhere has access to our most intimate thoughts, desires, and fears. My brother taught me that people will tell their search history things that they wouldn't even tell their spouse.

But I never search for anything for myself. I never type my thoughts out into the tempting clean white search bar. Not even in the middle of the night, when I'm the only one awake and my darkest thoughts tempt me to confide in someone.

"There are things you don't know about my wife." Waylen spoke the words, but even he doesn't know how true they are.

My footsteps echo in the empty, cavernous space. Gray concrete and shadows are all around me. There are no cars. The only life this place has seen in years is from the rodents that hide away in the darkness. My feet stomp in puddles of old grease and water that drip down from the rusty overhead pipes.

"Margaux, wait." Bertram has kept pace, impressively. Now he grabs my arm and spins me around. "Where are we going?" He's a bit out of breath. "This place is huge.

They could be anywhere. How do you even know they're here at all?"

"There are no security cameras in the parking garage," I tell him. "But they're turning the rest of the mall into storage units, so even though it's not set up yet, there are cameras. They're somewhere in here."

As though on cue, the sound of footsteps emerges from the top of the platform, accompanied by desperately heavy breathing. I expect to see Annie, coming to do God knows what. I know that she's the inevitable outcome of being here. But it's Waylen, rumpled and sweaty, with something trailing from one of his wrists. Duct tape.

If someone tried to bind him, he would know to let his captor think they have him, and then he would know how to slam his bound wrists over his knee to sever the tape. I tried to teach Collette once. She giggled at six years old as I bound her wrists with her neon pink duct tape that she used to make no-sew purses. I told her how she could use her own strength against her to escape if she ever needed to. But Waylen overheard us and came running. It turned into an hours-long fight about how I was going to scare her.

"She has to know what to do," I'd said. "She needs to be prepared."

"Prepared for what?" he'd cried. "Nothing bad is going to happen."

As always, I was right. It's a curse that has followed me all my life. Even as a child, born into the nuclear American dream: two parents, two children, a pretty little house, and an old barn cat that found his way into our yard all the time for table scraps. Even then, I carried an internalized sense of dread. The sunsets were too pretty. My father's jokes were too corny and they made us laugh too loud. I knew, somehow, that it was too good to stay that way forever.

I thought that I could prepare Collette the way I wish someone had prepared me.

Now Waylen makes his way to me, and I see a bruise that's forming on the side of his head. Someone hit him with a blunt object. Someone too small to overpower him themselves, so they knocked him unconscious and tied him up and put him out of the way. Someone slight and slender like Annie.

"Margaux, thank God," he says. "You're safe."

He grabs my shoulders and then pulls me into an embrace, but I feel my body tense up. Earlier he was chasing me out of the house, shouting for me to come back. He was warning Bertram about me. He lured me here.

"You told Annie about our meeting spot," I say, and I can feel that my accusatory tone stuns him. He draws back.

"Annie? That deranged woman who attacked me?"

Bertram seems to have the same thought I do, that Waylen and Annie are working together somehow, and that she'll descend like a wraith from the rafters at any moment.

But no one comes.

"I was so worried about you," Waylen says. "First you ran out of the house and I had no idea where you were going or what was wrong. Then the police came looking for you. They think you killed Bertram's sister. They refused to tell me anything. They wanted to search the house, but I wouldn't let them."

"You're not working with the police?" I ask, my voice trailing uncertainly.

"Of course not." His eyes meet mine, and I see the Waylen who made me fall in love with him. But this is the same Waylen who chased me in a decoy car to scare me out of my vigilante work.

I want to trust him. But I don't know what to believe. I don't even know if I can trust myself.

Bertram takes my arm. His grasp isn't forceful, but it is firm. He's telling me that he doesn't trust Waylen, and that I should trust him instead.

"Where is Collette?" I ask.

"Don't you have her?" Waylen says. The fear on his face tells me that he's surprised by my question.

I think of the anger in Elodie's voice on the phone when she realized I'd dragged her into more than she'd bargained for. She said the police were looking for me.

For a second, I allow myself to feel hope that Elodie is keeping Collette somewhere safe, somehow. Elodie didn't turn Collette back over to Waylen. Maybe she's still hidden somewhere. Or maybe, in desperation, Elodie gave her to the police, and that's where Collette was when she called me. It's not ideal, but maybe she's drinking hot cocoa in a police station somewhere, biding her time until I'm found to be innocent and this whole misunderstanding is cleared up.

Maybe it is as simple as Waylen bringing me here because he was worried about me.

Maybe Annie is just toying with Bertram, the way she

has been doing for years. The blood in her apartment is fake. She spoofed Erin's phone number. Maybe Skylar's death really was just an accident. All of this was done to scare Bertram, and I was just an unfortunate pawn in her revenge scheme.

And then I hear my daughter scream.

TWENTY-FOUR

I spin around, Bertram at one side and Waylen at the other, my two worlds standing in the same damp concrete space.

It wasn't real, I tell myself. *Collette isn't here.*

But then I hear it again. "Mom!" she cries. The color drains from Waylen's face, and I know that his fear, at least, is real. Collette is the one thing that was never an act between us.

We both shout her name and take off running in the direction her voice was coming from. There's darkness up at the top of this platform that leads to the next level. I'm only vaguely aware of Bertram running after us, saying words I'm not able to hear over the rush of blood in my ears.

"Collette!" I scream.

"Where are you?" Waylen shouts, cupping his hands to project his voice.

We're still running when Bertram snags my arm, causing me to tumble backward against his chest. I struggle as he coils his arms around me, keeping me from running. "Let go of me!" I demand.

"It's a trap!" he insists.

But I'm thinking of Skylar's dead body, and of the blood in Erin—Annie's—apartment. The woman who may have done these things has my daughter. I do everything I know to force Bertram to let go. Elbow him, stomp on his heel, bite him. But he's still winning, dragging me away from whatever is waiting for me in the darkness at the top of this platform.

Waylen is still running, and then I hear the loud crack. Even as I tell myself it can't be what I think it is, that I'm mistaken, I know that it was a gunshot. I can smell the gunpowder.

Blood puddles out onto the concrete. I can't tell where it's coming from or if he's still breathing. My breath hitches.

Bertram has lifted me off the ground now and is running for the exit, no matter how I fight him. Through my haze, I realize that he's just saved my life. I was going to be shot next.

There's a metallic rattle, like chains coming loose. And then the security cage slams down before us, right as we are coming up to the exit.

Bertram sets me down only so he can grasp at the bars and try to shake them loose.

There's a clap. Then another.

We both spin around to see the woman coming down from the top of the platform, sidestepping Waylen's body as she does.

I know her as Erin Casimir. But the sneer on Bertram's face confirms what I've already come to learn: This is Annie. The elusive ex-fiancée who he claims has been stalking him for years.

"Thank you for keeping things interesting," she tells me. "When I hired you, all I wanted was for you to take the bait I set out. Bertram would be implicated in Skylar's murder and go to prison."

I want to lunge at her, to throw her to the ground and demand that she pay for what she's done to Waylen and that she give me my daughter. But logic—frustrating as it is—comes flooding back to me, and I know that I'm of no use to Collette if I'm dead. And if Waylen is still alive, he needs me to find a way out of this so that I can get him help. If I run to him, she'll put a bullet in my back for sure.

So I tamp down my rage. "Why did you do it?" I ask. "Why hire us when you could have just filed a police report yourself when Skylar was killed?"

"Oh, come on, you're smarter than that, aren't you?" Annie says. "You and your brother have been running your little operation for years and nobody has ever figured out that you're behind all these mysterious criminals who got away with their crimes the first time. You always make sure they end up in prison." She shrugs. "So I made Bertram out to be a criminal. You'd get him put in jail, and that would be that. And then"—she smiles at Bertram sweetly, as though they're sharing a romantic evening over champagne and clams—"he would have no choice but to love me. What choice would he have, cooped up in prison with no pretty girls to fall in love with him?"

Bertram's jaw is clenched. "You're leaving out the

obvious part," he says. "Margaux puts away *guilty* people. I've never committed a crime."

But I'm still stuck on something else she said. She called Mr. X my brother. How did she know that?

Annie looks at me as though she's just read my mind. Her piercing gaze is so intense that I would believe she has the ability to do it. "But *you're* no stranger to the law, are you?" she tells me. "You and your brother killed your parents. Got a nice little inheritance. They had a tidy sum tucked away, and you found out about it, didn't you?"

I stumble back a step.

"Don't listen to her," Bertram says in my ear.

But Annie goes on. "I bet you thought nobody would suspect a poor, sweet, innocent little girl. Or is that what your big brother told you? Did he convince you to do it? Or did you already want to?"

"No." My voice comes out small, like I'm a child again.

"I've done my research," Annie says. "I like to know who I'm working with. And look at us now, all cozy." Her smile is so eerie.

"What do you want?" I rasp. "Where is my daughter?"

"How should I know?" Annie says. Then she laughs. "You mean this?" She holds up her phone, taps the voice memos screen, and plays back the scream I'd heard earlier. It *is* Collette's voice, but that's all it is. "I'm working on a new AI voice impression app. What do you think?"

My stomach is sick to think of Annie lurking about somewhere, collecting a recording of my daughter's voice to add to her program. It speaks to just how long she's been watching me.

She must have spoofed Erin's phone number in a similar way.

When Mr. X and I started our vigilantism years ago, we were ahead of the game on technology. But now it's so readily accessible that we aren't the only ones with a trick or two up our sleeves.

But Annie doesn't realize that she's just given me something valuable. She's told me that my daughter isn't here, which means I don't have to bargain for her safety. She's already left Waylen for dead. Which means I have nothing to lose.

I lunge for her, tackling her to the ground in a single motion. She doesn't fight me. I pin her arms behind her back and I straddle her with my knees, shouting for Bertram to find a way out. Maybe Waylen can still be saved.

And all the while, a nettling feeling starts to grow in the back of my head that Annie isn't fighting me. That she's gone to all this trouble to set me up, but now she isn't fighting me.

As this feeling rises, so too does the smell of smoke.

Annie is laughing, a low chuckle that grows to a keening, hysterical pitch.

"One more dead girlfriend ought to do it," she tells me.

Too late, I realize her plan. Her attempt to put Bertram in prison didn't work out according to plan, but Annie is adaptable. Of course. By ruining her initial plan, I've inadvertently handed her an even better one. She's going to set me up as having an affair with Bertram. I'm the last dead girlfriend in a pattern of dead or missing girls. Annie will slip back into the shadows, still technically missing. But

Bertram—it will look as though he lured me and Waylen here. By contacting Elodie and telling her to hide Collette, I've played right into it. Then I came here to de-escalate things. Bertram killed my husband in a jealous rage, and when that wasn't enough to win me over, he set this place on fire and killed me, too.

Annie will make sure that he escapes somehow. Then she'll disappear. The police will never believe him. There is no security footage to prove otherwise, apart from cameras on surrounding buildings capturing his car with a phony registration that won't be linked to either of us.

BILLIONAIRE CAN'T BUY LOVE. I can already see the headlines. It's so brilliant that I would believe it, too. He will pay the ultimate price for not being enough to fix what was broken in her when she came back to him. Worse than his prison sentence, he will spend the rest of his life telling a truth that nobody will believe.

I stagger to my feet. How long has the fire been burning? The faint smell becomes stronger. There must have been a car on the upper level that she set on fire, because I smell the singed metal and the rubber from the tires.

Bertram rattles the bars furiously. He doesn't realize that he's destined to live, in this game of Annie's. Waylen and I are the ones who are meant to die.

Years ago, I ran away from the flames. This time, I have to reach Waylen's prone form. Annie is right that I would take the bait because I will save my husband or die trying. Collette can't lose us both. The first time I was in a fire, I ran away and saved myself. This time, I run right into the flames.

TWENTY-FIVE

The smoke is already starting to thicken. I know too well how quickly a fire can spread. I know that the smoke will kill you before the fire touches you.

When I reach Waylen, I hear him groan. Was it my imagination? I drop to my knees beside him, my hand landing in a puddle. Blood? No. I smell the gasoline in the next instant. It's all over him.

"Wake up," I beg him. When I shove him, he rolls onto his back, and his eyes open, murky and confused.

He's alive. But I can't celebrate just yet, knowing that neither of us will be alive for much longer if I can't get us out of here.

Blood stains his shirt. The bullet could have hit him in the chest or stomach. Either way, nothing good. I shouldn't be moving him, but I don't have a choice.

He cries out when I wedge myself under his shoulder

and stagger upward, bringing both of us to our feet. He's deadweight at first, but then he manages to hold his own.

He rasps my name, his breath rustling the hair at the nape of my neck.

I look around us. Smoke in all directions, and behind that, the orange pulse of flames. Bertram and Annie are nowhere. If Annie meant for Bertram to survive, she's forced him out of here by now. She wouldn't have to work hard at that. The human instinct for self-preservation is stronger than our heroism. Once his lungs filled with smoke and he felt the suffocating threat of death, he would have moved in the direction that promised oxygen—even if he hated himself for it later. I can't fault him for that. And Annie will have made her own escape, ensuring she's long gone before the police arrive.

There will be no evidence that she was ever here. As always.

Sometimes criminals get away with it.

I'm sorry, I think. But the words aren't for Waylen, or Collette, or even for me. They're for my brother, who wanted this to be my shot at redemption. One last mission to prove that good triumphs over evil. But when he hears about this on the news, he'll know the truth. Sometimes, evil wins, and not only that; evil masquerades as the good guy.

When the firemen found me lying still in the yard behind my burning house, they thought I was dead. One of them said, "We have to try to save this one, at least."

It wasn't until hours later, after spending the morning at the hospital, that I learned Jeremy was still alive.

It didn't look good, the police officer cautioned me. He spoke to me like I was five, not twelve. He kept calling me "sweetheart" and pausing after each sentence, like he was telling me it was my turn to talk. But I never did. I didn't know what to say.

"I love you," I say to Waylen now, my voice strained. Despite my confusion about so much of our relationship, that much is true. "I'm sorry I didn't trust you."

He fights to stay conscious, both of us staggering in a direction that I think is the exit. It was blocked off earlier, but Annie must have gotten out somehow.

"I knew you were innocent," he tells me.

These are our final confessions because we know that we're about to die. Maybe that's why we're speaking so calmly, even as we cough. I feel an eerie sense of peace, and although I try to fight it, eventually I don't want to anymore. I drop to my knees and Waylen comes with me, breathing hard. He doesn't know the story of my past. He doesn't know what a fitting end this is for me. It all started with a fire, and now it's going to end with one.

After the fire happened, when I was a child, I dreamed about it almost every night at first. Eventually the dreams tapered off to an occasional haunt—the kind I never saw coming because it came after a period of tentative peace.

Did you do it? some asked me. But that was better than the ones who said nothing at all, because they'd already decided that I was to blame.

Something grabs my arm, reeling me away from Waylen. For a second, it's as though I'm flying, my spirit going up, up. This is what dying feels like, I guess. I watch Waylen still lying on Earth, among the living, as I start to slip away. He'll join me soon. I hope that we can at least look down on Collette from wherever we are.

My ascent stops, and I'm confused by the feeling of my feet on the ground. "Damn it, move, woman!" a voice says. An angel? I turn, and through the smoke I see the pristine platinum curls of my savior.

Not an angel. Elodie Blevins, cursing like a sailor in a most unladylike fashion.

I think I ask her what she's doing here. *How* she's here, and if she's some sort of oxygen-deprived hallucination. In any case, she doesn't answer. She only pushes me up, farther into the flames. *We're going the wrong way,* I think. *She's going to kill us.* But then she pushes open a door to the emergency stairwell that runs parallel to the elevators. The smoke is less intense in here, and I can almost think clearly.

"I didn't start the fire," I tell her.

"I know," she says.

"I don't mean this one," I insist, as she shoves me down the stairs.

Before she turns around to go back into the smoke to save Waylen, she nods, sweat beading her entire face. How is she always so ethereal, even when soot mars her cheeks? "I know what you mean," she says. "I know you didn't start it."

A week after the fire had killed my parents, I was able to see Jeremy. He'd been in a medically induced coma, they told me, because his legs were so badly burned they still weren't sure if they could be saved. But he was awake now, and he was asking for me.

As soon as I stepped into his hospital room, I started to cry. This scared the nurse, and she left us alone and closed the door. I had been imagining all sorts of horrible things when they told me he'd been burned. His face charred and peeling, his skeleton exposed, or his skin horrifically mangled like I'd seen in a horror movie I wasn't supposed to have watched.

But his face was spared, miraculously, and he looked the way he always had. Whatever horrific scars he bore were hidden under the blanket.

"Hey," he whispered. "Come here, kid, let me see you."

I shuffled toward him, my vision blurred. I was afraid to touch him. Afraid of pinching a wire or breaking a bone.

I was twelve, and he was fourteen, and we were all that was left. Just me and my brother.

"They told me you won't speak," he said. I nodded, wiped my soggy eyes with my fists. "Why not?"

I shrugged. The moment I woke up in the yard, I'd been bombarded with questions. Does it hurt anywhere? Do you know where you are? What's your name, honey? And it all came back to the same question, repeated over and over by everyone who came to see me: What happened?

"Because I don't know," I said, and my voice cracked. "I don't know what caused the fire."

He patted the side of his bed and made space for me to sit on the narrow mattress. "Listen to me, kid," he said. His voice was barely above a whisper, so I knew he was about to tell me something important. "I messed up. I—" He started to cry, which only made me more upset.

He told me that he'd been on a website that taught him how to take apart an old microwave and use the wires to burn patterns onto blocks of wood. From childhood, he'd had an engineer's mind. Our parents were always finding old electronics at yard sales and on eBay for him to disassemble.

Something went wrong. It sparked and he panicked, and the fire got out of control. He didn't know how to put it out.

"I'm going to tell them," he said. "It's my fault Mom and Dad are gone."

I begged him not to. They would send him to jail. He was older than me, and I knew enough to recognize that this made a difference. I imagined him being handcuffed and thrown into a jail cell, and it made me so hysterical that I couldn't breathe. Nothing he said could calm me, until finally he said, "All right. All right, Margaux. I'll tell them I don't know what happened."

For a small window of time, I believed it could really be that simple. But, of course, it wasn't.

When I woke up choking on smoke, I stumbled across the living room and tried to make it to the front door before I was overtaken by it. And the bottle of lighter fluid that spilled onto the carpet when I crashed into the coffee table, that splashed onto the couch and the wall behind it—that was bad luck. Something that had been left out after my father refilled his Zippo lighter to entertain his one vice, his evening cigar.

After helping me out of the house, Jeremy ran to a neighbor's house to call for help. But because he'd helped me, he smelled of the lighter fluid, too, and it was suspicious that he'd waited so long to go for help. The house was destroyed by the time he made it back to me, but he still went in to try and save them. I was screaming. I begged him not to.

When I realized they thought I did it, I didn't correct them. I didn't think it would matter, so long as Jeremy and I still had each other. He was older than me, and I knew he would go to prison for it if they suspected him. All I got was court-mandated therapy and a miserable adolescence.

Nothing came of the trial. My court-appointed attorney was worth his salt. He was able to raise enough reasonable doubt that the jury couldn't prove it wasn't *an accident, despite all the lighter fluid. My brother and I both received our share of our inheritance and our parents' life insurance policy when we turned eighteen.*

In the end, they separated us anyway. Our grandparents didn't want him to be burdened by his disturbed little sister, and they sent him to the best boarding school money could buy.

I got saddled with a therapist who thought I was a criminal, and I barely spoke for months. But my brother wrestled with the guilt of what he'd done in a silence of his own. By adulthood, he couldn't maintain it. He abandoned every opportunity that came his way, and when he abandoned all the scholarship opportunities his brilliance afforded, I was the only one who understood why.

When the ambulance comes for me this time, I feel myself freezing up. Something within me insists that the words I say won't matter. I won't be believed.

But then Waylen falls beside me after Elodie emerges from the parking garage like the badass hero in a 007 movie. She sees my bewildered expression and gives me a breathless smile. "You always underestimated me," she says. "Admit it. Just because I embezzled a little money from a leggings company."

She falls into an exhausted heap on the gravel beside me. I work Waylen's head into my lap. "Don't you dare die on me," I tell him.

He responds with a hazy smile. "And make it easy on you?"

Ambulances wail in the distance, and I know that they're coming for us. Elodie pats my hand. Her hair is in disarray, and soot stains her cheeks and rumpled clothes.

But it's the warmth of her expression that throws me. I've never seen this side of her before. Though I suppose she can say the same for me.

"How did you know where I was?" I ask.

She gives me a playful wink, despite everything. As the sirens grow louder, it offers a bizarre sense of reassurance. Some things never change. "While you were researching Bertram, I was researching you," she says. "Since, you know, you refuse to *tell* me anything. And once I figured out your past, it wasn't hard to figure out that Mr. X must be your brother. So I've been in touch with him at the hospital. Wasn't hard to find him there once I had a name."

"For how long?" I ask.

"Since the police came to my door accusing you of murder. You're a lot of things, but you're no killer. Just serially late to drop-offs and pickups."

She still hasn't answered my question. She was able to hunt down news of my past—something only a person with talents noticeable by Mr. X could pull off. But how did she find me here?

The ambulances are here now, and they're ushering Waylen onto a stretcher. He's grasping my hand. "Don't leave me," he says.

I know he's referring to more than just this moment. He means the years of turmoil between us. I let him hold on to me, and I stay beside him in the ambulance. "I'll stay if you will," I tell him.

TWENTY-SIX

There was only one wrench in Annie's plan: me.

Initially, she hoped for a clean revenge plot on Bertram. She would use me to investigate him for fraud with his app. But along the way, I would unwittingly discover that he was a murderer—this theory fed by breadcrumbs that Annie would throw along the trail. I would feel like a brilliant investigator who found Bertram to be more dangerous than anyone suspected. He would serve life in prison, and I'd add him to my scrapbook and call it a job well done. Elodie would have absolved herself of her own petty crime and go back to her life, feeling quite pleased with herself.

And Annie would stay missing, presumed dead. The blood all over her apartment is more than anyone can lose and still walk away. The police are still wrapping their heads around that one, but my theory is that she'd been drawing and then freezing a little bit of it at a time. Possibly for months, all to plan this out. It explains why she always looked so frail and gaunt when Elodie and I visited her, and the strange bruises on her face when we showed up unexpectedly.

Once she presented herself as the latest in a string of his dead girlfriends, she could reinvent herself as someone else and know that Bertram would be in a cage where he could never find love again. She would get letters to him, disguised as the words of a devoted fangirl, and trick him into loving her that way. Everyone would win.

Except Bertram. Lonely, heartsick Bertram whose story would never have been believed. Nobody in their right mind would pity someone who's risen to such success. The murder trial would have been covered by every podcaster in the digital space, the comments section calling for his head on a stick.

But I showed up the morning of her staged murder and stirred the pot, so she went to her plan B: setting Bertram up for my murder too.

In the week I spend at Waylen's side in the hospital, I have plenty of time to imagine how close things were to playing very differently. Rather than staying for an extended sleepover with Finnegan at Elodie's house, Collette could be attending our funerals. Worse, she would have inherited the generational curse of being the girl whose parents died in a fire. She would have wondered if anything in the papers was really true.

But then, she's a lot like me. I think she would have uncovered the truth eventually.

Seven days after the fire, Waylen is starting to emerge

from his honeymoon phase. As exhausted and in pain as he is, he's loved having me to dote on him. We've spent most of the time in content silence, or talking about podcasts and books, and the vacation we'll take when all of this is behind us. A nice cruise to the Riviera.

But now he wants to talk. A moment that I've been dreading, and yet I'm relieved that we're finally here.

"Why didn't you tell me about all of it?" he says. "The fire, and that you and your brother were blamed for it?"

Briefly, I feel like I'm a child again. A child with a long road ahead of me, and so many stories to tell.

He looks at me, and I know what he's thinking, even if he doesn't say the words: *Tell me the truth, Margaux.*

"I didn't think you would believe me," I say.

I'm sitting on the edge of his hospital bed, looking at the lone wire feeding an IV into his arm. "I thought you would leave me."

"Sometimes I think that's what you wanted me to do," he says. "But I already told you that we're stuck with each other. I don't want to go anywhere."

I've never understood his undying love for me. I've never understood why I feel the same way.

"You deserve to be loved," he tells me. "I know you think it's all about appearances, but I don't care about our reputation in the neighborhood, or if you quit the PTA and all that stuff tomorrow. Hell, do you want me to sell the house? I'll live with you in a barn in the country."

I laugh, even though I suspect he really means it. "We'll keep the house," I say. "But maybe scale back on some of the other stuff."

"What would your friend Elodie call it? A hard detox?

Maybe we should do that." He nudges my hand with his. He's being cautious, trying not to push me away again.

I stay with him until he falls asleep again. Then I venture out and afford myself the luxury of hospital cafeteria coffee. That's where Elodie finds me, beaming like she's just won the gold medal at the detective Olympics.

The peeling "visitor" sticker on her cardigan tells me that she's been here for a while. She must have been upstairs visiting my brother. She's right. I didn't give her enough credit. While I was trying to reconcile my instincts being at odds with the evidence, Elodie was leaning into leads of her own. That's how she discovered that the abandoned mall was due to be turned into storage units, and that the developer had set up a security system.

Everything that happened before and during the fire was recorded, stored on a cloud somewhere for the police to review. I never want to see it. I've had enough fire to last me a lifetime.

"How you doing, kid?" she asks me, and casts a wayward glance at my paper coffee cup. "I wish you'd let me bring you a nice mocha or something. You deserve it after all you've been through."

"I'm just happy to be alive," I tell her.

But Elodie refuses to let the conversation turn grim. She is many things, among which, a merciless optimist. "Your brother—I mean Mr. X tells me that he's planning to retire. He said he's been trying to talk you into doing the same."

I sigh. "If you'd asked me before this mission, I would have said there's no way," I tell her. "But now—Waylen would be happy. Collette probably would, too."

Elodie reaches across the table and puts her hand over mine. Her hand lotion smells like lavender and cream. "What do *you* want?" she asks me.

"You know, I can't remember the last time someone asked me that," I reply. "After the fire, when I was a kid, I was told where to go, what to say, which questions to answer, which ones to stay quiet about. And when my brother started this business, I found it empowering. It made me feel like I was one step closer to evening things out in the world. But now I look back, and it's like I was on a treadmill moving in place the whole time."

Elodie nods sympathetically. "The world will always be a mess," she says. "We can clean it up a little—and let's face it, it can even be fun—but if the goal is to make the world perfect, we'll always fall short."

I smile. "Thank you," I say. "You don't know how freeing that is to hear."

"How's Waylen?" she asks.

"Doing much better," I say. "But this isn't going to be one of those situations where a near-death experience changes our relationship." That may not be entirely true, but I'm still processing everything. "I don't know if I'm ready to give up saving the world. Call me an optimist, but I think things can improve if enough of us do the right work. But maybe switching it up a bit wouldn't be a bad idea."

Elodie nods. "It's a good time for a shift in motivations."

"Yes," I say. "I can stop trying to absolve myself of the past and focus on the future."

Elodie raps her manicured nail on the rim of my coffee cup. "That's poetic." She lights up. "You could teach an online course. A motivational summit. We could make an Instagram, memes—"

I hold a hand up. "Please stop."

"All right," she sighs. "Spoilsport."

"But I am open to your *other* offer," I say. She raises her eyebrow. "Friendship. Since you saved my life and all."

"Oh, honey, that's a given," she says. "You're stuck with me whether you like it or not."

The conversation shifts—mercifully—to our girls. They've struck up a friendship, and I'm grateful for the normalcy this brings to Collette's life. When all is said and done, and we're back home again, I'm going to tell her everything. The fire, her uncle—all of it. One thing I've learned is that you can't rid yourself of the past without first confronting it. I don't want her to grow up bearing any of my burdens. She deserves to know the truth.

That evening, for the first time all week, I step out of the hospital for some fresh air. The bitter early December cold has a cleansing effect, like the whole world has been scrubbed clean.

I sit at a coffee shop across the street, and I order a comically large cinnamon bun with extra frosting. I'm just taking my first bite when I feel the shadow looming over me. By now, I'm familiar with his presence, his carefully curated scent, and the uncertain shuffle in his otherwise confident gait.

Bertram Casimir is wearing a white cotton sweatshirt and jeans. His thousand-dollar haircut is mussed by the wind. He gives me a cautious smile.

"Still tracking me down, I see." I nod to the empty seat across from me. He slides into it tenuously.

"I swear I'm not stalking you," he says. "I called Elodie to see how you were doing, and she suggested I meet you here."

When I look at Bertram now, suddenly it all makes sense. I was questioning my instincts because I knew—I *knew*—that he wasn't what "Erin" was portraying to me. Just like his manicured hands, his record is impeccably clean.

"I'm sorry for everything that happened," I tell him. "That I had to lie to you, and that I caused you so much trouble."

"You didn't," he says. "If anything, you got pulled into my web. But now the truth is out. The police are looking for Annie, and I doubt she'll be stupid enough to try anything."

I snort. "For now, anyway."

He smiles. "Maybe I'll get lucky and she'll just wander off into the ether. Or find some other poor bloke to harass."

"I'd believe that."

The words hang in the silence between us, but it's not an uncomfortable one. Believe. The word at the heart of all of this. Because I believed him, I didn't quite play into Annie's hands. But when I think about how close I was to ignoring my instincts and blowing up my marriage on top of that, it's enough to make me question everything I've done in my adult life.

"I suppose it's wrong to play judge, jury, and executioner," I say.

"There's nuance," he says. "But if you ever wanted to take a break from saving the world, I was thinking it would be nice to write that book."

I look up from my plate. "I'm not really a writer. You know that, don't you?"

He shrugs. "You've heard a lot of stories. You even have a couple of your own. Why not write one of them down?"

"I'll think about it," I say. "Interior decorating has never really been my life's passion. You know, I'm not sure what is."

"Good time to find out. Better late than never." Although his appearance hasn't changed, he seems different somehow. Like he's letting me see the real him.

So I decide to let him see the real me. Just a little bit of it, anyway.

"You're the first person I'm telling this to, but I'm about to retire from vigilantism," I say. "I've decided to apply to law school."

Bertram leans back in his chair, crossing his ankle over his knee. "You don't say."

"I've been spying from the shadows for most of my life," I tell him. "I figured I'd try doing it under the unflattering courtroom lights instead."

"I'm surprised to hear you put it that way," he says. "You seemed to have zero faith in the legal system."

I hesitate. His observation isn't too far from the truth. When my brother and I were accused of killing our parents, I thought there was no way anyone would believe we did it. We were just kids.

But then, over the years, I've seen all sorts of cases where families are accused of crimes there's no way they could commit. The whole world will believe the story the media puts out, if it's covered enough.

"It's hard to know who to trust," I tell him. "But I know

I can trust myself. That's got to be worth something. Maybe I can't offset all the crooked judges and lawyers out there, but I can make their lives a lot harder."

"I've heard the bar exam can be a nightmare," Bertram says. "But I bet you know the law better than most. You'll do great."

His smile is not quite like that of the heartsick man I've come to know. He seems more at peace, not having Annie to worry about, at least for now.

"And you have a sponsor," he says. "I'd like to pay for your education."

"That's—"

He holds up a finger to stop me from protesting. "It's not a gift. It's an investment. When you're done, I'd like to hire you on retainer."

I raise a brow. "Why?"

"Do you really have to ask? I've seen how dedicated you are. Besides, I trust you. That's worth more than its weight in gold where I'm from."

"What's the catch?" I ask.

"No catch. Just fill that brain of yours with all the knowledge that you can, so I can sleep better at night knowing the world is a little safer."

In the weeks that follow, there's a sense that nothing is permanent. My brother is well enough to return home, though the police have seized most of his surveillance equipment. The rest, I arrange to be put into storage. Bertram—grateful for all we've done to relieve him of Annie's torment—shells out for his in-home caretakers.

My brother is in good spirits. I was worried that the absence of his tech hoard would upset him. But when we enter his home through the front door for the first time in years, he laughs. The living room is filled with empty shelves.

"Is this what a normal house looks like?" he asks me.

I ease him up the stairs. I've already been here earlier and made the bed for him. "I think normal houses have fewer shelves." Then I add, "I'll talk to Bertram about getting your stuff back. Or replaced, at least."

"No," my brother says, sitting on the edge of the bed. He looks around the room, at the plain walls. He watches me dig through my purse for the bag of prescriptions I've picked up at the pharmacy and lay them out on his nightstand. "I can't remember the last time I slept in here," he says. "I always worked at one of the computers until I was so exhausted, I just passed out in the chair."

I sit beside him. "Do you think about it? When you try to fall asleep and it's too quiet?"

He knows I'm talking about the fire. He nods. "You?"

"It's worse ever since Waylen started wearing those nasal strips to bed. Now he doesn't snore, and it's too quiet." I bump my shoulder against his. "Maybe we shouldn't have used spy work as a substitute for therapy." It gets a laugh out of him.

"I'm glad that you're going back to school," he says, his face turning sober again. "I know I won't be able to look out for you the way I used to. At least, not until this damned cancer goes away or kills me, whichever happens first."

"Stop that," I say. "You don't look out for me. We look out for each other. And that isn't going to change. The guilt that we both felt after—"

"After it happened," he says, saving me from having to say the words.

"Yes. We've spent our whole lives since then trying to make up for it. We both hid away from the world. I just did it in plain sight is all. I love the work we did, but maybe it's time to stop hiding." He said this case would be the big one. The one I'd retire off of. I don't know if this is what he meant.

As though reading my mind, he says, "When I researched Bertram's case, and when I did a background check on Erin, something didn't add up. I couldn't figure out what it was. Now I know it's because Erin really does exist, but that isn't who I was talking to."

"Annie is good," I admit. "She had us both going."

He shakes his head. "I knew you'd get it. And, not to brag, but I'm always right. I didn't know whether Erin was telling the truth about the Budgie app, or Annie was alive somewhere. Turns out none of it—and all of it—was somehow true."

"Give Elodie her credit," I say. "I'd be dead if it wasn't for her. Do *not* tell her I said that."

"Yeah, I'm working out a way to properly thank her for that," my brother says wryly. "She could have a bright future in surveillance engineering. Maybe I can pull a few strings."

I stay until he settles down and falls asleep. Before I go, I tidy up the kitchen and leave a note for him to remember to eat something with his pills. I write it in pen on old-fashioned paper. I think we could both use a break from the internet.

Waylen and I fall into a pattern that, to an outsider, would seem like domestic bliss. A happy couple, a beautiful child, and a glittering Christmas tree. He still walks tenderly as he heals, and needs carefully measured doses of pain medications, which I bring to him on a charcuterie board of tea and fresh fruit and toast.

Collette clings to both of us like we may evaporate if she turns her head away. Elodie and Finnegan come by for periodic playdates—coffee for the adults. There's no talk of curing the world's ills.

It's not a bad life, I think. I'll stay here for as long as fate will allow.

The morning after Christmas, Collette snuggles up against me on the couch. I'm reading a book—a cheesy romance novel loaned to me by Elodie. It isn't my usual cup of tea, but I need a break from the thrillers that fuel my usual drive to spy on others. Elodie was right—I do need a little bit of a pause before I dive into the browser tabs of college prep courses. I've never tried to relax before, and I have to admit that I don't hate it now that I'm giving it a try.

Collette taps distractedly at her tablet, moving the puzzle pieces of her relaxation game. There's the occasional chime of a text alert.

I glance at the screen. "Who's that?" I ask. "A friend from school?"

She shrugs. "Just someone," she says. "She said she knows you from work."

I gently take the tablet out of her hands, ignoring her confused look. I scroll through the messages, which go back for pages and pages. Vaguely I remember Collette telling me about this new app weeks earlier, right around the time she asked me if we could take a vacation to Oregon to see her grandparents' graves.

My blood runs cold as I read the latest message:

We haven't finished our game yet. Tell your mom to catch me if she can.

Annie ☺

I wanted to retire, I really did.

But it appears I'm not going to, after all.

Photo courtesy of the author

REN DeSTEFANO lives in Connecticut, where she was born and raised. When she's not writing thrillers, she's listening to true-crime podcasts and crocheting way too many blankets.

VISIT REN DeSTEFANO ONLINE

LaurenDeStefano.com
LaurenDeStefanoAuthor